TICK TOCK

Books by Fern Michaels

Fear Thy Neighbor
Santa Cruise
No Way Out
The Brightest Star
Fearless
Spirit of the Season
Deep Harbor
Fate & Fortune
Sweet Vengeance
Holly and Ivy
Fancy Dancer
No Safe Secret
Wishes for Christmas
About Face
Perfect Match
A Family Affair
Forget Me Not
The Blossom Sisters
Balancing Act
Tuesday's Child
Betrayal
Southern Comfort
To Taste the Wine
Sins of the Flesh
Sins of Omission
Return to Sender
Mr. and Miss Anonymous
Up Close and Personal
Fool Me Once
Picture Perfect
The Future Scrolls
Kentucky Sunrise

Kentucky Heat
Kentucky Rich
Plain Jane
Charming Lily
What You Wish For
The Guest List
Listen to Your Heart
Celebration
Yesterday
Finders Keepers
Annie's Rainbow
Sara's Song
Vegas Sunrise
Vegas Heat
Vegas Rich
Whitefire
Wish List
Dear Emily
Christmas at Timberwoods

The Lost and Found Novels:

Secrets
Hidden

The Sisterhood Novels:

19 Yellow Moon Road
Bitter Pill
Truth and Justice
Cut and Run
Safe and Sound
Need to Know

Books by Fern Michaels (Continued)

Crash and Burn
Point Blank
In Plain Sight
Eyes Only
Kiss and Tell
Blindsided
Gotcha!
Home Free
Déjà Vu
Cross Roads
Game Over
Deadly Deals
Vanishing Act
Razor Sharp
Under the Radar
Final Justice
Collateral Damage
Fast Track
Hokus Pokus
Hide and Seek
Free Fall
Lethal Justice
Sweet Revenge
The Jury
Vendetta
Payback
Weekend Warriors

The Men of the Sisterhood
Novels:

Hot Shot
Truth or Dare

High Stakes
Fast and Loose
Double Down

The Godmothers Series:

Far and Away
Classified
Breaking News
Deadline
Late Edition
Exclusive
The Scoop

E-Book Exclusives:

Desperate Measures
Seasons of Her Life
To Have and To Hold
Serendipity
Captive Innocence
Captive Embraces
Captive Passions
Captive Secrets
Captive Splendors
Cinders to Satin
For All Their Lives
Texas Heat
Texas Rich
Texas Fury
Texas Sunrise

Books by Fern Michaels (Continued)

Anthologies:

Home Sweet Home
A Snowy Little Christmas
Coming Home for Christmas
A Season to Celebrate
Mistletoe Magic
Winter Wishes
The Most Wonderful Time
When the Snow Falls
Secret Santa
A Winter Wonderland

I'll Be Home for Christmas
Making Spirits Bright
Holiday Magic
Snow Angels
Silver Bells
Comfort and Joy
Sugar and Spice
Let it Snow
A Gift of Joy
Five Golden Rings
Deck the Halls
Jingle All the Way

FERN MICHAELS

TICK TOCK

KENSINGTON
PUBLISHING CORP.

www.kensingtonbooks.com

KENSINGTON BOOKS are published by

Kensington Publishing Corp.
119 West 40th Street
New York, NY 10018

All Kensington titles, imprints, and distributed lines are available at special quantity discounts for bulk purchases for sales promotion, premiums, fund-raising, educational, or institutional use.

Special book excerpts or customized printings can also be created to fit specific needs. For details, write or phone the office of the Kensington Sales Manager: Attn.: Sales Department. Kensington Publishing Corp., 119 West 40th Street, New York, NY 10018. Phone: 1-800-221-2647.

The K with book logo Reg US Pat. & TM Off.

Library of Congress Control Number: 2022935870

First Kensington Hardcover Edition: September 2022
ISBN: 978-1-4967-3711-3

10 9 8 7 6 5 4 3 2 1

Printed in the United States of America

TICK TOCK

Prologue

Texas

He was determined to get even with the people who put him behind bars. It didn't matter that he was guilty. He didn't care about that. All he cared about was revenge. Fourteen years of his life in prison had made him a very angry man, and he was hell-bent on tracking down the people who put him there. He was going to show them who was more cunning. More clever. He was going to make them wish they'd never laid eyes on him.

But the fourteen years weren't a total waste. The prison program encouraged the inmates to learn new skills. And he did. Now he was about to put them to work. He learned a lot about computers, programming, and best of all, 3D printing. All of those newly learned abilities were perfect companions to his past proficiencies. He wasn't going to let a miscalculation stand in his way. Not this time.

One by one, he was going to show everyone just how talented he was. He knew he wasn't the capo mastermind of the crew, but between his skills and the others', their plans would come to fruition. With the help of his fraternity of former inmates, Darius was about to unleash the pent-up wrath he held for those who took away years from his life. He felt no remorse. The only thing that mattered was punishing the punishers.

Virginia

Sometimes listening to other people's advice could land you in the slammer. But when you did something stupid on your own . . . well, you had no one else to blame. Leroy knew it was a long shot, but it could have changed everything for him. He could have gotten out of the dump he was living in. But it didn't happen the way he planned.

There was an upside to all of it. He befriended—if you could call inmates friends—a dude who claimed he had some cash stashed away. Now that he was out, he could help his pal and make his fantasy come true. He just needed to wait until he got his orders. But he had to be careful. He didn't want to blow his parole. Again.

Los Angeles

It was tough in the beginning for him to adjust to a more modest lifestyle. But that would end soon. Once his fellow former inmate arranged for the transfer of funds, he could leave the country. And that would be fine with him. Eventually he would work his way to a no-extradition country and live the life of luxury again. But first, Eric and his cohorts had a few things to do. As long as they stuck to the plan, life would be very different in a short time.

Las Vegas

Lucky for him, he was able to move from Ohio to Nevada. He still had to register with the state, regardless which one he was in. He didn't think it was fair. Why him? Other ex-cons didn't have to register anything or anywhere once they finished their parole. *Why is child pornography worse than bank robbery or murder?* He didn't know the answer, but he was about to change his life and name for good. He patiently waited for the rest of his cronies to get out and get settled, and then the plan would roll.

When they were in prison, he took a liking to the white-collar-crime dude who had scammed millions. The guy was so out of his element that Bennie almost felt sorry for him. Almost. The Gucci-loafer fella needed some protection while in the slammer. He was a little too pretty and was an easy mark. Having played and coached football, Bennie was large enough to become the guy's bodyguard, and the man promised him a bonus when they got out.

They all had their own agenda, but the payoff would be the same for each of them. $50k. Not bad for two weeks' work. Better than what Bennie got in the slammer: $7.23 a month. It was almost unfathomable to calculate how much it was per hour. Bennie was relatively certain there would be a few "detours" before he could become anonymous. At this point in his life, he knew there were always detours. What they would be? He did not know. All he knew was that he would be responsible for setting up the logistics.

Chapter One

Pinewood

It had been ages since Myra, Charles, Nikki, and Jack had dinner without the rest of the sisters. Annie and Fergus were visiting friends in Bar Harbor and wouldn't be back for a week. At first, Myra thought she might have separation anxiety. She and Annie were hardly ever apart. But Myra also welcomed the quiet time she would have with Charles. No other couple had their kind of unique relationship. It was truly unconditional love. Love, passion, understanding, support. Myra appreciated the way Charles always had her back. Regardless. Regardless of how mad and outrageous a mission was, Charles was always at the ready to do whatever it took to get the job done. And because of everyone's devotion to one another and the cause, "Whatever it takes" became the slogan of the group.

The group. An avenging selection of women who were cheated justice. Several years earlier, Myra's daughter was killed by a motorist as she was crossing the street. Myra's unborn grandchild was also lost. But the driver had diplomatic immunity and was secreted away and never brought to justice. For months, Myra anguished over the loss of her daughter and grandchild until she spotted a newscast about a woman who was another victim of injustice. That's when Myra decided it was time someone took matters into their own hands. With the aid of her confidant and lover, Charles; her best friend, Annie; and all their connections—both legal and behind the scenes—the Sisterhood was formed. Each woman brought her own unique skill to the group. When an injustice was at hand, so were the women of the Sisterhood, who stopped at nothing—apart from murder—to avenge the sins perpetrated on innocent people. Though murder was never their goal, by the time the Sisterhood finished their mission, the perpetrators just might wish they were dead.

But tonight was going to be a quiet evening filled with several of Charles's culinary creations.

Myra's adopted daughter Nikki had just finished a big case with her law firm, and Jack rested the prosecution's case in a different legal matter. Between their two schedules, they rarely had time to eat, let alone have a real meal with family.

Myra had been looking forward to this evening for weeks, needling Charles about the menu. His signature dish was a crown roast with popovers, but Myra knew one should never use the American vernacular of Yorkshire pudding in front of him. Not if you wanted a taste of one. But Charles had other menu ideas. He wanted to try something new.

"It just better be delicious." Myra playfully tapped her finger on Charles's collarbone. He immediately took her hand into his and kissed it. Myra pulled it away and gave him a playful pinch on the cheek.

"My love. Would I offer anything less than scrumptious?" Charles replied in his British accent, which occasionally morphed from traditional Cockney to West Midlands to RP, which is what one commonly heard on the BBC. Charles's background was a bit hazy. He was retired from MI6, but no one knew exactly why he could no longer enter the UK without stirring up the local authorities. Now he served the Sisterhood with his contacts, networks, and expertise. Even though he was no longer welcome in his homeland, his former colleagues and allies were always willing to assist when requested.

"I don't suppose you're going to tell me what you're planning?" Myra gave him a sideways look as she stroked her pearls, a habit she had developed several years ago.

Charles gently moved her hand away from her neck. "What are you fretting about?"

"Fretting? Nothing." Myra was aware her "tell" was showing.

"You can't play that game with me." Charles put his hands on each of her shoulders. His eyes locked with hers. There was nowhere for her to go.

Myra sighed. "I can't say."

"Can't or won't?" Charles pressed.

"More can't." Her brow furrowed.

Charles peered closer. "Tell me you are not having one of those 'gut feelings.'"

"That's the problem, Charles. Something isn't sitting right with me. I can't explain it."

"You usually can't. But within time, whatever it is comes to the surface." Charles kissed her on the forehead.

"I suppose you're right. But I hate when this happens. It feels so uncomfortable," Myra said, pouting.

"Perhaps it's because it's been several months since you and the Sisters were on a mission. It fuels you. The adrenaline takes over. And when the mission is over, you deflate like an old mylar balloon that's run out of air."

"Old balloon?" Myra jerked her head back.

Charles knew he had unintentionally hit a sore spot. "Oh, love, I don't mean you're an old balloon. What I meant was . . .

oh, bugger that." He put his arms around her and started humming a few lines from one of her favorite love songs, "All the Way."

"You are no Frank Sinatra, buster." Myra snickered as she swayed back and forth in his arms.

"Okay, lovie, leave me to my work." Charles gave her a peck on the cheek. "The dough for the ravioli is getting hard."

"Is that a euphemism?" Myra snorted.

Charles let out a howl. "My, aren't you the cheeky one?"

Myra gave him a sly grin and winked before she turned and retreated into the atrium.

Charles went back to preparing his homemade ravioli, rolling the dough into long sheets. He took small scoops of a mixture of porcini mushrooms, mozzarella, and ricotta, placing them on the rows of dough, then topped it with another sheet of pasta. He pulled out a pasta wheel and rolled out a few dozen square shapes. Most people were accustomed to round ravioli. "But this is the traditional way," he would explain to confused onlookers. Once cooked, the ravioli would be finished with a sauce made of butter and sage, sprinkled with truffles. That was the first course. Next up would be a salad with arugula, radicchio, and fennel, drizzled with a light lemon vinaigrette. After the salad, Charles planned for osso buco as the main course, accompanied by French green beans and polenta. He knew he'd get a little grief about all the carbs, but it was a must. The sauce from the veal shanks deserved something to soak in. He thought about dessert, but knew he'd get grief about that, as well, so he opted for fresh raspberry sorbet. Normally it was served between courses, but it would have to suffice for after dinner.

About an hour later, Myra walked back into the kitchen. The aromas were beckoning. "Oh, Charles, you have outdone yourself. Again. I know I say that every time you cook a meal like this. Nikki and Jack will be salivating as soon as they walk in the door." She came up behind him and put her arms around his waist. "May I kiss the chef?"

Charles stiffened. "Not now, dear. I have my hands full."

Myra took a step back. "What did you say?" Never in their history together had he denied her a kiss.

He turned quickly and said, "My hands are full. Of you!" He dipped her backwards, like the famous photo of the sailor kissing the nurse in Times Square, and planted a big wet one on her lips.

"Unhand me, you brute!" Myra pretended to fight him off.

"Never." Charles gently tipped her upright and patted her on the fanny. "Now please, let me get back to my work. Unless you want to be part of the cleanup crew."

Myra sighed. "Where is Fergus when you need him?"

"Sailing on Frenchman Bay, I suppose," Charles answered.

Myra grunted. "I miss them."

"Love, they've only been gone for two days."

"I know. You're right. I'm being silly. But it's that strange feeling I'm having. Something foreboding." Myra reached once more for her pearls.

"Remember that expression: Worry is like paying a debt you don't owe."

"I do, but it's still difficult wrapping my head around."

Charles smiled. "You're thinking about something that does not exist."

"Not yet, anyway," Myra replied in a stubborn tone.

Chapter Two

Los Angeles

Eric Barnett had it all. At least that was the impression of anyone who met him. Head of a hedge fund with a large double-digit-million-dollar income—in a bad year—with a former supermodel wife, a 10,000-square-foot house in Calabasas, a beach house in Malibu, a Tesla (so everyone would think he's cool) and an Aston Martin (so everyone knew he was rich).

Even though he wasn't technically a Wolf of Wall Street, the financial moguls were a different breed, regardless of where they lived. It didn't matter how much money or things you had. You had to have *more*. More than anyone in your circle of friends. And neither he nor his peers took the time to enjoy the riches they had. They were obsessed with more. More of everything. More expensive watches. More expensive cars. More expensive vacations. And when the circle of friends became lower than your pay grade, you moved up to the next circle of social inequality. It was excess within excess.

Los Angeles was the perfect setting for such conspicuous

consumption. It bordered on obscene, which made his job as a hedge fund manager easy. Just the idea of being accepted into a hedge fund was something to brag about. But the hedge fund business was exactly that—hedging that the person you entrusted with your savings was going to invest the money in something that would yield a big return.

There were two caveats to participate. First, the investor's net worth had to exceed one million dollars or be part of an institutional investor. The second was that it was very risky. Hedge funds were managed by an individual or small group of individuals who invested the money in stocks, bonds, and securities, with a higher chance of reward. Eric preferred the individual investor. Those were the people who wanted to get richer fast. There weren't as many questions to answer. More often than not, they didn't succeed to the extent of the pitch they were given about high yields. Yet every day, Eric found someone who wanted in.

Unfortunately for Eric, the money train jumped the rails when it was discovered he had misrepresented details about a company. He gained over 100 million dollars from 800 investors, but he also landed in a federal penitentiary and owed 250,000 dollars in fines. At least they didn't get him on wire fraud. He was careful about that. It was all checks or cash. No online exchange of funds from his clients. None of them protested. Lucky for him, his fines did not outweigh his profits, and he was able to stash away a few cool million before his stint at the Gray Bar Hotel. He hoped he would get released early for good behavior. Besides, he hadn't killed anybody. No, he simply stripped innocent people of their life savings. It was *their* fault. They knew it was a risk. At least that's how he justified it to himself. As expected, he served just five years of his sentence, and learned a lot more about computer technology while serving time.

After his arrest, they raided his bank accounts, where very

little was left. They confiscated all of his personal posses-
sions, sold them off, and portioned the proceeds out among
his victims. No one, including his now ex-wife, knew he had
carefully squirreled away five million dollars in an offshore
account. The only problem was getting to the money after his
release. He knew the feds were watching him, so he had to
find a patsy he could trust to fetch the funds. Of course, the
flunky wouldn't physically handle the money. They would
bring the proper paperwork to the bank and have it diverted
into another account.

Eric had found the perfect stooge, a man who had been
busted for falsifying information on a background check for
firearms. As if no one was going to notice. Leroy Crenshaw.
Such an idiot.

Chapter Three

Nikki and Jack

It seemed like it had been months since the two of them spent the evening together. In the beginning of their relationship, Jack suspected something was awry with Nikki and her group of friends. There were too many coincidences pointing the finger of vigilante justice toward Nikki's stepmother and her best friend, Anna Ryland de Silva. As a federal prosecutor, Jack faced a serious dilemma, but his love for Nikki had outweighed the consequences of his job. Now, as a freelance attorney, he had no one looking over his shoulder. Or so he thought.

There was a time during one of the Sisterhood's crusades when the women were caught. Thanks to the whip-smart legal mind of Lizzie Fox Cricket, a compelling argument was made, and the women were released and put under house arrest. Then, with the guile and guts of the Sisterhood, they managed to unshackle themselves by putting the ankle monitors on barn cats. Once Jack realized what the women were doing, he founded a like-minded group of men who worked under the same directive to see that justice was served. It was often a slippery slope, but Jack's conscience had always been his guide. Some laws just weren't fair, and sometimes, the system failed.

Jack was sitting on a bench in the master bedroom, pulling on his socks, when Nikki walked in. He blinked several times.

"What?" Nikki asked innocently.

"You." Jack smiled. "You are as beautiful as ever."

Nikki made her way over to the bench and sat next to him. "Thank you, Mr. Emery." She rested her head on his shoulder. "As much as I want to see Mom and Charles, I wouldn't mind if you and I had a quiet dinner alone one of these days."

Jack stood and walked over to a chair, where his blazer was draped. He pulled an envelope out of the inner pocket. "You and I are going away for a long weekend in Irvington."

"But my work!" Nikki immediately protested.

"Ha. I spoke to Alexis. She said the caseload is light right now." Nikki tried to interrupt, but Jack kept talking. "And I spoke to Lizzie. She said if anything comes up that your firm can't handle, she'll step in. Besides, we'll only be gone for four days. Not much can happen in four days." Jack rested his case.

Nikki sighed. "You are too good to me." She got up and slipped on her shoes. "Ready?"

"I am. It's going to be good to see Myra and Charles. I'm looking forward to discovering what he's cooking for dinner."

"Oh, so am I." Nikki cocked her head. "Let's go."

They hopped in their golf cart, which served as their local mode of transportation from their house to Myra and Charles's. They could have walked, but Nikki always got a kick out of zipping across the farm, laughing as they bounced along their way.

Chapter Four

Virginia

Leroy Crenshaw kept looking at the burner phone, waiting for it to ring. He never had much patience. He was already spending the money in his head. First, he'd buy himself a new Winnebago motor home. Maybe not brand new, but it would be new to him. Then he'd take it up to Pennsylvania, where his cousins lived. He was sick and tired of hearing them brag about all the fine vacations they took. *Show-offs.* He could spit bile every time he spoke to them. But soon, he was going to show them who had the bucks. Maybe he'd even get himself a gold tooth—even if he didn't need it. He just liked the way it looked. Yeah. He had big plans.

He remembered back when he went on a road trip with George and ended up in the hoosegow. Dang that George. George thought there might be money hidden in some furniture he had moved from an estate. According to George, a couple of people were looking for it, so it had to be valuable. Turned into an all-night drive to some hoity-toity art place in North Carolina. When they got there, they parked in the back of the parking lot, waiting for an opportunity to sneak inside by the end of the day. Leroy also remembered he got some kind of stomach disruption—probably from all the fried chicken he ate on the trip. After that episode, he could never look at a piece of chicken again. But he did miss it in his mind. Even though the smell would make him gag.

But that was long behind him. As stupid as that trip had been, he knew he had done himself one better. He shook his head, continuing to remember that night and what followed.

He and George both got six months in jail for breaking and entering. They were lucky no assault charges were filed, even if they were on the receiving end of a fire extinguisher that some nutty hippie chick used to keep them at bay. After they were released from jail, Leroy got himself another idea. In his mind, it was almost foolproof. He was going to rob a liquor store with another one of his buddies.

The plan was to target a liquor store on the edge of town. That way, they'd have enough time to get away before any cops arrived. Being a regular himself, Leroy knew the flow of customers. He would wear a ski mask, like they did on all the TV shows. Get some camouflage duds and walk with a limp. He saw that on one of those true-crime shows, too. He figured his disguise and wobbly walk would do the trick. Part of the scheme was to leave one of their vehicles a few miles down the road from the store. Then they would steal a car from one of the dealerships right after they closed and head to the liquor store. Leroy knew every inch of his hokey town and the dimwitted people who lived there. He fancied himself smarter than the rest of his chums, thinking he was a few IQ points higher than the average person. Sadly, the average people he knew weren't all that bright, either. Thus, the second big mistake came when he had to figure out how to get a gun. With his criminal record, it would take a bit of lying, an area where he showed a modicum of talent. But not enough.

Again, sadly for Leroy, his higher-than-average IQ was still a few digits short. He didn't want to buy a gun on the black market. Too expensive and too dangerous. He figured he could fake parts of the application to get a firearm. Nobody checked. Or so he thought. Two weeks later, he was back in jail, then on trial, and subsequently convicted. He spent three years in a federal penitentiary for being a dumbass. He actually thought it was a lucky break. He could have been locked up for armed robbery had his foolish plan gone through. He could have been in the slammer for fifteen years. Life's little blessings.

According to Leroy's way of thinking, it really had been a blessing in disguise. Prison was where he'd met the slick talker who was serving time for some kind of money fraud. He told Leroy that when they got out, he had a plan to get some money. Enough money so that neither of them would have to work again. All Leroy had to do was get on a plane, go to a bank, give them some papers, and come back. Then he would get a cut of the dough. Leroy never bothered to ask what that amount was. He just figured it was a lot. He continued to pace, waiting for the phone to ring. Dreaming about all the places he'd visit, traveling the highways and byways of this grand country. Yessiree. It was his time to get in on the good life.

Chapter Five

Pinewood

Nikki was howling with laughter as she tried to hang onto the golf cart with one hand and steady the huge bouquet of white peonies on her lap with the other. Jack made a quick turn at the back door of Myra's farmhouse, kicking up rocks in their wake.

"I forgot how much fun this is!" Nikki gasped for breath. "We have had our noses to the grindstone for too long, Jack. We should try to ratchet it down a bit, don't ya think?"

Jack came around to her side of the cart and held out his hand. Nikki passed him the flowers and grabbed his other hand, hoisting herself down from the cart. Jack put his arm around her and kissed her on the cheek. "Do you know how happy it makes me to hear you laugh?"

"Yes, but tell me again." She smiled up at his handsome face.

"I love your laugh. And you need to do more of it." He opened the back door to the house that led to a small entry area. One part led to the kitchen. The other was a stone staircase that led to the Sisterhood's area of operations. It once served as part of the Underground Railroad, and the Sisters had made good use of it over the years.

Nikki burst into the kitchen, giving Myra a huge hug. "Mom! I cannot believe we are actually doing this!" She handed Myra the bouquet.

"Yes, darlin'. It's been too long." Myra pressed her nose into the flowers. "Oh, these are lovely. Thank you." She gave Nikki another hug.

"I can't take all the credit. Jack actually picked them up." Nikki headed toward where Charles was cooking.

Jack followed, giving Myra a kiss on the way. "Hello, Myra. It's nice to be here." She returned the affectionate gesture.

Nikki was now arm in arm with Charles, peeking into the pots on the stove. "Everything smells divine." She fanned the aromas in her direction.

"Okay, Little Miss Nosey, you go pour everyone a glass of wine and let the master work," Charles teased in his very best RP British accent.

Nikki saluted and went into the butler's pantry, where a nice white Bordeaux was chilling in a wine bucket. "Ooh . . . fancy," Nikki called over her shoulder.

Charles chuckled. "Nothing is too good for our girl."

"A-*hem*," Jack chimed in.

"Of course, you as well, old chap." Charles took a moment from sautéing to pat Jack on the back.

Nikki began to pour the wine into a mismatched set of glasses.

"Just one moment." Charles wiped his hands on the sop-towel that was tucked in the front of his apron pocket. "You seriously think you're going to serve such a delectable beverage in a jelly jar?" Charles folded his arms and feigned annoyance.

Nikki chuckled. "You are so right. What was I thinking?

We're not generally fancy around here. But I agree. We should honor this elixir of the gods more appropriately."

"Spoken like a true orator." Jack nodded and followed Myra into the dining area, where they pulled out the special Waterford crystal goblets.

"This feels like a special occasion." Myra smiled and handed two glasses to Jack.

"Yes. It does," Jack agreed. "Nikki has been working very hard these past few months. It's nice we can get together and relax."

"Were you able to get the accommodations you wanted in Irvington?" Myra asked.

"Yes. Thank you for the introduction. Everything is all set." Jack beamed. "You should have seen the look on Nikki's face when I told her we were going to escape for a few days, and I wasn't taking no for an answer. I told her everything was under control and Lizzie was backup if something urgent came up."

"I'm so glad you're doing this," Myra said.

"I would have liked to have made it a longer, more exotic trip, but I knew Nikki would get too antsy if she was more than a few hours' drive from home. And work. And you. And Charles."

As they reentered the kitchen, Charles turned. "Were you two gossiping about me?" He took a fencing stance, pretending his wooden spoon was a sword.

Jack grabbed a spatula and challenged Charles to a spatula duel. "Present arms!"

Charles spun around and countered with, *"En garde!"* They commenced to dance around the kitchen in mock-fencing style.

Nikki and Myra were doubled over in laughter. It was heartwarming and hilarious to see two relatively serious men having good old-fashioned fun. The kitchen timer signaled the end of the match. All agreed it was a tie, even though there was never a tie in traditional fencing.

Charles patted his forehead with a clean towel. "My dear young man, you gave this old goat a run for his money."

Myra sidled up next to Charles. "But you're *my* old goat."

That brought a few more laughs. Nikki finally finished pouring the wine. Charles made a toast: "May the best of the past be the worst of the future."

"Hear! Hear!" came from Jack. "It is my utmost pleasure and honor to be part of this remarkable family."

Myra's eyes misted. "When Barbara died, I thought I would never again live a day of joy, love, or happiness. But you . . ." She lifted her glass to Charles. "And you," she said, pointing to Nikki, "have given me even more." She looked over at Jack. "And you aren't so bad, either." The short, somber mood was broken by laughter.

Nikki held up her glass. "Here's to all of us. I love you very much." She wiped a small tear from the corner of her eye.

"Enough blubbering. Let's start with some hors d'oeuvres. Actually, tonight it will be antipasto!" Charles pulled a tray from the oven. On it was baked clams oreganata, shrimp scampi, and small eggplant rollatini. Just enough to whet everyone's appetite. He plated the food and handed it out to everyone. "Let's sit at the kitchen table for now. I still have to prepare a few things, and I don't want to miss any chatter."

In anticipation of the small repast, Myra had set both tables earlier. The kitchen table was arranged for the appetizers, and the dining room table was adorned with her fine china, linens, and crystal. As Nikki had acknowledged, normally they weren't a fancy bunch; pulling out the luxury items wasn't standard operating dinner procedure. That was reserved for wrap-up dinner parties and special occasions.

But Myra was right; the evening was a special occasion. Nothing in particular. Being together was special enough.

Nikki held the plate up to her nose. "Oh, my goodness. This smells divine." She quickly took a seat. Jack pulled out a chair for Myra, then sat next to Nikki.

"Charles, aren't you going to join us?" Myra looked up.

"I'm right here, my love." He was busy, carefully placing the ravioli into the boiling water.

"Well, that just won't do." Myra pushed out her chair and carried her plate over to where Charles was cooking. She stabbed a piece of eggplant on her fork and held it up to Charles's mouth. He graciously accepted.

"Not bad, if I say so myself." He smacked his lips. Myra scooped out a clam and waved it under his nose. Again he graciously accepted. Once he swallowed, he insisted she take her seat and enjoy the food. "Myra, if I can't watch you enjoy the food I prepared, I would be greatly dismayed."

She stitched her eyebrows together and gave him a quizzical look.

"Darling, I appreciate this, but please go put your fanny in a chair." He shooed her back to the kitchen table.

"Well, I hope you don't plan on spending the whole evening in the kitchen." Myra made a face.

"Not at all. I timed everything so we can all be together." He gave her a *tsk-tsk*. "I don't know why you underestimate my culinary skills."

"I do not. But you usually have Fergus here as your souschef, busboy, and potato peeler."

"The good news is we're not having potatoes. But I believe I can manage." He turned back to the stove and mumbled. "Ye of little faith."

"I heard that," Myra blurted.

"You were supposed to." Charles chuckled.

Groans of gastronomic delight filled the kitchen as everyone consumed the first course. Nikki then cleared the table as Charles was plating the ravioli with the butter sage sauce.

More accolades and words of wonder followed as everyone brought their plates into the dining room. Before anyone could dive into the pasta, they said grace. As they held one another's hands, Myra spoke the simple words: "It is a blessing to be here. Thank you, Lord, for this moment together."

*Amen*s went around the table, followed by more coos, groans, and unidentifiable words as the group dug into the pasta. The salad was served and then the pièce de résistance, the osso buco, on top of the polenta Charles had painstakingly cooked earlier that day and finished with the green beans.

The look on Nikki's face was priceless. It was her favorite dish. Charles had tried to keep this from Myra because he wanted it to be a surprise.

"So this is why you didn't want me wandering in the kitchen?" Myra gave him a look.

"More like lurking." Charles grinned. "*Buon appetito!*"

Nikki raised her glass. "To the best dinner ever! *Cin cin!*"

The others heartily concurred.

Chapter Six

Las Vegas

Benjamin "Bennie" Weber pulled out a twenty-dollar bill and collected casino coins to throw in the one-armed bandits known as slot machines. He was getting antsy just staying in his motel room. Sure, it had a TV and a hot plate, but the walls were starting to close in on him. He should be used to living in a confined situation, but now that he was out of prison, being inside for too long made him anxious. He worried he would never be able to leave. He referred to it as Post-Traumatic Small Space Disorder. *PTSSD*, he'd joke with the two friends he had left. Well, they weren't actually friends. Just a couple of guys he met playing the slots. They didn't know about his child pornography conviction.

As far as Bennie was concerned, she was no child. By any means. She was a fifteen-year-old who had flaunted her long legs and ample breasts in front of the team. In front of a crowd. Despite the fact that she was a cheerleader, and part of her "job" was to get the crowd excited, he thought she was aiming her enthusiasm directly at him. That's what he told himself. That's what he told his lawyer. It was *her* fault.

She was too evocative. Yeah—*evocative* was the right word. He liked using it. He blamed her for seducing him. Except there was no evidence beyond the photos of her on his phone. Photos he actually took himself. Photos he procured through the peephole in the wall of the girls' gym. It was so easy. Too easy. But then again, sometimes life gives you a gift. Then, when he found out he could sell the pics online, he was all for making a few extra bucks. But life sometimes catches up with you. Especially when you're careless.

Yes, it became too easy. He was getting careless. It was during a game when he had taken off his jacket and left his phone in the pocket. When the game was over, he didn't notice that his phone had fallen to the ground. One of the players saw it under a bench and picked it up. Most of the time, people lock their phones, but on that particular day, the odds were not in Bennie's favor. Before the game, he had been busy taking covert photos of the girls changing into their uniforms when his phone rang. Bennie got spooked, shoved the phone into his pocket, and sneaked out of the janitor's closet that served as his personal photo booth. It was a narrow escape. He couldn't remember the last time he'd been shaken up like that.

As Bennie had scurried toward the field, one of the referees stopped to chat. Then the team came out, and he wasn't able to mess with his phone. The phone he should have locked immediately. The phone with dozens of incriminating photos.

When the game was over, he walked toward the locker room and felt around in his pocket for the phone. Gone. He patted himself down. Nothing. More panic. As he retraced his steps, he came face-to-face with the linebacker who'd found it. Next to the linebacker was a referee and the superintendent of schools. By the time they got to the other side of the field, several police cars were waiting.

His lawyer argued that the police had no right to confiscate his phone. The judge thought differently. And so did the jury. He was found guilty and served five years of a fifteen-year term. But all was not lost. He made a few acquaintances in prison. Acquaintances that could prove very valuable. His only obstacle now was having to register as a sex offender wherever he resided. But it was Vegas. Land of deviance, debauchery, and vice. It was a city where he could remain anonymous. Except for the sex offender thing. But soon he could move about freely. That's what the pretty boy had promised as payment for his protection.

Chapter Seven

Leroy and Darius

Even though he had been waiting for the call, Leroy jumped several feet when his phone clanged.

"Huh . . . hullo?"

"Hey, man. How's it goin'?" a rather pleasant voice replied.

"Is that you, Darius?" Leroy asked.

"No. Sorry. Wrong number." Darius huffed and disconnected the call. How many times did he have to tell Leroy not to use his real name? Even though they were using burner phones, he still didn't want them identifying themselves. There would be plenty of other information they would have to exchange. Leaving their names out of it was minor but important.

Darius waited a few minutes and then redialed.

"Huh, hullo?"

"Hey, Mike. Todd here."

Leroy gave the phone a strange look. Then the light bulb went on in his head, and he giggled. *Just like being spies.* "Well, hello, Todd. Yes, this is Mike. Yep, it's Mike all right."

Darius wondered why he aligned himself with such a misfit. But there had to be one in the crowd. The other two were relatively normal. Normal for a financial fraudster and a child porn offender, that is.

Darius continued. "I sent you a postcard with an address and a description. I want you to follow the mark and keep me posted."

"You mean like on a stakeout?" Leroy was all atwitter.

"Yeah. Whatever."

"When should I start?" Leroy asked excitedly.

"When you get the postcard." Darius hoped he hadn't made a big mistake enlisting this numbnut.

"Yeah. Right. Okay, boss," Leroy responded. "How long do you want me to do this?"

"Until I get there."

"Where?"

"Wherever *you* are."

"Oh. Wow. So you're coming here? To Virginia?"

Darius wanted to strangle him. "No names. No places."

"Sorry, boss." Leroy gulped. "I meant West Virginia."

Darius was hitting himself on the head with his phone at this point. "No. *Louisiana.*"

"But I'm not . . . oh, right." It finally dawned on Leroy.

"The info should arrive today or tomorrow. I should be there in two to three days. I'll keep you posted." Darius hung up before Leroy could blurt out more stupidity.

Fourteen years ago, Darius Lancaster was a better-than-average-looking forty-year-old man. He grew up on a ranch and had a sexy, rugged image that he maintained working as a foreman on construction sites. A likable guy with a set of smarts. Except when it came to women. He fell under the spell of a Texas beauty who was fifteen years his junior. She also had very expensive tastes. She was all his—as long as there were gifts, flowers, and trips to Vegas. He liked playing the sugar daddy, and she was his arm candy. Over time, his funds dwindled. He couldn't keep up with her wanting and spending. When he told her they had to cut back, she made a stink. He knew there were plenty of men who could and would easily take his place, so he did whatever he could to keep her happy. He maxed out his credit cards to the tune of $50k. Then there was the big ticket of another $50k to the loan sharks. They had loan sharks in Texas—some of the biggest in the country. It was Texas, after all.

He started pulling a few heists in small towns in the Panhandle. Gas stations, mostly. A convenience store now and again. No one ever got hurt, and he managed to escape the authorities several times, but he was smart enough to know his luck would run out in that pursuit. But he was in deep. He needed more than a few hundred bucks per robbery. He was desperate.

The loan sharks had given him two weeks to come up with the rest of the cash, or he might be spending weeks in an intensive care unit. If they let him live.

His first legitimate job was working for a local demolition company, but it was dirty work, so he moved on to commercial construction, instead of destruction. Now he could put his experience to good use. Rob a bank. His employer had recently finished building a strip mall on the outskirts of town in anticipation of suburban sprawl. It included a branch of a local credit union. As the foreman, he had access to the plans, and he put his photographic memory to the test. He knew which of the walls were steel-clad and which were normal commercial partitions.

The bank shared a wall with a franchise coffee shop. The east wall of the storage room in the coffee shop backed up against the break room of the bank. He patronized the shop a half-dozen times, casing the joint as he drank eight-dollar cups of coffee. He frequented the men's room to get good sight lines. After each visit, he would tweak his rudimentary sketches of the floor plans he pulled from his memory. He kept track of the baristas and the bus person. He watched the clock as the flow of people came through, noted the busiest time and the lulls. After two weeks, he knew everyone's schedule, including the delivery trucks. He kept to himself, only occasionally nodding at the regulars. He tried to remain inconspicuous by acting as a normal patron. The fake wig under the western cowboy hat he wore was a good enough disguise that no one would be able to give an accurate description of him—if it came down to that.

It didn't take long for him to build his confidence. He had everything planned down to the minute. One evening, Darius showed up at the coffee place with a hunting backpack. No one seemed to think anything of it. He had carefully packed a small battery-operated hacksaw and some plastic explosives. He casually walked to the men's room and slipped inside the storage area, where he crouched behind a pallet of paper cups. He checked his watch. Almost closing time. He listened to the chatter as the few workers said their good nights and locked up. He checked his watch again. It had been almost half an hour. Anyone who left anything behind would have come back by then.

He moved to the wall that separated the storage area from the break room in the bank. He pulled out a small device that would check for metal and studs. So far, he was at the right place. Now, nothing was standing between him and the interior of the bank except a few layers of Sheetrock. He listened again for any sounds. Nothing. He began to put the saw together, assembling all its parts. A simple click here. A click there. Then it was ready to go.

He carefully and meticulously cut an opening between the studs. It was just wide enough for him to fit through sideways. There was no room to spare. Good thing he fought off the beer belly by going to the gym several times a week. He shimmied his way through the opening and pulled out a small flashlight. Scanning the room, he saw the door that led to the lobby and another door that led to the electrical boards. That was the first thing he had to do: disarm the grid. Once that happened, he had less than ten minutes to get the job done. Under normal circumstances, the system would allow for one recycling for it to reset. If it didn't, then the backup alarm would sound at the security center—the place that monitored all the alarm systems.

He quickly packed the doorjamb with a small amount of plastic explosives. Just enough to loosen the lock. In an instant, a poof of smoke was discharged, and the door was free. At the entrance to the vault, he checked the panel of the security door. He tripped the wire to mimic someone getting buzzed in. So far, so good. He quickly moved over to the steel-encased safe and packed the turnstile with more plastic explosive material. According to his calculations, the fuse would burn in a coil-like pattern, and the wheel would come off nice and clean. That's what was *supposed* to happen.

In an instant, his world literally exploded and sent him sailing across the room, while the shriek of alarms bounced off the walls and the ceiling. His head was reverberating in sync with the pulsating sound. He was dazed. He couldn't feel his feet. He panicked, thinking he may have blown them off. He tried to move, but the room was spinning. He was losing his focus.

The next thing he saw was a flashlight shining in his face. The next thing after that was waking up in a hospital bed, handcuffed to the railing.

He wiggled his toes, flexed his fingers. Everything was still intact. He wasn't sure if he was happy he was still alive. The goons would be looking for him and the money. A few days later, he was taken into custody. Once he was arraigned, bail was set at 50,000 dollars. He wasn't sure if he could raise the money. Even if he could get his hands on the funds, would he use it to get out of jail or to hand over to the sharks? The only person who could help him—and would be willing to help him—was his sister Kate. She had a soft spot for her brother.

Instead of calling his lawyer, he phoned Kate. Luckily for Darius, his sister had money in an IRA, and she was able to arrange for a cash advance on a few credit cards. After she amassed the $50k, she drove the two hours on the interstate to get to the jail where they were holding him. The two decided there was no sense in Darius getting out of jail, only for him to be beaten within an inch of his life. They opted to use the money Kate had amassed to pay off the thugs. A few months behind bars wouldn't kill Darius.

Bank robbery was not an unusual crime. Not in the least. It had become so rampant, the FBI developed an app just in case someone witnessed or heard of a bank robbery being committed. Because it was his first offense—at least the first one where he got caught—Darius thought they'd go easy on him. Cut a plea deal. Regrettably, that was not the intention of the new federal prosecutor. He was going to use Darius Lancaster as an example. The use of explosives in the attempted burglary was underscored. This prosecutor and his associates were going to make their mark on the legal system. And Darius Lancaster was their target. But now, he was about to turn the tables on them.

Chapter Eight

Irvington, Virginia

Nikki leaned her head out the window of their vehicle. The wind lapped at her face. She tried to remember the last time she'd felt this whimsical. Jack reached over and patted her hand.

"Enjoying the ride?"

"I feel like one of Lady's pups when their ears are flapping in the breeze!" She turned and gave him a brilliant smile. "I am so happy you planned this getaway." She squeezed his hand. "Out of curiosity, what made you think of doing this?"

"All the things you and I haven't done. The hours of work you put in. And just wanting to spend some alone-time with you. Away from everything. At least far enough away."

"Four hours is my comfort zone." Nikki laughed.

"Yes, I made sure I was within the perimeter of your 'comfort zone.' " He made a one-handed air quote. "We should be there in about a half hour."

Jack was referring to The Tides Inn. It had been built in 1947 by a couple who purchased the area originally known as Ashburn Farm, nestled between a creek and the sea. It was very upscale, but with a rural ambiance. Nikki had never been to the hotel, and Jack thought it was a good blend of luxury and relaxation—and romance. He'd booked the Ashburn Suite, with a coastal view. He made reservations for dinner on the terrace at the Chesapeake Restaurant. He didn't want Nikki to have to exert a single one of her brilliant brain cells.

Upon their arrival, the valet cheerfully opened Nikki's door and extended his hand. She smiled and thanked him. Jack popped the trunk, and the bellman removed their bags and placed them on a luggage cart. All that was left was to walk into the lobby and pick up the key from the concierge. The décor inside was casual with a spa-like, modern feel.

"Welcome to The Tides Inn, Mr. and Mrs. Emery. My name is Anthony. Please let me know if I can be of service," the concierge said as he handed two key cards to Jack. "Enjoy your stay."

"Thank you, Anthony." Jack nodded, and Nikki followed with a smile and a nod.

"Oh, I just love the smell of this place." Nikki took in a long inhale. "White tea?" she mused.

Anthony couldn't help but overhear her and ordered a scented candle to be sent to her room with a note indicating it was compliments of the house.

Anthony wasn't the only one observing Nikki and Jack. A skinny, nervous guy watched the two of them cross the lobby and walk down the far corridor. He shuffled to a section of the lobby where no one could hear him. He parked himself behind one of the potted plants, as if no one could see the conspicuous man crouched under a palm tree. He dialed a number.

"Hey boss. They just checked into The Tides Inn." He listened for a moment. "They walked to the other side of the building, and I watched the bellman bring their bags down the hall just like you said." He listened some. "Got it." Another pause. "Okay. I'll meet you at the motel tonight." He slipped the phone into his pocket and left his posh surroundings.

Nikki strolled into the bedroom of the suite. Jack followed. "This is beautiful." She turned and put her arms around his neck.

"I wanted something private but also with amenities, so you can be pampered."

"Really, it's spectacular. Look at this view." She motioned to the beautiful trees and vegetation that surrounded the creek that led to the bay. She gave a sigh. "The best part is that we are together. Alone. Far away from the chaos."

Jack held her close. A knock on the door indicated their luggage had arrived. "Okay, sport. Let's unpack, freshen up, and head to the veranda and have a glass of champagne."

"I love the way you think." She pecked him on the cheek.

Jack went to the door and ushered the bellman in. There was a small shopping bag atop the two suitcases. The bellman handed it to Jack. "Mrs. Emery mentioned she liked the scent in the air. This is from the concierge. Compliments of The Tides Inn."

Jack was impressed. "Thanks very much." He motioned for the man to bring the bags into the bedroom. Upon his return, he handed the man a twenty-dollar tip.

"Thank you, sir. Enjoy your stay."

Nikki emerged from the bathroom.

"Look what they sent." Jack handed her the shopping bag with the scented candle.

Nikki took a deep inhale. "I'm loving this place already."

*   *   *

Leroy got in the rental car and drove to the motel a mile away. He knew something was going to go down, but he wasn't sure what it was. He chewed his nails in suspense. Then his mind wandered to the money they were going to make. He wondered when that was going to happen. Maybe Darius would know. He'd ask him later.

Chapter Nine

Pinewood

Myra walked into the atrium, where Charles was tinkering with one of his laptops. "What are you doing, dear?" she asked.

"Something isn't right with this." Charles pointed to the screen. "It keeps fuzzing up."

"What do you mean 'fuzzing up'?"

"I wish I could replicate it, but it seems to happen periodically." Charles sat back and crossed his arms. "These machines are supposed to be bugproof." Charles shook his head. "They have been through the most stringent tests, and the firewall is supposed to block out everything." He flipped the computer shut. "I'll have Fergus take a look when he gets back. I'm stumped."

Myra looked at him in surprise. "You? Stumped? I don't think I've ever heard you utter that word."

"Technology moves incredibly fast. We've been radio silent for several months. Much can change in a short period of time."

Myra stood behind Charles. She stroked her pearls. "Charles, I'm getting that odd feeling again."

He took her hand and kissed the back of it. "You just have the jitters because Nikki and Jack are on a long-overdue holiday. You don't like it when your chicks aren't in the roost."

Myra chuckled. "Oh, you know me too well."

"Did they check in with you?" Charles asked, referring to Nikki and Jack.

"Yes, she sent a text. They are settling in."

"There now. Feel better?"

"No, not really. She said she and Jack are going to put their phones in the safe."

Charles let out a guffaw. "I can't say I blame them!" He could tell Myra was uncomfortable with the inability to instantaneously contact her adopted daughter. "The hotel has phones, my love. Please try to relax." Charles stood. "Come, I'll fix us something to drink."

Several hundred miles away in Alabama, Cooper, a very unusual dog, was pacing the floor. His owner, Julie, knew that meant something was not right. "What's the matter, boy?" She crouched down and looked him in the eyes. He gave a soft woof. Julie motioned for him to follow her into the kitchen, but he wouldn't budge. He hunkered down on all four paws. "Coop? Are you okay, pal?"

He gave another woof and scurried toward the closet, where his "go-bag" was stashed. Julie knew that was a sign of trouble. The dog was known for his psy-tracking ability. Most tracking dogs were trained in one of several areas: drugs, cadavers, weapons. But Cooper had extraordinary talents. He could sense something from miles away. It was as if he possessed some kind of psychic ability. Some people thought it was absurd until he helped solve a few situations with the Sisterhood. Julie tried to keep his special talent under wraps. She didn't want to be harassed by the media or put Cooper in any kind of jeopardy. There were a lot of crazy people out there.

Cooper began the ritual of piling his gear by the front door. The only option Julie had was to call Myra. Maybe something was going on and they needed help.

Myra was beginning to relax when the phone in the kitchen rang. That meant it had to be one of the Sisters or someone closely affiliated with them. Her hands started to shake.

"Hold on, love—I'll get it." Charles kissed her on the top of the head and walked into the kitchen.

Myra could hear Charles's voice in the background. "Hello, Julie. How are things?" There was a minute of silence. "I see. When did this start?" More silence. At that point, Myra was by Charles's side. She had a look of panic in her eyes. Charles put his hand on her shoulder and continued to speak. "Of course. Jack is away for a couple of days. I'll ring Harry to see if he can meet you in Atlanta. Right-o. Will do." He hung up.

Myra was about to burst. "What is it?" She clutched her pearls.

"Evidently, Cooper is pacing. Julie said he pulled out his gear and piled it by the door."

"Oh, my. What do you suppose it means?" Myra was starting to shake.

"It means the old boy is on to something. Let me call Harry and make arrangements. Once Cooper gets here, maybe he can tell us."

"Don't be funny, Charles."

"Myra, darling, you know what I meant. You have been very jumpy lately."

"See—I told you I was having a bad feeling about something. Now Cooper is, too, and he's over eight hundred miles away! I'm calling Nikki." Then she remembered their phones were locked away. "I'll leave a message with the front desk. They couldn't have wandered too far."

Charles pulled up the phone number of The Tides Inn and dialed. "Good evening. Can you connect me to the Emerys' room, please?" The phone rang several times, but no one answered.

The operator returned. "I'm sorry, there's no answer. Shall I take a message?"

"Yes, please. Can you ask them to contact Myra and Charles?" Myra gave him a wide-eyed look. He punctuated his sentence with "It's important." He listened for a moment. "Yes, that would be much appreciated. Thank you." He hung up and turned to his nervous wife. "She is going to have someone check the loggia and the restaurant and hand-deliver the message."

Myra let out a long exhale. "Now, please, call Harry."

Charles pulled out his phone and hit the speed dial for Harry Wong. Harry was married to Yoko, one of the Sisters. He specialized in training law enforcement officers for the FBI and CIA. He had a love-hate relationship with Jack. The source of their complicated dynamic went way back, but they would both kill for each other. Not all that different from many brother-to-brother relationships, although they were not brothers in blood. Only in spirit.

"Harry? All good with you? Yes, it's been a while." Charles smiled at Myra. "Listen, old boy, we need you to fetch Cooper." Charles listened for a few seconds. "That's just it. We don't know what's gotten into the pooch, but Julie insists he's pacing and is ready to go." Charles was nodding his head. "Let me see if I can get Annie's plane ready. That should get you back here in time for your afternoon training session. Right-o. Will do."

He turned to Myra. "He has a training session tomorrow

afternoon. Can you get in touch with Annie so Harry can borrow the plane? That would make this a whole lot easier. Otherwise, I'd have to drive to Atlanta, and I have some important tech work to catch up with."

Myra pulled out her phone and punched in Countess Annie de Silva's number. After two rings, she answered.

"Myra? Everything all right?" Annie's voice was tense.

"Annie, I'm not sure what's going on, but we just got a call from Julie. Cooper is pacing. He piled his gear by the door. Jack and Nikki are away, and Harry's schedule is in a crunch. May he use the plane to fetch Cooper?"

"You know you never have to ask," Annie said calmly. "I'll send it down tonight. Tell Harry to be at the airport by six o'clock. That should give him plenty of time to get to Cooper and turn it around."

"Thank you, Annie." Myra's voice was still shaky.

"Myra? What is going on?" Annie knew her friend all too well. "Tell me you're not clutching your pearls."

Myra brought her hand down from her neck. "Oh, Annie, I had one of those goose-bump feelings earlier today, and now this thing with Cooper has me a bit spooked."

"I'm sure it will be fine. Maybe Cooper just needs a change of scenery." Annie was trying to soothe her friend's anxiety. Annie knew when Myra had one of her spooky feelings, something always followed. Good and bad. "Call me tomorrow. Call me anytime. Stop fretting, please."

"I'll do my best. Thank you, my friend." Myra clicked off the phone. "The plane will be back from Maine and ready to go by six o'clock tomorrow morning. Harry should be back well in time for his session."

"See? That worked out." Charles put his arms around her. "Let's not worry about something until something happens to worry about." Charles guided Myra back to the atrium, where Lady and her pups were lazily wagging their tails.

"You're going to have company," Charles said in an upbeat tone. The dogs jumped up and gave howls of approval. Yes, dogs could have a vocabulary of 200 words. "Company" was one they understood.

Charles poured Myra and himself a glass of sherry. "Come, sit. We'll wait to hear back from Nikki and Jack."

Myra sat in her favorite chair, her dogs gathered at her feet. Charles pulled a cashmere throw from a nearby bench and wrapped it around her. He rubbed both her shoulders. "Don't worry, love."

But Charles knew something was indeed afoot. It was simply a matter of time.

Chapter Ten

Darius and Eric

While in prison, Darius had spent many hours studying the mechanisms and instructions for 3D printing. A 3D printer cost about 2,000 dollars. He didn't ask why Darius wanted a printer, but Eric fronted the money. He'd deduct it from the final payout. Eric had some cash stashed somewhere. Not a lot. Just enough to get them to the next level. Tying up loose ends and then getting away.

The things Darius needed to manufacture to do the job weren't complicated. In order to fly under the radar, they knew they could not leave any kind of trail, whether it was on paper or footprints, digital or actual. They each had their agenda, and one wrong move could blow the entire operation.

Darius was almost giddy when the carton with the 3D printer arrived. A new toy. A toy to make toys with. It couldn't get better than this when it came to tinkering. He could create almost anything with that fine piece of technology. And the parts he would create were almost impossible to trace. He nodded his head as he popped the bubble wrap between the thumb and forefinger of his latex-gloved hand. This was going to be a whole barrel of fun.

He shredded the carton and all the packing materials with a Sheetrock knife and divided it into several piles, shoving the pieces into separate trash bags. Later, he would drive around town, depositing the bags in commercial dumpsters in different locations on the north, south, east, and west outskirts of town. No fingerprints, either. The plan was that they would be long gone before anyone could put it together. Timing was everything. Speaking of which, he wondered when he would get the call from the once-and-probably-still-rich pretty boy.

He turned on the local news. Nothing much to report. That was good. It meant everyone was in a more relaxed state. The past couple of years had been hellacious, whether you were incarcerated in prison or at home during the lockdown. People were bouncing off the walls. Mass shootings, drive-by shootings, stabbings. Road rage. It was crazy. For those who got caught, you prayed you didn't end up in a maximum. That meant everything from murderers, rapists, thieves, and perverts.

He considered himself fortunate to have been transferred to a medium-security facility, but he still had to watch his own back while watching someone else's back. He needed to form an alliance, and the two new dudes presented that opportunity. Then came Leroy, and things started to fall into place. Each had a goal for when they got out, and they either gained a new skill or perfected one. Compared to everyone else, they were saints. At least none of them had murdered anyone. Not yet, anyway.

Eric

Not too long before he got caught, Eric knew his luck might run out, so he made a contingency plan. He rented several storage units under his wife's maiden name. The paper-work was easy enough to fudge, and the storage facilities were more than happy to take a few years' rent upfront. In cash. He stashed $250k across five different locations through-out Los Angeles County. He also packed a set of clothes in each bag. He didn't want to look like a schlub when he got out. He needed to be better-than-normal respectable.

After his arrest, he gave his lawyer specific instructions to continue to pay the storage rental fees should he not be re-leased within the next five years. He told his lawyer it was personal stuff he didn't want his wife to know about. Attor-ney-client privilege.

Once Eric had been released from prison, he made his first stop at the Budget Car Rental in Pasadena. He didn't want his own vehicle passing through the security cameras at the storage facility. He wore the obligatory baseball cap and sun-glasses, and a fake mustache, just for the heck of it.

Pasadena was an upscale community. Very little crime. The storage company was almost as impenetrable as the prison where he'd spent a good chunk of his time. He figured out the math. Almost fifteen percent of his life had been spent behind bars. He was only in his late forties now, actu-ally closer to fifty, but he had plenty of time ahead. He had planned to retire by age fifty, so in some ways, he was still on track.

He punched the passcode into the box, and the security gate opened. He looked around. There was no one in sight. He went to the small unit and opened one lock with a key and a second with a combination. Sure, the town was safe, but he wanted to be doubly sure; hence, the double locks. Looking around, he realized he wasn't the only one who felt that way. Make it harder for the criminals. He chuckled to himself. *You're the criminal.*

He pulled the duffel bag off the only shelf in the unit. Unzipped it. Everything was exactly the way he left it. The clothes needed to go through a wash—maybe also the cash—but that was minimal in the scheme of things.

He hadn't counted on shelling out a couple grand for a 3D printer. Darius said he needed it. Eric didn't question him. He wouldn't dare. When you are in jail, you have to reassess your situation, and project future situations. This was one of those future situations. Eric didn't want to cross Darius. The guy had too much rage.

Thinking back five years, Eric recalled how much his plans had changed after meeting the other three. But it was a matter of necessity. He had to make friends, or he could easily have become mincemeat.

The inmates were rough, but not murderous. He hoped. There was a small handful of tattoo-covered good ol' boys who liked to mess with those who were a bit shorter, thinner, prettier. The thought made Eric's knees weak and his stomach turn. Nope. He didn't want to become anyone's substitute girlfriend. Eric had thought he might end up in one of those "country club" detention facilities. Nope. And what was worse, he was in with the general population. He didn't know what to expect. It could mean a bevy of bad guys. A crowd of criminals. So Bennie had served as Eric's protection. Then there was Leroy. A bit dim-witted, but not a terrible person. He never hurt anyone.

And Darius. Out of the three, Darius was the one Eric feared the most. He had the most anger. Plus, he had been in the place more than twice as long. Five years was grueling enough. Eric understood how someone could become embittered. Darius had an ax to grind. Probably several.

All Eric cared about was getting out, getting his cash, and getting the heck out of the country. He had known his time in jail was finite. He simply needed to keep his head down and work on his computer skills. He would come out with a boatload of money and then disappear into the sunset. There was no time for bitterness. He was on the move. The only sketchy part was relying on Leroy to follow instructions. It was unclear what Darius's ultimate plans were, but Eric knew they couldn't be anything close to benevolent.

Eric locked up the unit and returned the rental car. He drove his car to a second car-rental company so he could go to another storage unit and pick up more cash. He'd already gone through half of the $50k from the first bag. Eric knew Leroy needed to hotfoot it to the island, which meant new identities had to be formed.

Before he got arrested, Eric had already created a false identity for himself. He searched through public records for someone no one would look for and requested a copy of Gregory Masters's birth certificate. That would be his new name when he got out of jail. At some point, he would need fake IDs made for himself. Now he needed them for three others.

He searched along the same vein as he had for himself in the past. It took several hours, but he came upon several wards of various states. Once Eric got the basic information, he would arrange for the fake passports and driver's licenses.

Eric pulled out Julio's mother's address. He would meet up with her in about two hours. Once he got the package of new identities, he'd send it with the debit cards to Bennie, who would then forward it to Darius and Leroy.

Chapter Eleven

Pinewood

Charles waited until Myra was fast asleep. He crept toward the kitchen and then down the concrete steps that lead to their mission control center. The Sisters would joke about calling it that, but for all intents and purposes, it was their control center. It was packed with the most up-to-date, state-of-the-art technology: computers, scanners, high-definition monitors. And the computers were equipped with everything that was also available to the CIA and FBI. Well, almost. Sometimes Charles and Fergus would seek outside help from their former colleagues, who were usually more than willing to lend a hand.

Charles listened to make sure Myra hadn't followed him. He pulled out one of the anonymous cell phones and dialed.

A groggy *hello* answered.

"Sorry to bother you, old chap, but I think something is afoot." Charles spoke in a whisper.

"Eh? What's the matter?" Fergus's voice began to sound normal.

"I really can't say," Charles sputtered.

"Can't or won't?" Fergus was wide awake now.

"Can't as in that I *don't* know, but Myra is in one of her foreboding moods."

Fergus tried to stifle a chuckle. "Surely that can't be all of it. You wouldn't be calling me at this hour babbling as if you lost the plot."

"Precisely." Charles let out a half-growl, half-moan. "It's Cooper."

"Cooper? The dog?" Fergus was surely confused at this point.

"Yes, as in canine."

"So what of it?"

"Didn't you think it odd that we asked to use the Gulf-stream pronto?"

"Well, I suppose. But I didn't have many details. Annie said Harry needed to pick something up in Atlanta. I surmised it had something to do with his job. You mean to tell me he is picking up Cooper?"

"Yes. As in now." Charles realized he had been raising his voice. He stopped for a moment and listened, hoping he hadn't awakened Myra. Fortunately, Lady and her pups were snuggled together, and none had even picked up their heads when Charles tiptoed past them. "Listen, mate. When Myra is clinging to her pearls, and a dog with remarkable and uncanny abilities starts pacing at the same time, eight hundred miles apart, well, I don't need to tell you, as puzzling as it is, we need to stand by and pay attention." Charles paused again to steady his voice. "To make matters worse, or perhaps it's just a bizarre coincidence, my laptop is getting a bit wonky."

"As in how?" Fergus pressed.

"There is a delay. It's ever so slight, but you know how your systems work, and when they do something out of the ordinary, however slight, you cannot help but notice."

Fergus remained silent.

"Are you still with me, old chap?" Charles asked.

Fergus hesitated. "Now that you mention it, I went online this morning to check the weather forecast, and I thought there was something . . . off. Can't quite put my finger on it."

"Fergus, we have the highest-rated security systems in place. But I wonder if we could have been hacked somehow." Charles had deep concern in his voice.

"Well, it is possible. Highly unlikely, but possible." Fergus paused. "Let me check Annie's computer. She doesn't use it very often, but hang on a sec." Fergus went to get Annie's laptop. It was in the same place, under the same scarf, since they had arrived a few days before. He powered it up. "The only thing on my end is I wouldn't know the difference on hers, and I hesitate to bother her. She was planning on finishing reading a novel she started. I was too knackered to stay up." He heard footsteps coming in his direction. "Here she comes now."

Charles winced. He didn't want to get Annie involved, not just yet. Because that would mean getting Myra involved, and she was already nervous.

"Who are you talking to, darlin'?" Annie entered the room. "And what are you doing with my laptop?" She came around to Fergus's side of the bed.

"It's Charles." Fergus remained unruffled.

"At this hour?" Annie pulled the phone from Fergus's grip. "Charles? Everything all right?" Annie asked sweetly.

"Annie. Dear. Yes, everything is fine." Charles was very good at concocting stories instantaneously. It harkened back to his days working for MI6. "Myra was talking about some photos she couldn't find. I was hoping you might have copies on your computer. I want to surprise her." *Brilliant.*

"Probably. Photos from where?" Annie asked.

"She said they were from the last trip you went on together." Charles's brain was in overdrive trying to recall the last time the two women traveled together. Then he thought about Charlotte in London. "When you were in London."

"That was several trips ago," Annie replied.

"Yes, you're correct. She said the last trip you took to see Charlotte." Charles sounded convincing.

"Let me give a look." She motioned for Fergus to hand her the laptop, and she handed the phone back to him.

"So's that all you need?" Fergus asked plainly.

"Right." Charles knew the conversation would have to come to an end to avoid any suspicion from Annie. "I'll give you a shout tomorrow morning after Cooper arrives."

"Right-o." Fergus pushed the red button and disconnected the call.

"What was that all about?" Annie looked up over the computer screen.

"Charles wants to surprise Myra with some photos. I can't really say what else." And he really couldn't. Just like Charles couldn't. "Maybe they're bored without us. Maybe Myra is putting a photo album together." Fergus shrugged. He knew he had become part of a ruse. He just didn't know how deep, how wide, and for how long.

Charles was trying to quell his frustration. He would have to wait another eight hours before he could discuss anything with Fergus. That is, if he actually had anything to discuss. He consoled himself knowing Cooper would arrive in the morning. That should give this riddle a clue. Or perhaps result in more riddles.

Charles looked around at all the electronic equipment that covered the walls, including huge screens where any map or photo could be projected. It rivaled the War Room at the

Pentagon. But even the United States government got hacked. The State Department and, ironically, the Department of Homeland Security—the department that oversaw cybersecurity. He thought again. More than ironic, it was horrifying. He took some comfort knowing he had the best people on his team. It was the *other* teams that posed a threat. Threats that no one knew about. New versions of wars and disruptions that they rarely saw coming. Charles shook his head. The world had gone mad.

He powered up the system, each monitor coming to life, each with its own special functionality. This way, if one system went down, it wasn't the entire system. Charles noticed one of them had a slight delay. It was the one connected to the server for their VPN, virtual private network, only accessible to the Sisters and their male counterparts. In theory, it was impervious to hacking. But nothing truly was.

Charles began a security scan, which would take up to a few hours. He decided to let the scan run, and he would return upstairs and pour himself two fingers' worth of Highland Park eighteen-year-old scotch. He settled into one of the big, overstuffed chairs in the farmhouse living room, stepping over the piled-up pups. He, too, was beginning to think something quite devious was about to go into play. But what? He finished off the single malt and carried the glass into the kitchen. He thought he would go downstairs one more time to check the scan. When he reached the bottom of the stairs, he was stunned to see the screen had gone dark. He pressed a few buttons on the large control panel. Nothing. He tried to reboot it. Still nothing.

He didn't want to alarm anyone at that late hour, but he felt it necessary to tell them to avoid using the network and only send text messages through their burner phones. He debated whether or not to wake Myra. It would only cause her more worry. He began to type into the phone:

Please do not use the VPN for any reason. Text only but not until tomorrow AFTER 8:00 AM.

He checked his watch. It was slightly before midnight. They would all check the time it was sent.

He made his way back to the bedroom, where Myra was still asleep. He curled into bed and tucked himself behind her like a spoon.

Chapter Twelve

The Next Day

It was early in the morning. Darius sat in the passenger seat as Leroy drove to The Tides Inn. They circled back to the rear area near the employee entrance and parking lot. It was also where the valets parked guests' cars. He looked at the scribbled, misspelled note, a la Leroy:

Silver Range Rover, Verginia Plate with United We Stand

One would think he would know how to spell his home state correctly. When Darius pointed it out to him, his excuse was he had been driving at the time. He didn't want to stop in case anyone saw him. Darius could at least buy that logic.

Leroy pulled in front of the Range Rover to block anyone's view of it. Darius hopped out of the truck and ducked behind the car. It had been less than three minutes when he jumped back into the cab, scaring the bejeezus out of Leroy. He managed to gulp back a squeal. Darius rolled his eyes. This was going to be the longest week of his life. "Let's move," he grumbled. With that, Leroy pulled out of the parking lot.

Nikki and Jack planned to have breakfast in their room and then take a drive along the shore. Nikki emerged from the bedroom wearing a pair of red capri pants, a white jersey T-shirt, white pull-on Top-Siders, and a wide-brimmed straw hat with a matching straw bag.

"You look absolutely stunning." Jack beamed. "I seriously married up."

Nikki flashed a smile. "And don't you forget it, either." She popped on a pair of white sunglasses.

Jack phoned ahead to the valet, asking if they could bring the car around, but he wasn't available. When they reached the lobby, Jack asked the doorman if he could get the keys and they would fetch the car themselves. He turned to Nikki. "I want to check the Eagle Room for a sec. See what kind of vintage bourbon they have. I want to bring home a bottle for Charles."

"Okay. I'll meet you in the car." Jack handed Nikki the keys, and she turned and exited through the lobby. She was within arm's reach of the vehicle when she pushed the button for the trunk.

The explosion rocked the building. Pieces of metal flew through the air. Flames shot out of the wreckage, lapping at the fringe of what was once a straw hat. Nikki's body lay crumpled on the ground.

Pandemonium broke out in front of the hotel. People were running to and from the scene. Jack was one of the first. He ran to Nikki's side. He checked her pulse. It was barely there. He reached for his cell phone, then remembered it was locked in the safe in their room. "Somebody call 911!" he screamed in horror. Staff and guests huddled in the driveway, shouting questions at each other.

"What happened?'

"Did anyone see anything?"

"Did someone call the police?"

Jack gingerly took his wife's hand. He didn't want to cause any more harm. For one of the very few—if ever—times in his life, he felt utterly helpless.

Darius and Leroy were a block away when they heard the explosion. Leroy jumped out of his seat.

"What in the Sam Hill was that?"

Darius had an evil smile on his face. It gave Leroy the willies.

Jack rode in the ambulance with Nikki, trying to answer the questions being thrown at him. He stared down at his wife's tattered clothes, burn marks on her arms, and an oxygen mask on her face. The paramedics were calmly hurrying to give her fluids, take her vitals, and stop the bleeding from the lacerations caused by flying metal. Jack took Nikki's hand and leaned as close as he could without compromising her. "You are going to be okay. You have to be. You are my everything." He could swear she squeezed his hand, but then he noticed both her hands were trembling.

"Her body is in shock," one of the EMS technicians told Jack. He lifted one of her eyelids and shined a light. He then checked the other. "Her vitals are weak, but not dangerously so. Her respiratory system is stressed. The oxygen will help. They are going to run a CT scan on her as soon as we bring her in."

Jack knew what that meant. Possible brain injury. "Do you think she suffered a concussion?" He also knew there was an obvious answer.

"Any type of concussive incident can create a number of issues on the human body." That was cover-your-ass speak for *I'm not making any kind of diagnosis here, pal.*

As a former prosecutor, Jack was very familiar with dancing around a question. "Understood."

Realizing he didn't have his phone, he asked one of the medics if he could use theirs. He had to call Myra and Charles. He dreaded it.

Jack knew that Myra's daughter Barbara and her unborn child had been killed, and the driver had gotten off on diplomatic immunity. Myra had fallen into a pit of darkness for months. Nikki told Jack stories about how both she and Charles tried everything to help pull her out of her depression. She was despondent. It wasn't until Myra saw a newscast on television that her spell was broken. It was about a woman who had been raped, and the men went free because of some technicality. It breathed new life into Myra. If she had her way, those who were guilty would pay. Such was the beginning of the Sisterhood. Bringing women together to right a wrong. Jack feared that the news about Nikki would send Myra back to that dark place.

Jack decided to dial Charles first. Better to have someone there who could help steady Myra. Jack could taste bile coming up the back of his throat. He wondered if Charles would even answer a call from a number he didn't recognize. "What's the caller ID on this?" Jack asked the medic.

"Irvington EMS."

Charles would definitely answer. The phone rang twice.

"To whom am I speaking?" Charles's deep British accent was in full force.

"Charles. It's Jack." He took a gulp of air. "There's been an accident. It's Nikki."

"How bad is it?" Charles stiffened.

"They don't know yet. Her vitals are weak, but stable. It's her head they're worried about."

"What in blazes happened?" Charles was still calm, but not for long. At this point, Myra was standing next to Charles. She was almost choking herself with her pearls.

"What is it?" There was panic in Myra's voice. Charles put his arm around her. He continued to listen as Jack conveyed the few details he knew. Nikki went to the car two minutes ahead of him, and it exploded just before she got in. It threw her onto the ground. They were in the ambulance now. Her vitals were weak, but stable. They would run tests. Jack omitted the part where she was mentally unresponsive. He hoped there would be good news after the tests, so why burden Myra with more troubling news now?

Jack could hear the screeches coming from Myra as Charles was explaining the situation to her. It was chilling. "Charles, I'll call you as soon as I have more news. We're pulling into the hospital now." Jack continued to hold Nikki's hand as they removed her from the ambulance.

It was chaos outside the emergency room doors. The news of an explosion spread like wildfire. A crowd of reporters had already gathered, shooting off questions. Two police officers were on the scene, keeping the group away from the entrance. They kept repeating the same answer: The only thing they knew was that it wasn't a typical auto accident. There was an explosion. The nature of the incident was not yet known.

As they wheeled Nikki into the hospital, people were firing questions at Jack. His first instinct was to tell everyone to bugger off. Instead, he held up his hands and announced, "People. Please give me a moment to speak with the doctor, and I will answer your questions to the best of my ability. Please excuse me." One of the deputies cleared the path of onlookers and reporters and brought Jack to the area where they were prepping Nikki for tests.

One of the doctors approached Jack. "Mr. Emery?"

"Yes."

"I'm Dr. Pecora. The explosion threw her backwards, and your wife suffered several head injuries. We are going to run a series of tests."

"Is she conscious?" Jack held his breath.

"I'm afraid not. But that can be temporary. Let's see what the results are, and then we can discuss her diagnosis and prognosis." The doctor put his hand on Jack's shoulder. "She seems like a strong young woman. Stay positive." He held out his hands and clasped Jack's with both of his. "We are going to do our very best for Nikki, and if we can't, we'll find someone who can."

Just hearing the doctor speak her name made Jack woozy. It was his Nikki being wheeled into the depths of the hospital to be zapped and scrutinized. It had been a while since he actually prayed.

In Pinewood, Myra was writhing on the floor, screaming. Charles kneeled down to comfort her, even if it meant her beating him with her fists. She shrieked and continued to pound him until she was spent.

Leroy pulled to the side of the road and waited as the fire engines screamed past them. Darius couldn't contain his glee. "Ha. That'll teach 'em."

Leroy was befuddled. "Teach who what?"

Darius rolled his eyes. "What do you think that was, a Fourth of July celebration?"

"You mean it was a bomb?" Leroy's eyes were bugging out. His hands started trembling. He thought Darius was planting a GPS tracking device under the car. Not a gosh-durned bomb!

"Just drive." Darius folded his arms and leaned into the back of the seat. As they made their way to their motel, they stopped for a couple of sub sandwiches.

When they got back to the room, the first thing Darius did was turn on the television. He was excited, anticipating the news.

"Do you think they'll have a special news report?" Leroy

chomped into the onion-filled hoagie made with bologna, American cheese, ham, hot peppers, ketchup, and mayo.

Even with his iron will and stomach, Darius was wincing as he watched his partner in crime wolf down the smelly, gross mess.

Darius checked the cheap tabletop clock on the end table. "Maybe." Darius smiled to himself. He didn't know if the media in Irvington was quick enough, or if they even had media. He doubted they had their own television stations. He sat back and picked up the equally cheap remote. He clicked on the TV. So far, it was the usual national shows— *Today, Good Morning America.* Then there was *Good Morning Virginia.* He focused on that one. It was local enough. Just as the clock was about to hit nine, a beeping sound came over the air.

"We interrupt this program to bring you this breaking news. A car exploded in front of the historic The Tides Inn. The cause of the explosion is not yet known. A spokesperson from the hotel said that one woman was injured and rushed to the hospital. No names have been released. We hope to have more details at the noon hour."

Darius sprung up from his chair, the sub sandwiches toppling to the floor. "Did they say a woman?" His eyes were bugging out.

Leroy licked some of the ketchup from his lips. "Yep. I think so."

Darius tried several buttons on the remote, hoping one would be rewind. No such luck. He let out a growl that would rival a grizzly bear's and began to pace the floor.

"I don't get it." Leroy had a stupefied look on his face. More stupefied than usual.

"Damnation! It was supposed to go off when *he* got in the car." The piece he constructed had consisted of a switch, steel wool, and a 9-volt battery. It was set to detonate when there was a vibration. He hadn't counted on someone popping the trunk. Everything had been carefully fabricated with no paper trail, well-planned and executed, except the execution itself. Darius knew she might be collateral damage, but *she* wasn't the target. He was furious. "It was supposed to be for him." He kicked the dilapidated chair in the corner, turning it into a pile of splinters.

"Holy cow! I didn't know you were going to kill somebody!" Leroy had raw onion stuck to his chin stubble. His eyes were watering. "Holy cow," he repeated. Leroy might not be playing with a full deck, but he had enough sense to know he was now an accomplice. He kept shaking his head. "Oh, mercy me. Now what?"

"We move on. We don't have time for a do-over for this one. But I will have some comfort if she dies. He'll still suffer." Darius stuck a toothpick into his mouth and began to chew, working on the next plan.

"But what if they find out it was us? We need to get out of here!" Leroy was becoming a little unglued. This was not what he signed up for. But now he was in it big-time. His only consolation was the money, and under the circumstances, it had to happen pronto. "So when do you think we'll get some money?" Leroy finally wiped his lunch off his face.

"I have to call him later." Darius never shared his ultimate goal with Eric or the rest of them, and Eric didn't want to know anyone else's plans, either. It was an exchange of money for services rendered. What they did with the money was up to them, although Eric suspected Darius had some kind of revenge planned.

But Darius wasn't finished producing more bodily harm. He was focused on the people who put him in the concrete palace. Like his ex-girlfriend. She dropped him like a hot potato after his arrest. Didn't he do all of this for her? She was on the list. Thanks to technology, they were able to locate her after fourteen years. She was married and had moved to Austin. Now all they had to do was get details. Eric and Bennie were on it. Darius liked Austin. Too bad he'd be in and out in a few hours. But first, he'd deal with his former lawyer. A public defender. Probably graduated at the bottom of his class. Didn't even try to make a deal on Darius's behalf. And wasn't that what lawyers were supposed to do?

Darius wasn't sure what he was going to do in the long run. For the short term, he was heading to a small town on the Gulf and taking a boat to Mexico. Growing up on a ranch in Texas made him almost fluent in Spanish. Enough to get his ideas across, and enough to understand most. He was still in good shape, thanks to the great workout equipment they provided in jail. Eric had promised them all $50k, which would buy him plenty of time to find work. He'd figure it out when he got there. The main thing was to get out of where he was now.

Leroy had no interest in revenge. Not in the usual sense. His idea of revenge was showing off a Winnebago to his cousins and making them jealous. Yep, that sayin' was true: *Living well is the best revenge.* Leroy heard an actor say that in a movie. Leroy's idea of living well was living in a vehicle and being able to drive anywhere he pleased. Leroy would be the courier, like in *Mission: Impossible. Or was it one of them Jason Bourne movies?* he wondered.

Bennie's participation was to help coordinate their plans without leaving any traces. It was as if he were orchestrating a silent symphony. It was rather exciting. Pulling strings. And for his efforts in and out of jail, he, too, would receive a sum of cash. His plan for the money was to start over somewhere with people less perverted than he was. A midsize city, maybe in the Carolinas. No one would know who he was. He would use the new false ID Eric arranged for him. He would live anonymously in a small city with a million people. Technically, he was supposed to register wherever he lived. But who would know he moved? No one in his family spoke to him. None of his friends wanted anything to do with him. He could start over. His own version of a witness protection program. People didn't take kindly to perverts. His only saving grace was that he never touched anyone. But what he had done was creepy, nonetheless.

Eric's plan was simple. Once the funds were transferred and verified, he would work his way south to Ecuador. Specifically, to Cuenca, the third largest city, with a population just under half a million. It had several universities, where he could blend in with his chino pants and button-down shirts. His plan was to wire money for a large one-bedroom flat he'd found on the second floor of a private home within walking distance of the main town. He would tell them he was a writer. Not a real stretch. After all, he'd made up one heck of a hedge fund story.

Now he was just waiting to hear from Darius and Leroy before moving on to the next step.

Chapter Thirteen

Pinewood

Charles lifted Myra from the floor and helped her to the atrium. She was trembling uncontrollably. He poured some of the same whiskey he had the night before. He knew it was still early, but Myra needed something to steady her nerves, even if it meant simply focusing on holding the glass. With all the upheaval, Charles forgot Cooper was about to arrive. He remembered as soon as he heard the familiar bark. "Myra, my love, Cooper is here with Harry. Let me go fetch them." He patted her on the knee and kissed her on the forehead.

Charles opened the door. He couldn't hide his concern from Harry.

"Charles? Everything okay?"

Cooper brushed past them and headed straight over to Myra and put his head on her lap.

"It's Nikki. There's been some kind of accident. Jack said the car exploded," Charles explained.

Harry's eyes went wide. "What? How is she? Where are they?"

"Irvington. Jack surprised her with a long weekend at The Tides Inn." Charles motioned for Harry to follow him inside. "I was just in the process of calling Annie and Fergus."

"I have a little time. What can I do to help?" Harry walked into the atrium and gave Myra a hug. She looked up and gave him a weary smile, tears running down her cheeks.

Charles nodded in the direction of the kitchen. He walked over to Myra. "Love, I'm going downstairs to contact everyone."

She blinked several times. Charles wondered if she was in shock and decided one of the calls he made should be to Dr. Falcon.

Charles hurried down the stairs, with Harry following him.

"Will she be all right up there alone?" Harry asked.

"She has Cooper. He's smarter than both of us." Charles smiled for the first time since receiving Jack's call.

"Speaking of Cooper, why the rush to get him here?" Harry asked.

"Ask Cooper. Evidently, he was pacing, and he pulled his gear from the closet like he usually does and plopped it at their front door. Julie called, and here he is." Charles stopped suddenly. "And Myra was having some bad juju feelings."

"She's never been wrong," Harry recalled.

"Indeed. I also have another issue I need help with, but let's get the texts rolling."

"Why don't you do a group call?" Harry was confused as to why Charles chose texting rather than their usual means of communicating.

"That's the other issue I am going to have to deal with." Charles shook his head, and he punched in Fergus's number.

"What's up, mate?" Fergus was much more awake than he was the night before.

"There's been some kind of accident. Nikki is in the hospital, and we don't know what her status is except she is stable." Charles rushed out as much information as he had.

"As soon as the plane gets here, we'll turn it around and come home," Fergus promised.

"Thanks, mate. Myra could use Annie right now."

"I'll get things sorted on my end. We'll see you later today. Keep me posted on Nikki's progress."

Both men clicked off at the same time. In the meantime, Harry wrote a group text to the list of Sisters in his speed dial:

There's been an accident. Nikki is in the hospital in Irvington, Virginia. She's stable but that's all we know for now. They're running tests. Jack is at the hospital. I'll text when I know more. Stand by.

Before Harry hit *send*, he asked Charles, "Do you want them to come here?"

"Not yet. Not until we know more." Charles took in a deep breath. He dialed Dr. Falcon's number next and explained what little he knew, including that he feared Myra was going into shock. The good doctor told Charles he would be there within the next half hour.

As they were about to head back up the stairs, Charles snapped his fingers. "Can you see if you can get Abner on the phone? I suspect something is amiss with our VPN."

"You sure do have your hands full." Harry gave Charles a hefty pat on the shoulder. "Whatever you need, you know you can count on us."

"Thanks, mate."

When they got back to the atrium, Myra was sitting up tall and looked quite lucid. She stared at Charles. "I told you."

"Yes, you did." Charles took her hand. "I didn't doubt you, my love. I simply didn't want you to worry until something really happened."

"Well, now it has." Myra wiped a tear with her sleeve. "I want to see her."

"Right now, she's at Rappahannock General. It's a three-hour drive. Let's wait a bit. At least until we know something. They may have to transfer her to a different hospital. Please, Myra, try to stay calm. Think good thoughts. Dr. Falcon will be here shortly."

Harry stood in the kitchen, trying to answer all the text messages that were bombarding his phone. Isabelle, Yoko, Kathryn, and Alexis, the other members of the Sisterhood, were all frantically responding to Harry's text:

"What?"

"What happened? Where is she?"

"What about Jack? Is he all right?"

"Where's Myra? Charles?"

"Are Annie and Fergus with them?"

"Should we come?"

Harry typed back:

Rappahannock Hospital. Jack is okay. He's with her. Waiting for tests. I'm with Myra and Charles now. Cooper is here. Will let you know when we know.

He walked back to the atrium and gave Charles a look that said, "Uh, boy . . ."

Several minutes later, the doorbell rang. It was Dr. Falcon.

"Thanks for coming so quickly." Charles ushered him into the atrium. and explained what had happened, concluding with, "We're waiting for test results."

Dr. Falcon approached Myra. "Hello, Myra. I heard you had some disturbing news this morning. I can assure you, the doctors at Rappahannock are top-notch, even if it's a rural community. Who wouldn't want to live on the bay?" He was trying to get her to ease up with some casual banter. As casual as one could be, knowing your patient had just received devastating news. "I'm going to take your blood pressure. Is that all right?"

Myra nodded. The doctor wrapped her wrist with a new device that no longer required pumping or using a stethoscope. Her blood pressure was 140 over 90.

"It's elevated, but that's not a surprise," the doctor stated.

Myra finally spoke. "It's the not knowing. I can't stand it."

"Yes, it's normal to feel the way you do," Dr. Falcon said in his most kindly manner. "How about I give you something to help calm your nerves?"

"No!" Myra shouted. "I want to be compos mentis when we hear from Jack."

"This isn't going to knock you unconscious. Just calm you a bit." Dr. Falcon turned to seek help from Charles. He nodded at the glass of scotch Myra was still clutching in her hand.

Charles took the glass and noticed she hadn't had any of it. He shook his head, indicating to the doctor that Myra hadn't consumed any alcohol. "What is it you want to give her?" Charles asked.

"Half a milligram of Xanax. It's an anti-anxiety drug," Dr. Falcon explained. "Most people can function normally with that dose, although I wouldn't recommend driving a car or one of your souped-up golf carts." He gave a slight smile and looked at Myra straight on.

"Myra, I promise you, this will make you feel a bit better. You won't be trembling. Your mind will be more at ease. You'll be able to think more clearly, even though it's an anti-anxiety drug. It's not a narcotic."

Myra took in a long, deep breath. "Well, I don't have anything else to do." She rolled up her sleeve.

"We don't even have to do that." The doctor smiled. "Charles, can you get us a glass of water, please?"

Charles dashed into the kitchen and returned with a pitcher and two glasses. "I didn't know if you wanted one as well," he explained.

Dr. Falcon tapped out a pill from a prescription bottle. "Here," he said to Myra, "take this now. You should feel a bit less stressed in about twenty minutes." He handed the bottle to Charles. "There are two more in there if she needs them tonight or tomorrow."

"Thanks, mate." Charles put the bottle on the buffet, hoping it wouldn't be needed again.

"I have to get going." Dr. Falcon stood and packed his bag. "I'll check in with you later. Keep me posted on Nikki's condition, and if there is anything I can do, please do not hesitate to call me."

"Right-o." Charles shook the doctor's hand. "Thanks again." He walked Dr. Falcon to the door. Cooper went back to his previous position, with his head on Myra's lap. Lady and her pups were still at her feet.

Charles motioned for the dogs to move as he helped Myra to the sofa. He propped a few pillows behind her head and wrapped a blanket around her. He kissed her on the forehead. "It's going to be okay. Try to get some rest." The dogs repositioned themselves, as if they were guarding a precious gem. And they were.

Charles went into the kitchen, where Harry was still fielding text messages from the Sisters. "Listen," Charles said, "I am having some issues with the VPN. I need to get Abner here ASAP."

"He's out of the country right now. What about Izzie? She's really a good substitute."

"Yes, she is, but I don't know what I'm dealing with yet. I need someone who knows our system inside and out."

"Let me check with Izzie and see if she can contact Abner." Harry sent off a text to Isabelle.

The kitchen phone rang. Charles jumped to answer it. "Yes?"

"Charles, it's Jack." He was calling from one of the hospital phones. He could barely speak. "She's suffered a severe brain injury and is in a coma. The good news is that she can still breathe on her own. They said it's a good sign." Jack's voice was quivering.

"Jackson University Hospital in Philadelphia is one of the best neuroscience facilities in the country. Do you think she would be able to be moved there?"

"I . . . I don't know." Jack was on shaky ground. "The doctor is going to meet me in a few minutes, after his rounds. I'll discuss it with him and get back to you. How is Myra?"

"Quite upset, but Dr. Falcon gave her something to calm her nerves. Jack? It's going to be okay. Let's all think positively."

"Right." Jack sighed. "I'll be in touch."

Charles hung up the phone. He was hesitant to say anything to Myra just yet. If the doctors thought it was feasible to move Nikki, then Charles would arrange everything and then let Myra know. He peeked into the atrium and saw she was dozing. He then turned to Harry. "Any word from Izzie?"

"There was a colleague of Abner's in school. She works for the DOD on highly classified projects. He recommended we get in touch with her. Coincidently, she, too, suffered a coma and memory loss. Some kind of accident. But she's good to go. Her real name is Libby Gannon."

"What do you mean, 'her real name'?" Charles quizzed him.

"Izzie didn't get into it, but Abner swears by Libby's techno-talent. He's going to send an intro text to both of you."

"If Abner thinks she's top-notch, well, that's good enough for me." He paused for a moment. "But that is an odd coincidence, don't you think? That she was also once in a coma?"

"Not for this group." Harry smiled.

Charles chuckled for the first time that day.

A few minutes later, the kitchen phone rang again. It was Jack. "Charles. The doctor said she is stable enough to be medevacked."

"Splendid." Charles felt a sense of relief. They were moving in the right direction. "Get me all the information, and I'll arrange for transport."

"Thanks, Charles. I don't know what we would do without you and Myra." Jack's voice cracked.

"Likewise, Jack." Charles hung up the phone and explained to Harry they were going to arrange for Nikki to be taken to Philadelphia.

"What do you want to do about the computer issue?" Harry asked.

"I'll reach out to Libby as soon as I get Abner's text. First thing is to get Nikki's transport settled."

Harry checked his watch. "I have to get going. Let me know if there is anything else any of us can do."

Charles walked Harry to the door. "Thanks for everything."

"Anything. Anytime. Anywhere." They shared their first fist bump in a long time.

About an hour later, Charles received another call from Jack, with specific instructions as to where and when the helicopter should arrive. The transport would be later that day. Jack would ride with Nikki and the medics in the chopper. Charles and Myra would drive to Philadelphia and meet them at the hospital. Depending on when Annie and Fergus returned, they would accompany them.

Charles walked softly over to where Myra was sleeping.

He gently touched her shoulder. She immediately sprang up, dogs tumbling over each other.

"What is it?" Her voice was frantic.

"They are going to transport Nikki later this afternoon. They're taking her to Jackson University Hospital in Philadelphia. We'll meet them there."

"How is she?" Myra clenched the tissue she was holding.

"She has a traumatic brain injury." He hurriedly added, "But she is breathing on her own. That's a good sign." Charles put his arm around her. "We're sending her to one of the best neurological institutes in the country."

Myra sat up and looked Charles straight in the eye. "How bad is it?" She was steeling herself for the worst.

Charles let out a sigh. "She's in a coma. They don't know how long it will last. They are going to be testing her constantly and recommending treatments. It's going to be a waiting game, I'm afraid."

Myra took Charles's hand and squeezed it tightly. "I cannot lose another child, Charles. I just can't."

"There, there, now. She is going to be okay."

"You don't know that. You can't promise that!" Myra was agitated from fear and frustration.

"My dear, all we can do is pray and stay positive. Think good thoughts. I know it's difficult, but what other choice do we have?" Charles was certainly not about to divulge his concern about the VPN. That could push Myra over the edge. It was best to keep that from her for as long as possible. Nikki was the number-one concern right now. But maintaining security could not be overlooked. He would get Fergus on it as soon as he could. As soon as he heard from Libby Gannon.

Myra sniffed and stared ahead. "Do we have any soup?"

Charles did a double take. "Soup? Did you just ask me for *soup*?"

"Do you have a better idea?" She squeezed his hand again. He kissed her on the cheek. "That's my girl. Come." He hoisted her off the sofa. They linked arms and went into the kitchen with the pack of dogs following, Cooper in the rear. He had their backs.

Chapter Fourteen

Virginia

Leroy and Darius stared at the TV. It was true. A woman had been approaching the car when it exploded, sending her backwards. She was in stable condition. Names were being withheld for now.

Darius stifled the urge to punch the wall. The explosion hit the wrong mark. Nothing he could do about that now. His cell phone buzzed. It was Bennie. Bennie, the guy who made all the arrangements.

"Hey, man. How's it goin'?" Darius asked. He nodded. "Us? I took care of some business." He kept his cool with Bennie. He didn't want any of them to know what he was up to. Unfortunately, Leroy was not only a witness; he was also now an accomplice. But better Leroy than Bennie or Eric. Neither of them would let Darius push them around like he did Leroy. If Eric knew what the 3D printer was going to be used for, he probably wouldn't have fronted the money.

Darius snapped his fingers at Leroy, indicating he wanted the pad and pen sitting on the wobbly table. Leroy jumped and handed them to Darius. Leroy might seem like he was oblivious, but Darius's mood could not be ignored. Leroy was keenly aware the man he was sitting with was a ticking time bomb. The word *bomb* sent shivers up his spine.

Darius proceeded to write down information. "Got it. Yep. Uh-huh. Will do." He listened for another minute. "Okay, man. We're on it."

Leroy's excitement was like that of a kid about to go on an adventure. He was bouncing up and down on the bed. "Whaddhesay? Whaddhesay?"

"Easy, man." Darius looked at the instructions. "Tonight, we drive to D.C. We're staying at a motel near the airport. Tomorrow, we go to the DHL counter, where an envelope will be waiting for us. Inside will be passports, driver's licenses, your airline ticket, a hotel reservation, and a letter of introduction. You're to get on a plane to Grand Cayman Island. You'll check into The Hideaway."

"Wait! The place is called The Hideaway? For real?" Leroy's imagination was running wild. He felt like James Bond.

Darius continued. "You will go to Cayman National Bank and give them the letter that will be in the envelope. It will instruct them to transfer the funds to Banco de Guayaquil."

"But . . . but I don't speak Cayman!" Leroy was getting nervous.

"They speak English, you twit." Darius continued. "Once the transfer is done, they will give you a letter of confirmation and will send a copy electronically to Eric. Once you get the letter, you get back on a plane and come home."

Darius copied the list of instructions onto another sheet of paper. He didn't want to worry about someone, namely Leroy, losing the list. Darius handed it over to him.

"Let's go over this again," Darius instructed. "Oh, and we'll have to pick up some kind of better clothes for you. You can't go looking like that."

Leroy ruffled his hair. "Like what?"

"Like a hick who just got out of jail."

"Huh." Leroy slumped his shoulders.

The week before, Eric and Bennie had arranged for everyone to get 3,000 dollars cash for supplies, food, clothes. Eric had also arranged for new passports and driver's licenses. During his stay behind bars, Bennie became acquainted with a gentleman named Julio, who was locked up for forgery. Bennie and Eric cut a deal with him. Once Eric got out, he would be put in contact with an associate of Julio's. Eric had to personally deliver the cash to Julio's mother in San Pedro. Then Julio's associate would arrange for the new identities, to the tune of 8,000 dollars.

"So what are you going to be doing while I'm in the Caribbean?" Leroy asked.

"You won't be gone more than a day, day and a half." Darius pulled out a cigarette. He had quit many times before, but now he needed an outlet for his nervous energy.

"I thought you gave those up?" Leroy asked.

"I did." He lit the end of the Lucky Strike.

Leroy snickered. "I like your brand. Luck-ee Strikes! Don't they call that some kind of omen or something?"

"Maybe. I suppose." Darius took a long pull. As soon as Eric and Bennie had the coordinates, he was going to track down the half-baked lawyer who had represented him. This time, he would hit his mark. Then he would take care of his ex-girlfriend. She had dumped him the second he got arrested—and he had been doing it all for her. Every time he thought about it, his blood would boil, even after fifteen years.

"Come on. Let's pack it up. We gotta three-hour drive, and we gotta get you some clothes."

Leroy was atwitter. This was probably the most exciting thing he had ever done in his life. Not probably—it *was* the most exciting thing. He tossed the few clothes he'd brought into a brown shopping bag.

"That, too, has got to go." Darius looked at the pathetic thing that Leroy was using as a suitcase.

"What?" Leroy looked confused.

"The big brown bag luggage. We'll get you a carry-on. There has to be a Target or Walmart on the way. Come on." Darius zipped his duffel bag shut and hauled it over his shoulder.

Darius got in his vehicle, and Leroy followed. It was going to be a bit challenging keeping two vehicles in sync. They'd have to keep a good eye on each other. They took Route 17 to Fredericksburg and got on the interstate. Darius dialed Leroy's cell to let him know he was going to take the next exit, where it looked like there might be one of the big box stores nearby. They both needed gas, and after stopping, they asked the attendant for directions. Once they filled their tanks, they drove another mile and came to a Target. They parked their vehicles far enough away from the main entrance. Both donned baseball caps and sunglasses. They were wearing jeans and T-shirts emblazoned with obscure band logos.

Darius grabbed a cart and proceeded to blend in with the rest of the shoppers. They stopped in the men's department first and picked out two pairs of trousers, two shirts, and a pack of underwear. God forbid something happened to Leroy; he didn't want to be found with ungodly undies.

From there, they went to the shoe department and got a pair of Top-Siders.

"Man, I don't like these shoes. They make me look like a poof," Leroy complained.

"Don't be ridiculous. You need to look realistic. You know, like a guy who would actually have money in an off-shore account. And please, please do not engage in any conversation with anyone. No 'Hello, how do you do.' Nothing. Got it?"

"What if they ask me what I'm doing and where I'm going?"

"You're checking on a resort for your employer."

"Which one?"

"Several. We'll pick up a travel guide so you can fake it. But please try to limit the chatter."

"Yeah, yeah." Leroy kept checking his feet in the shoe department mirror. "Socks?"

"No socks."

"No socks?" Leroy exclaimed loud enough for a woman nearby to give him an odd look. She quickly ushered her grandson out of the department.

"No socks. It's a thing. Okay?" Darius was trying to be patient. It was like being with an eight-year-old. The departing grandkid seemed better behaved.

"Can I put powder in them?"

"Since when have you been so foot-conscious?"

"Since I am going to the K-Man Islands."

"Keep your voice down."

Leroy saluted Darius and placed the shoes in the shopping cart. They moved on to the luggage department. A small duffel bag with wheels was on sale. "Forty-nine bucks." Leroy pointed to the tag.

"Fine. Let's get outta here."

Darius told Leroy to go on to his truck. No need for both of them to stand in line. Plus, it was better if they split up. Harder to give a description. Darius kept his head down, attempting to hide from whatever cameras might be spying on him. Once he was done paying, he wheeled the cart out to his car and tossed the shopping bags into the back. He got in his vehicle and signaled Leroy to follow him. As they were leaving the parking lot, Darius tossed his baseball cap into a dumpster.

Leroy had the address of the motel, just in case they got separated, but Darius liked it better if he could check on Leroy in his rearview mirror.

It took just a little over an hour before they reached the motel. It was still early in the day, and there wasn't much for them to do. Leroy was going to try on his clothes. Darius knew he would have to supervise the entire makeover. "We need to find you a good barber shop."

"What's wrong with my hair?" Leroy ruffled it again.

"Well, that, for one thing." Darius mimicked Leroy playing with his hair. "Stop messing with it." Darius scrutinized him. "A good shave, trim those bushes that double for eyebrows. Check your ear hair. Remember, you have to resemble the photo on the ID."

"Oh, is that why Eric made me wash the gel out?"

"Duh." Darius gave him a look.

"Whatever." Then Leroy smiled, thinking that he might look decent after all.

Darius called the front desk and asked if there was a barbershop nearby. There was one within walking distance. Darius thought maybe their luck was finally moving in the right direction.

Chapter Fifteen

Pinewood

The farmhouse was a flurry of activity. Myra had gathered enough wits about her to organize a travel bag. She suspected she would be away for an undetermined amount of time, and so packed ten days' worth of clothes. She could always find a way to do laundry. Annie made arrangements for adjoining suites at The Kimpton Hotel. It had all the amenities and was a short walk to the hospital. Annie and Fergus would catch up with them in the evening. The only hitch was Cooper. All systems had to be a "go" if the big dog was going to be traveling with them. Annie assured Myra that the hotel policy allowed for service dogs, which is exactly what Cooper was. He had every kind of identification a canine could collect. He was almost human, but better. He had special abilities. His sixth sense was off the charts. Since Nikki would be in a private room in a special wing, Cooper could visit any time he was accompanied by a person. Or was it the other way around?

Charles was relieved to see Myra a bit more lucid and controlled. He smiled to himself. *She's dealing with this as if it was one of their missions. Good. That will keep her focused. I suppose I should be doing the same thing.* He still had not let on about his suspicion of their system being breached. He was waiting to hear from Libby.

Myra smiled at him. "This is going to be like a mission."

Charles let out a snort.

"What's so funny?"

"I was just thinking the same thing."

"Of course you were." She patted him on the cheek.

Charles hoped Myra would remain in this cogent frame of mind. He threw his Dopp kit into the suitcase and turned to Myra. "We are going to get through this."

"Yes, we are, and we are going to find out who was responsible. They will never see the light of day again. That much I can promise you."

"That's my girl." Charles patted her on the rump.

"What time will Annie and Fergus arrive?"

"Around seven o'clock. We should be there by four o'clock if we can beat the traffic." Charles continued to pack a few shirts. "I doubt they'll have Nikki settled before then."

Myra sighed. "She *is* going to be all right, isn't she?"

Charles wrapped his arms around her. "Right as rain."

Earlier, Charles had sent a group text to the Sisters:

Nikki in stable condition. Moving to Jackson U. Hosp. in Phil. Meeting Annie and Fergus later. Will send more info after we arrive. Pray.

Another flurry of texts arrived on Charles's phone. Some asked why they weren't using the VPN. Charles ignored the question. He hoped he would hear from Libby before they parted. He didn't want Myra to overhear the conversation. No sense in adding more worry.

His phone chimed. It was a text from Libby:

Hello. It's Libby. Can we chat live?

Charles replied:

5 minutes. Is this a good number?
Libby responded:
Yes.

"Who was that, dear?" Myra asked.

"Harry. Checking in. He needs something from the war room. I'll be back in a jiff." Charles hurried to the basement steps. He hated lying to Myra. It wasn't right, but it was for her own good. He kept telling himself that.

He dialed Libby's number. "Hello, it's Charles."

Libby chuckled. "Yes, I know. Aside from knowing it was you, I have a special program for caller ID."

"I hear you are quite the techno wizard. Abner speaks highly of you."

"As he does of you." Libby had a sweet-sounding voice. "So, Charles, what can I help you with today?"

"I've been getting little, almost indiscernible, glitches on my monitors. I think there is a problem with our VPN."

"I understand you have some of the highest-performing security."

"Well, at least I thought I did. Would you mind taking a look? Is it malware? Spyware?"

"Really." It was more of a statement than a question.

"Yes. I need an outside assessment."

"I'd be happy to," Libby replied.

"What do I need to do?" Charles asked.

"Nothing. I'll be doing everything on my end," Libby explained. "I will attempt to hack into your system. If I can do it, then it's likely someone who is highly skilled has breached it, as well."

"How long do you think it will take?" Charles was getting concerned that Myra would come looking for him.

"As long as it takes, Charles. I don't have to tell you that."

"Yes. You are correct. I'm a bit distracted right now. Myra's daughter Nikki was in an accident, and we are about to leave for Philadelphia."

"Oh, my goodness. What happened?" Libby sounded genuinely concerned.

"Car explosion. She's in a coma." Charles stopped short, remembering Libby had been through something similar.

This time, it was Libby who stopped short and was silent for a moment. "Wow." Another pause. "You know, I was in a coma year before last. Six weeks. When I regained consciousness, I had memory loss. Only partial. Just the few hours leading up to the incident."

"That's terrible. How are you feeling now?" Charles was looking for any silver lining he could grasp.

"I'm right as rain."

Charles paused before saying, "Do you believe in coincidences?"

"Like synchronicity?" Libby asked.

"Precisely!" Charles chimed back. "A remarkable concurrence of events. Something that cannot be explained."

"*Inexplicable* is the word I use," Libby added. "Why do you ask?"

"Because, not an hour ago, I told Myra that Nikki would be 'right as rain'."

"Holy guacamole!" Libby exclaimed. "That is *too* bizarre."

"Don't use the word 'bizarre' around Myra. She has deep feelings about such things. Feelings. Premonitions. Telepathy. We even have a psychic dog working with us!" Charles was amused at the turn of the conversation. Again, he realized he was taking too long. "I better log off. Keep me posted. I'll be in Philadelphia for an undetermined amount of time, but I can have one of my colleagues work with you if I'm out of reach or if you need to come to our headquarters, so to speak."

"Sounds good. I shall be in touch. And stay positive."

Charles chuckled. "That's exactly what I was saying to Myra."

Libby laughed. "Of course you were. Bye now." She clicked off the line.

Charles stared at the phone for a few seconds. *Did she just say, "of course you were?"* It was a little spooky. But in a good way. He was relieved to hear Libby talk about her experience and that she was now back to normal. And considering the type of brainpower she had to use, well . . . miracles did happen.

Charles scurried back to the bedroom, where Myra was closing her suitcase. "Did you find what Harry was looking for?" she asked.

"Hmm?" For a moment, Charles forgot his white lie to Myra. It was something he was not accustomed to. "Yes. He needed me to send him an old document." He quickly changed the subject, for fear the conversation would get out of control and he'd have to make up more lies. "Is Cooper packed?"

"Yes. I hope Lady and her kids are okay. They're worried. They can sense trouble."

"They'll be fine. Everyone will be fine and dandy. Right as rain." He smiled, thinking about his conversation with Libby. He felt it was some kind of omen. He wanted to share it with Myra, but that, too, would have to wait.

Charles grabbed their suitcases and loaded them in their new Range Rover. It was the same model Jack and Nikki drove. *Was.* Charles ran his overall "to-do list" in his head. *Get Nikki sorted. Get the computer thing sorted. Get the maggot who did this . . . get him sorted for good.*

Myra, Cooper, and Charles piled into the SUV. Charles punched the address of the hotel into the GPS. "Should be there in about two and a half hours." Before they pulled out, he reached in the back, pulled out a picnic basket, and handed it to Myra. "I know you didn't have much of an appetite, so I packed some things to nosh on."

"Oh, Charles, I don't know what I would do without you—except to eat all of these luscious-looking sandwiches by myself." She dug into the basket. Brie and roast beef; tomato and mozzarella with basil; avocado salad; water bottles with fresh cucumber. "This is wonderful. And you made my favorite—caprese!" She was referring to the tomato and mozzarella on a ciabatta roll. "You are such a love." She took a whiff of the sandwich. "I love the smell of basil. Divine." She began to unwrap it.

Charles laughed. "We've barely left the driveway."

Myra wiggled her shoulders and took a huge bite. She began making sounds of delight. "Mmm . . . mmm . . . mmm . . ."

"I don't suppose I should expect you will save any of it for me," Charles teased.

"Too bad, buster." Myra elbowed him. "For some reason I'm feeling very positive right now. It's as if a cloud was lifted."

Charles reached over and patted her on the hand. "Good. That's what we want."

Myra slapped his hand away. "Don't even think about stealing this from me." She turned her back from him as much as she could, bent over, and continued to eat.

Charles laughed again. He had to agree. Something *had* shifted. He didn't know what, but he knew they would soon find out.

Chapter Sixteen

Darius and Leroy

Leroy stepped out of the barber shop looking like a different person. His hair was clipped short, the unibrow under control, ear hair removed, and he'd had a really clean, close shave.

"Not bad, Leroy. You clean up real good," Darius noted.

Leroy strutted down the street. "I'm feeling real good." He thought he might spend some of his money on more clothes. It had been a very long time since he looked or felt spiffy. Yep. He'd set some money aside so he could look good in his Winnebago.

They walked over to a burger joint on the way back to the motel. An older stocky woman wearing a pastel pink uniform greeted them. "How y'all doin'? Come for a bite to eat?"

"Sure did." Leroy was inhaling the smell of the fried food. Then he remembered the last time he overdosed on fried chicken.

She showed them to a booth. "Can I get y'all something to drink?"

"You got any Dr Pepper?" Leroy asked.

"Nope. Pepsi and ginger ale." She pulled a pencil from behind her ear and perched it on her pad.

"I'll take a Pepsi," Darius said.

"Me, too. And a grilled cheese and bacon sandwich," Leroy said.

"I'll have the barbecue chicken," Darius added. As the waitress walked away, Darius mumbled. "I don't know why I ever order barbecue when I'm not in Texas."

"We got some decent barbecue around these parts." Leroy defended the area's culinary arts.

"I doubt in *these* parts." Darius pressed his thumb on the old Formica table, emphasizing where they were.

"You never know. Some places can surprise you." Leroy was fidgeting with the salt-and-pepper shakers.

"Can you sit still for more than a nanosecond?"

"I'm just kinda excited. I never done nothing like this before. Last time I went on a trip, I almost got clobbered with a fire extinguisher. That was after I puked my guts out from eating a bucket of fried chicken."

"A whole bucket? Serves you right." Darius shook his head.

"It was a long ride, and I was hungry." Leroy stopped fiddling with the condiments and turned his attention to the kitchen area. "I should have asked for American cheese."

"I'm pretty sure that's all they have here."

A few minutes later, the waitress returned with their food. Much to Darius's surprise, the barbecue wasn't bad.

"See, I told ya." Leroy had cheese grease on his finely shaven chin.

"Oh, geez. Do you know how to use a napkin?"

Leroy quickly wiped his face. "Like I said—I'm excited."

"If you do eat in public while you're on this trip, please mind your manners, okay?"

"Okay, boss!" Leroy polished off the gooey bread and cheese combination. He diligently wiped his face and his hands. He held them up. "See? All clean."

He's like a five-year-old, Darius thought to himself.

Chapter Seventeen

Philadelphia

Traffic started to get heavy as Charles, Myra, and Cooper got closer to Philadelphia. Myra looked at the slow-moving cars ahead. "I don't remember this many people commuting. I cannot imagine sitting in a vehicle for hours each day."

"Nor can I." Charles got off the main highway that was going nowhere. His GPS recalibrated, and they moved slightly faster on the side streets. "It's odd. But if I am going to be in traffic, I'd rather be moving slowly than just sitting in one place. It may take just as long, but I feel like I'm getting somewhere."

Myra gave him a wry smile. "I agree, even if it sounds silly. I suppose being in motion gives you the sense of being in control."

"I believe you are onto something. For example, we are doing something right now to help Nikki recover. Even though so much is out of our control, we can still have some influence on the outcome."

"So true. Look how many missions we've completed. Going in, we had little idea where it would go, how long it would take, and if we would succeed. But each and every time, no matter what, we kept to our 'whatever it takes' motto." Myra let out a huff of air. "Of course, having the resources we have certainly doesn't hurt. We could never do what we do without them."

"Correct, but there is still never a guarantee."

Myra sighed.

Charles didn't want her to go down the dark road again. "But in the case of Nikki, I believe we'll get the results we want." He reached over and patted her hand. "Anything left in that basket, or did you wolf down all of it?" He chuckled.

Myra lifted the basket from between her feet and peeked inside. "There's the roast beef sandwich."

"Can you hand me half? I just need a smidge."

Myra wrapped a napkin around half the sandwich and handed it to him. She placed another napkin on his lap.

"You are the best chum." Charles grinned.

"And you are the best pal." Myra pinched his cheek.

"You are going to make me blush."

"I'll pinch the other side to make it even," Myra joked.

"That's not what I meant." He chuckled. Charles peered closely through the windshield and turned at the next corner. "And here we are." They pulled in front of the reimagined historical Lafayette Building with its whimsical and bold décor. It was a beautiful combination of globally inspired treasures in a majestic setting.

"Good afternoon," the doorman said as he pushed the revolving door ahead of Myra and Cooper.

"Thank you." Myra entered the building first, followed by Charles. "Such a lovely place," she stated as they entered the chic lobby filled with antique replicas from around the world, highlighted by unusual wallpaper designs. They strolled over to the front desk.

"Reservations under the name of Ryland de Silva, please,"

Charles spoke to the wispy gentleman at the counter. The desk clerk stood at attention immediately.

"Of course. I have two adjoining suites. Is that correct?" The guy was starting to break out in a sweat.

"You all right, mate?" Charles furrowed his brow.

"Oh, yes, sir." He leaned in and whispered. "It's just that Ms. de Silva is, well, let's say a 'legend' here."

Myra bit her lip and rolled her eyes. She could only imagine what kind of shenanigans her friend had been up to. "Was she wearing her tiara?" Myra asked with a straight face.

The hotel associate blinked several times. "Tiara? Not that I recall."

Myra chuckled. "Just kidding. It's a private joke between us. Right, Charles?"

"Right-o." He addressed the clerk. "They have several private jokes. Most are not shared with me or Annie's partner." Charles signed the electronic guest registry.

The young man giggled. "I don't suppose they would. So who do we have here?" He looked at Cooper, standing at attention.

"This is Cooper. Dog extraordinaire. I'm sure everyone says that about their dogs, but he is rather special." Myra reached down to scratch Cooper's ears. Then she leaned into the counter. "Don't you dare tell my dogs at home what I just said."

The young man was clearly trying not to be flustered by the interesting trio. "Okay. Now, the bellman will bring your bags to the room." He tapped an old-fashioned bell sitting on the counter and handed two key cards to Charles. "If there is anything you need, please do not hesitate to ask. My name is Kurt. Enjoy your stay."

"Thank you, Kurt." Charles turned and took Myra by the elbow.

Myra looked back at the desk clerk. "You're going to have

to share the details of how my best friend became a legend, Kurt." She gave him a quick wink.

They took the elevator to the penthouse floor, where two adjoining suites awaited them. A beautiful arrangement of peonies was positioned on the cocktail table in the living room area. It had a note from Annie: *See you soon, my friend. Keep your chin up. Much love, ADS.*

Myra's eyes welled up with tears. She had been fixated on the travel plans and the drive from the farm. Now, in their hotel, the exact reason why they were in Philadelphia hit her once more. Her shoulders began to tremble.

Charles pulled her close. "It's okay."

"I don't want to be a slobbering ninny," Myra protested.

"You can still be emotional without being weak. You're human, my dear." He pulled out his handkerchief and dabbed Myra's face.

She took a gulp. Breathed in and out. "I'm okay. I just wasn't expecting this." She placed the note on the table.

"It's Annie. Would you expect any less?"

"Not really."

The bellman showed them where the thermostat was and pointed out the amenities, which were aplenty. Annie always knew how to travel well. Charles handed him a twenty-dollar bill. "Thanks, mate."

"Thank you, sir. Enjoy your stay." He backed out of the room.

"Come, let's unpack and unwind. I'm a bit stiff from all that driving." Charles took Myra's hand, and they moved into the luxurious bedroom with a view of the park.

"Should we call the hospital?" Myra asked absently as she moved her clothes from the suitcase to the closet and the dresser. More often than not, she just lived out of her suitcase, but she knew it could be weeks before they could go home.

"Jack said he would phone when she was settled in. I'm going to take a shower and wash the road off of me."

"Okay, dear. I'll finish unpacking." A few minutes later, Charles's phone chimed. Myra looked at the caller ID and did not recognize the number. She hesitated to answer, so she brought it into the bathroom. "Charles? Your phone is ringing, and I don't recognize the number. Shall I answer it?"

Charles froze for a minute. "Let it ring. If it's important, they'll leave a message."

Myra set the phone on the vanity. She gave it a dubious look. No one except the Sisters and the guys had that number, and it was blocked for any kind of spam. She shrugged and went back to hanging up her clothes. Several minutes later, Charles exited the spa-like bathroom with a towel wrapped around his waist. Myra took a long look at her husband. Still handsome and fit. She counted her lucky stars she'd hired him years ago to be head of her company's security. Even though his resume had been a bit vague.

The light on Charles's phone indicated there was a message waiting for him. Myra pointed. "You have a message."

"Oh, yes. I'll get it in a bit." He donned one of the hotel robes and slipped the phone in the pocket. He hoped Myra hadn't noticed. It was difficult to hide anything from her. He was already anticipating the thrashing he would get when he finally had to tell her. That is, if there even was a problem. But *his* sixth sense told him there was.

While Charles was in the shower, Myra freshened up and donned a pair of wide-legged pants and a crisp white cropped shirt, along with sensible shoes. She ran a brush through her hair. She peered closely in the mirror. She'd need a touch-up soon. She realized she was fidgeting. "Charles, should we just head over to the hospital? I'm getting anxious waiting around to hear from Jack."

"I would think this is a much nicer waiting area than the

hospital, but if it will make you feel better, we can leave in a few minutes." Charles returned to the bathroom and sent off a text to Libby:

Can't talk now. Will call later.

He got an instantaneous response:

Ok. FYI malware link on J. Emery system.

Charles froze. A breach on Jack's system? That was almost impossible.

He texted back:

Got it. Will call ASAP. Crack on.

Now he was positive he had to share this news with Myra. Someone had been able to break through Jack's security wall. Charles thought about what he'd said in an earlier conversation with Myra. Technology advancement was in a state of perpetual motion. It was constantly changing and often not in a good way. The idea that many government institutions were breached was unnerving. The hackers were stealthy, and you didn't see it coming. You could only hope you had the best weapons to protect your data. It was difficult to fight an invisible army. If not impossible.

Charles decided it was best if he discussed this with Myra before they went to the hospital. Having it hanging over his head would be too much of a distraction. He would have to handle it *tout de suite*, which meant getting everyone involved. It was quite a dodgy situation. He walked into the living area, where Myra was pacing.

"Love, please sit for a moment."

Myra gave Charles a worried look. "Is it Nikki? Is she all right?" Her voice was quivering.

"No. It's not about Nikki." Charles walked closer. "Please." He motioned to the sofa and took her hand. "Last night, I mentioned I thought something was a little wonky with the system?"

"You said your laptop. You didn't mention the system." Myra winced.

"Yes, well, it turns out it is the system." He paused.

"Does Abner know? What about Isabelle?" Myra's voice was rising.

"Abner is away, but he recommended a woman he went to school with. Her name is Libby Gannon. She works for the DOD, and her job is cybersecurity."

"With all the breaches they've had, how good could she possibly be?"

"That's the point. They need someone to constantly test their systems. It's her job to find the back door."

"Huh. I hadn't thought about it that way."

"I suppose you could call it quality control, or some such. The point is, I had her check the system."

"And you didn't tell me?" Myra's voice was getting even louder.

Charles took her hand. "All of this happened this morning. I was suspicious, so I asked Harry to reach out to Abner. This was while Dr. Falcon was at the house. You can see why I didn't think it was the most opportune time to tell you I had suspicions. I didn't want to worry you further until I had more information."

Myra's shoulders began to relax a bit. "And what is the information?"

"The leak came through Jack's system."

"Jack's?" Myra was incredulous. "But how? Why?"

"That's what we have to find out. Libby is going to do some deep dives and see what she can find."

"Charles, this is horrible." Then something occurred to her. She grasped at her pearls. "Oh, my Lord. Do you think it has anything to do with the explosion?"

"That's entirely possible. I don't believe it's a coincidence that these two things happened simultaneously."

"But why?" Myra was dumbfounded. "Why Jack? Or was someone trying deliberately to get to us?"

"Again, I do not know the answer to that, but we are going to have to find out."

Myra thought for a minute. "I would bet one has something to do with the other. This was no coincidence." Cooper moved over to Myra and put his head on her lap. "See? He agrees with me."

"Myra, I want you to know it pained me all day to have kept this from you, but I was doing it for your own good."

Myra touched his face. "I know, Charles. You always have my back, even if it means going behind it." She gave him a wry smile.

Charles gave her a peck. "Come, let's get this situation sorted."

Myra grabbed her purse and Cooper's leash. He wore a vest indicating he was "official." The three got into the elevator with a few other people. One uptight woman gave a sneer. As they exited the elevator, Cooper farted in front of her. Myra and Charles doubled over in laughter, as did the other passengers. Yes, Cooper was an extraordinary dog.

They waved at the concierge on their way out. Charles arranged for a nice bottle of cognac, fresh strawberries, and chocolates to be delivered to their room later. Charles thought they might need it to unwind after whatever kind of day it turned out to be.

As they walked the several blocks to the hospital, several people commented on how handsome Cooper was. After the third comment, Charles grunted.

"Jealous, dear?" Myra elbowed him.

"Of a dog?" Charles feigned indignation.

Cooper gave him the dog version of the stink eye.

"You apologize." Myra stopped on the sidewalk.

Charles leaned over and took Cooper by the head and looked him in the face. "You know I am kidding, right, ole boy?" Cooper gave a woof of approval. "I must say, your air biscuit leaving the elevator was brilliant!" Charles did a double take. He could have sworn Cooper smiled.

They continued walking arm in arm. As they got closer, they could hear the sounds of police and ambulances. Myra took in a deep breath.

"They are going to be landing on the helipad at Jackson and then transfer her to the neuroscience building," Charles said. Myra tightened her squeeze on Charles. He nodded to the front of the building. "Here we are."

Myra noted the sign that said WORLD CARE. "I like that."

They entered the building and were greeted by a cheerful middle-aged woman. "Good afternoon. Welcome to Jackson University Hospital for Neuroscience. How can I be of assistance?"

Charles took the lead. "Good afternoon. We're Nikki Quinn Emery's parents. She is being medevacked from Virginia."

"Please follow me." The woman walked them to an elevator marked PRIVATE. "As soon as you exit the elevator, someone will meet you and give you your visitors' passes."

"What floor?" Charles asked.

"This is a private elevator, sir. There is only one way on and one way off." She smiled. When the car arrived, she motioned for them to get in. "Have a good evening. She will be in the best hands."

The doors closed, and all three of them looked at each other. Then they looked at the elevator panel to see if it indicated a floor. Nothing except a button indicating UP or DOWN, and an emergency call switch. If Cooper could shrug, he would have.

After the car arrived on the mysterious floor, a well-dressed security guard greeted them. "Good evening. I'm Edmond. You are Myra Rutledge and Charles Martin." He didn't ask. It was a statement. "And Cooper." The dog stood at attention. "Please step over here." Edmond directed them to a kiosk. "Because this is a high security and privacy floor, we will have custom identification badges made for you. You will then have access to this floor, provided the patient is cleared for twenty-four-hour visitation. Ms. Quinn will be evaluated upon admission, so it will be several hours before you can see her."

Myra looked dismayed. "What about her husband, Jack Emery?"

"He is already in the suite. Shall I escort you?"

"Yes, thank you," Charles answered.

Myra followed with, "Yes, please."

Edmond led them into a large open area with a circular nurses' station in the middle. Corridors led off in four different directions. He stopped to introduce them to the woman at the desk. "Connie, this is Myra Rutledge and Charles Martin. They are Nikki Quinn Emery's parents." Cooper gave a soft moan. "And this is Cooper." The guard bent down. "Sorry, pal." Cooper thumped his tail against Charles's leg. The guard turned to them. "This is Connie Hatch. She is the head nurse."

Connie extended her hand. "Nice to meet you. I know these are very troubling times, but I can assure you, your daughter will get the best care available."

"Thank you." Myra was trying not to get choked up.

"Edmond will show you to the suite Countess de Silva arranged. If you need anything, please let me know. I will introduce you to the rest of the staff as soon as you get settled."

"Right-o. Thanks," Charles said, and then he, Myra, and Cooper followed Edmond down one of the halls. Myra noticed that it didn't have the usual glaring, blinding light. It was softer. More calming.

Neuroscience. They ought to know what works best for the brain, she thought.

At the end of the hall was a suite of rooms. Once inside the entry, to the right was a living room with a sofa, matching club chairs, coffee table, end tables, and floor lamps.

On the far right wall was a Murphy-style kitchen complete with a sink, a sizable toaster oven, and coffee maker. A counter-height refrigerator sat underneath. A small café table and two chairs rested between the kitchen wall and the living room. A beautiful arrangement of sunflowers sat on the table. The left opposite wall was actually two large sliding wooden-paneled doors that opened up to a sleeping area with a queen-size bed. The large glass windows spanned the rooms and looked out on the park in the distance. It could have been a hotel suite. A very fine hotel suite.

To the left of the entry was a short hall that led to a full-size guest bathroom on one side and a walk-in closet on the other. At the end was the patient's room. Aside from the mechanical bed, the machines, and monitors, the room also looked like part of a high-end hotel, complete with a daybed-style sofa along the window area.

Edmond walked them through, pointing out the amenities.

"This is very impressive," Myra noted. She prayed the medical care was equal in quality.

"Often family members take turns staying here. It depends on the situation. The prognosis of the patient."

"I see. That's a wonderful option you offer."

"This is the finest hospital I have ever worked in." Edmond nodded.

Footsteps could be heard coming down the hall. Myra turned and saw it was Jack. They both ran toward each other. "Oh, Jack! What on earth happened?" Myra was close to hyperventilating.

Jack gave her a huge bear hug. "We're not sure." He let her go and gave Charles an equally large squeeze. "Come. Let's sit." They walked back into the room and positioned themselves in the living area. He looked up at Edmond. "Thanks, Edmond."

"My pleasure. If you need anything, just pick up that phone." He pointed to a desktop. "Red button is for me; blue button is for the nurse."

"Thanks, mate." Charles shook his hand.

"My thoughts and prayers that everyone goes home safe and well." He grinned.

"Amen to that," Myra muttered.

Jack, Myra, Charles, and Cooper settled into the modern furniture. Jack poured each of them a glass of water from a carafe that was sitting on the coffee table.

Jack sighed. "First, let me say I am hopeful. The latest CT scan shows some bleeding in the brain, but they think they will be able to manage it. Obviously, they will keep a close eye on her."

Charles leaned in and rested his forearms on his legs. "So what can you tell us about what happened?"

"Not a whole lot. Forensics will take over a week. They have to separate what they believe are the pieces of the explosive device from the wreckage of the car."

"Do they have any idea? Anything at all?" Myra asked.

"They think it was an IED. Improvised explosive device. Not much different than any other random homemade bomb. It ignited the gas tank. Or so they believe."

"But why *your* car?" Myra asked.

"I haven't the vaguest idea." Jack shook his head. "The one good thing is that we weren't inside the car when it happened. If not, we would both be dead."

Myra's hand flew to her face. She had a wave of dizziness. "I don't understand. Who would want to harm you or Nikki?"

Jack looked at Charles and then back at Myra. "You're serious, right?"

"Dead serious." Myra gave him a stoneface.

"Think about all the misfits and miscreants we've encountered over the years. Individually and collectively. It could fill a stadium."

"He has a good point." Charles pursed his lips.

"So where do we begin looking?" Myra asked in earnest.

"As I mentioned, we are going to have to wait for the lab results to see if there is some kind of signature from the bomber. They all have one. They keep making the same bomb over and over because of the materials and resources they have. That being said, sometimes they never find the bomber, because he either stopped voluntarily or someone nailed him. Remember the kid who was in Central Park? He was a tourist. He jumped off a rock and landed on an IED. It blew off the kid's leg. It's been over five years, and they still don't have a lead. So unless this person has done it before or plans on doing it again, we may never find out."

"And you said it will take over a week to get forensic results?" Myra's wheels were turning.

Jack knew exactly where this was going. He lowered his voice. "If we leave it to the authorities."

Charles cleared his throat. "I'm afraid I have more troubling news."

Jack sat up straight. "What is it, Charles?"

"It appears our VPN has been breached. We don't know how deep the breach is yet. All we know is that someone, shall we say, visited our portal."

Jack looked confused. "What are you talking about?"

"Last night, when I opened my laptop, there was a very brief flicker. A nanosecond, but it caught my eye."

"You're saying someone tried to hack us? Are you sure it just wasn't some kind of glitch?"

"I'm afraid not. Abner is on a job. This is a bit more complicated than Izzie can handle on her own, so Abner recommended a former classmate. Her name is Libby Gannon. Her job is to hack into high-security systems so they can be proactive in maintaining their firewalls. And with all the breaches, it requires deep divers to stay on top of things."

Jack nodded. "Oh, believe me, I get it. I'm stunned that someone would try to hit us."

"That's the issue. It's not necessarily us. It could be you. It came from your computer. "What?" Jack sprung up out of his chair. "How is that possible? All of us have the same up-to-the minute security software." He began pacing. Then it hit him. "Do you suppose this has anything to do with the car?"

"I would think it's quite likely," Charles continued. Myra was nodding in agreement. "I asked Harry to send a text to the Sisters telling them to stay off the VPN. That's how we've been communicating. By text. No FaceTime, no Zoom, Meetup, WhatsApp. Once Fergus gets here, we will contact Libby again and see if she has discovered anything else."

Jack took a seat. He was shaking his head. "Someone really wants me dead."

Chapter Eighteen

Las Vegas

After going through his self-imposed gambling allotment, Bennie strolled over to the dumpy-looking raised platform that served as a cocktail lounge. It was far enough away from the constant dinging and cacophonous sounds of the slot machines. He laughed to himself, remembering the rules the state set for wearing masks and smoking in casinos: PLEASE REMOVE MASKS WHILE SMOKING. *Have we come to that? Are people that stupid they need to be told not to put a lit cigarette next to a facial mask?* He shrugged. Maybe the world *had* come to this. He'd only been away for five years. Anything was possible. He blamed the Internet. After all, that was one of the reasons he got locked up. He used it to his advantage until it was no longer a good idea. In prison, he had limited access, but his skills were sharp.

He and Eric were partners in the technological end of their plan. Eric had a lot of know-how, wheeling and dealing online, but Bennie knew how to go deeper into the dark web. He used his coaching skills to teach Eric how to get there and back.

He felt his phone vibrating in his pocket. It was Eric, sending a text:

Tomorrow. 5:00. Best Western Desert Oasis.

They agreed that any use of the Internet should be done in a different state. And each time they got together to work, it was in a different town. They always tried to pick a spot that was an equally distant drive for both of them, usually somewhere on the Arizona side of their state line.

Bennie threw back a shot of whiskey, paid his tab, and walked the five blocks to his motel. He felt a sense of relief. Something was starting to happen. He was getting antsy. He shoved a change of clothes and the basic toiletries—deodorant, toothbrush, toothpaste—in a backpack. His beard had grown in nicely. Once this caper was over, he would shave it off. And his head. A whole life makeover. He was going for the Bruce Willis look.

He flipped on the small TV. Five channels. Basic, *basic* cable. He zeroed in on the very young, very pretty, bubbly local newscaster. That described most of them. It was Las Vegas. It was Sodom and Gomorrah. Such a paradox. From strip clubs to water parks. A place the whole family can enjoy.

In California, Eric was in a similar mode, carefully packing the most innocuous clothing he owned. He purchased a cheap pair of moccasins and purposely scuffed them up. They said you can tell a lot about a man by looking at his shoes. He was going for bland. Worn. He let his beard grow out for a couple of days. Also bland. Worn. Scruffy. He colored his hair dark brown and began letting it grow a few months before his release. Once he was out of the country, he planned to cut it short and strip the color.

Before he had the fake IDs made, they decided everyone should change their appearance. They had instructions to do the opposite of however they normally appeared.

He thought about Darius and his bright red curly hair. And his fair skin and freckles. Dying his hair darker would have looked bizarre, so Darius had opted for straightening it and coloring it gray. It was just a tad more believable.

Then there was Leroy. He had a black pompadour, all of which was fake. That meant Leroy had to go back to his normal shade of medium brown and leave the hair products on the shelf. A good cleanup would change his look entirely. He wondered if Leroy was going to revisit his idea about walking with a limp. He hadn't yet had the opportunity to play out his fantasy, but he was under strict orders not to try it on his trip to the Cayman Islands. If anything, it would draw more attention to him.

What a crew.

Eric packed two new laptops in a separate duffel bag. He didn't want to use the normal carrying case for them. Too easy to spot: *Yeah, I saw two guys carrying something like computer bags.*

Their last meetup had been a few days ago, when they found the whereabouts of the guy Darius was looking for. It was their first successful crack. They were able to hack into the guy's personal computer and get his address. After that judge's son was shot, the laws were pretty tight on revealing personal information about judges and prosecutors. Eric didn't want to know the reason why Darius needed the information. He could only guess, and it wasn't pretty. Yes, Darius was the one he feared the most, but he was part of the deal.

Eric thought hard for a moment. Why *had* they included Darius in their group? Bennie was there because he covered Eric's back. Leroy, because Eric knew he could trust him to follow instructions. Leroy wasn't very good at thinking on his own, but give him a list, and he'd obey. That's what Eric needed. A lapdog. Eric's goal was to retrieve his money and get the hell out of the country, and he would pay what he promised the other men. His modus operandi of deception worked on a lot of people, but he was not going to try to pull anything on his pack of ex-cons.

He pursed his lips. *But why Darius?*

He recalled the first time he'd met Darius. It was in the prison cafeteria. Eric and Bennie were sitting together, finishing up dinner. Darius nodded at them and sat down. "How y'all doin?"

"Fine," Eric responded.

"Okay," grunted Bennie.

"Name's Darius."

Eric and Bennie looked at each other. Bennie had been incarcerated only a few weeks before Eric, but he already knew what to expect. Especially with his conviction. He knew there were those who thought what he did was an atrocity, and then there were others who were curious. Bennie discovered that the longer the inmates were there, the more perverted they became.

Bennie nodded at Eric as he said, "Bennie. And this is Eric."

"What, Eric can't speak for himself?" Darius asked menacingly.

"Yes, he can. He's my friend." Bennie stared straight at Darius.

Darius cracked a smile. "Oh, I get it."

"No, I don't think you do," Bennie replied and puffed up his chest a bit. He knew he was pushing his luck, but the guy did not outweigh Bennie, and Bennie was in good shape.

"I must have misunderstood." Darius pursed his lips. "No offense."

"None taken," Eric finally spoke.

The conversation centered on how and why they were in the pen. It was cordial enough. The next day, Darius latched onto them again, which became the routine for the next two years. That's when Leroy arrived. He looked like a deer in headlights. Bennie and Eric befriended the goofy-looking guy, knowing he might become someone's human punching bag. They soon discovered Leroy was severely lacking in common sense.

For the next three years, the four of them shared their meals. The routine was: Wake up at 4:30 A.M. Breakfast at 5:00. Report to work at 6:00; lunch at 11:00. After noon, they would either work, go to the gym, or take a class. Dinner at 4:00; 6:00, more classes, TV, or dominoes. Inmates had to return to their cells by 9:30 for evening count. They were allowed to have a light on to read up until 10:30.

The place was not packed with hardened criminals. The really, really bad guys went to ADX super maximum security in Florence, Colorado, home to heads of international drug cartels, terrorists, and serial killers. It was something to be thankful for.

Chapter Nineteen

Philadelphia

It was almost 7:00 P.M. when Annie came rushing into the suite. She ran to Myra, practically knocking her over.

"Oh my Lord! What on earth has happened? How is she? How are you?" Annie stopped to catch her breath. "Jack? Are you all right? Charles?"

Myra untangled herself from Annie's grip. "We don't really know much. We're waiting for the doctor."

Charles added, "And we don't know much about what happened, except there was an explosion."

"It was meant for me. I'm sure of it," Jack said grimly.

Myra and Annie took a seat on the sofa. They were clutching each other's hands. The three men paced. Cooper sat at the women's feet.

"The wreck is on the way to a lab in D.C. I was able to pull a few strings, but it's still going to take several days," Jack informed them.

Annie elbowed Myra. They scanned each other's faces. Everyone knew what they were all thinking: *Get the sonofabitch who did this.*

"Fergus, we have another problem." Charles began to deliver another piece of bad news.

Fergus gave him a concerned look. "What's up, mate?"

"It appears our VPN has been hacked."

A resounding "What?" came from both Annie and Fergus.

"We don't know the extent of the breach yet. Abner recommended a woman named Libby Gannon. They went to school together. She's top-notch. She checked our security, and she was able to break in."

"That's terrible!" Annie cried out.

"What's worse is that it came through Jack's laptop," Myra interjected.

"Jack's laptop?" Fergus squinted in disbelief.

"Yes. Someone hacked into Jack's system and wormed their way into our portal."

Fergus scratched his head. "This is bloody awful. All of it."

"So what happens next? What's the plan?" Annie asked.

"I'm afraid we are in a holding pattern until we get more information," Charles explained.

There was a soft knock on the door. It was Connie, the head nurse. "Sorry to interrupt. Dr. Jarmon is on his way to see you. They'll be bringing Nikki in a few minutes."

"How is she?" Myra sprung out of her seat.

"She's in stable condition. Dr. Jarmon will fill you in on all the details." She turned and went back to her station.

Dr. Jarmon entered, carrying a tablet that replaced the old clipboards. He was smiling. "Good evening." Salutations went quickly around the room before he resumed. "Nikki is in stable condition. She is still unconscious. She suffered a fracture of the occipital bone. There is some swelling of brain fluid. We are going to check her again in an hour before we decide on a craniotomy."

Myra gasped, and her knees went weak. Annie grabbed her on one side, and Charles, the other.

Dr. Jarmon continued. "I know it sounds horrifying, but it's a routine practice. One of the downsides is that she would need to be intubated. She is on oxygen now, but not a respirator. That's the good news."

"What's the bad news?" Charles put his arm around Myra, bracing for something horrific.

"The usual concerns that accompany any surgery." Myra was close to hyperventilating. "But we won't have to make that decision yet," the doctor added.

Voices and the sounds of wheels were getting louder as the hospital aides shuttled Nikki into the room. Myra was frozen in place. Annie thought they were both going to faint. Fergus put his arm around Annie, and Charles did the same with Myra. Jack stood helplessly, with Cooper by his side.

In less than three minutes, Nikki was settled into the room designated for the patient. Myra rushed to the side of her bed and gently took Nikki's hand. "Oh, my dear girl." Tears were flowing down Myra's cheeks. Charles pulled out a clean handkerchief. He had the forethought to bring several. Surely the hospital would be rife with boxes of tissues, but there was something comforting about a real cloth hankie. Myra looked up at Charles. He was placid. But only on the outside. Inside, he was raging. Charles noted all the machines monitoring Nikki's vitals. Her pulse was weak, and her blood pressure was low, but the doctors thought she was within the range to be determined "stable."

"We'll bring the portable CT scan down here so she won't be disturbed," Dr. Jarmon said.

Myra turned to him. "Thank you, Doctor. Is it all right if I sit with her?"

"Absolutely. And talk to her. I'll leave you for now," he said, and shook Charles's hand.

"Thank you," Charles replied.

Annie walked with the doctor. She reminded herself of the Sisterhood slogan. She spoke to him in a hushed voice. "Whatever it takes." He nodded. He understood. She was Countess Anna Ryland de Silva. No price tag for Nikki's care was too high. Even if they had to fly experts in from Switzerland. She prayed it wouldn't come to that.

Myra and Jack stayed in the room with Nikki. Cooper rested his head on the end of Nikki's bed. Charles, Annie, and Fergus went into the living room to discuss the breach and what to do next.

"I'll text the Sisters and give them an update on Nikki's condition," Annie offered. She pulled out her phone and sent a quick note:

Nikki is stable. We are at hospital. More tests. Pray.

Dozens of texts flew back:

"Can we come?"

"Can we meet?"

"How is Myra? Charles?"

"What can we do?"

"Deadheading back. Leaving Cal. now. s/b back 2 days."

The last message was from Kathryn, whose main occupation was driving a long-haul eighteen-wheeler.

Annie replied to all of them:

Hang tight. Stand by.

Annie, Fergus, and Charles huddled in the living room. Fergus was the first to speak.

"I think we should have the Sisters meet at the farm. Granted, we won't be able to use our systems until we find the leak."

Charles chimed in. "Perhaps we should invite Libby Gannon to join us. She might have better luck if the electronics are at her fingertips."

"Good point," Annie said. "Let me go speak with Myra. Be right back."

Annie softly entered the room where Nikki lay unconscious, Myra holding one hand, Jack holding the other.

Annie put her hand on Myra's shoulder and motioned her to stand and walk into the hallway. Myra looked weary as she asked, "What is it?"

"Fergus and Charles suggested we bring Libby in. Have her come to the war room and see if she can sort this mess."

"According to Abner, she is one of the best, and he trusts her." Myra paused. "Did you know Libby also suffered a head trauma and was in a coma for six weeks?"

"My goodness!" Annie exclaimed. "That is a bizarre coincidence."

"You know how I feel about coincidences." Myra gave a wry smile. "And, according to Abner, Libby doesn't seem to have any long-term issues, either. That gives me hope."

"Indeed." Annie gave Myra a hug. "It's a good sign."

"Tell the men I am totally fine with inviting Libby. She's in Missouri, though."

"I'll send the plane," Annie offered. "Let me get back to the gents and get this show on the road." Annie walked briskly into the living area of the suite.

"Myra is fine with asking Libby to join us. I can arrange for the jet. Charles, can you see how soon she would be available?"

"Right-o." Charles quickly dialed the number he saved. After two rings, Libby answered.

"Hello, Charles. How is Nikki?"

"She's stable. Thank you for asking. Would you be able to come our way anytime soon? As in tomorrow?"

"Fortunately, I just finished a project, so I have some free time. I'll check the airlines," Libby responded.

"Never mind that. We'll send Annie's plane to fetch you. Just get me the name of the nearest airport."

"That's great. I can be ready in a few hours. Jackson City is probably the closest. Just need to make sure someone can watch my dog, Buddy."

"Do you want to bring him with you? We are very dog-friendly," Charles offered.

"That is very kind of you, but I think he'd be less stressed if he hangs around with the kid down the block."

"Even if it's a private jet?" Charles chuckled for what felt like the first time in two days, although it seemed more like a lifetime.

Libby laughed. "I appreciate it, but I don't want to spoil him, either."

"Very well." Charles smiled. How about ten A.M. to-morrow?"

"That would be fine."

"The plane will take you to a private airport in Virginia. Someone will meet you and bring you to our farm, Pinewood. Tomorrow evening, there will be a meeting with some of our group members."

Libby interrupted. "Group members?"

"Fergus, my best friend and colleague, will meet you at the farm. He will explain more upon your arrival," Charles continued. "You mentioned you went through something similar. A head injury?" Charles stopped. "I don't mean to be cheeky—er, personal."

"Not at all," Libby responded. "I'm a walking, talking, computer-hacking miracle. There is a lot to the story, which I would be happy to share after we get things figured out."

"Splendid." Charles nodded. "When you get to the airport, ask for Annie de Silva's pilot. He'll get you to Pinewood straight away."

"Roger that." Libby had an obvious hint of enthusiasm. As much as she loved her home and neighbors in Hibbing, Missouri, it would be a nice change of scenery for her, and nice to meet new people.

Charles turned to Fergus and Annie. "Jackson City municipal airport. Tomorrow at ten A.M."

"Excellent. I'll ask Maggie to pick her up and bring her to the farm," Annie replied.

They stopped and stared at each other for a moment before Fergus spoke up. "I'll gather the Sisters at Pinewood. Whomever is available. The rest will have to use one of their cell phones. We can't risk any other technology until Libby gets under the hood, so to speak."

"Agreed," Annie and Charles said in unison.

"We'll get a helicopter to take you to the airport. This way, you can ride to the farm with Maggie and Libby," Annie offered.

"Splendid idea," Fergus said. "I'll phone one up and see if I can take off from the hospital helipad."

"I'll go tell Myra what we're up to. I know this may be a slow process. All of it. But, one foot in front of the other," Annie said, before she headed back into Nikki's room. No one had moved an inch. Jack and Myra looked up as she entered.

"Fergus is calling the Sisters to Pinewood for tomorrow. We're sending the jet to pick up Libby in Missouri. Fergus will helicopter to the airport where Libby is landing, and Maggie will meet both of them and bring them to the farm." Annie stopped to catch her breath. "I'll stay here with you and Charles."

Myra stroked her pearls. Tears welled up in her eyes. "I don't know what I would do without you." She gave Annie a bear hug.

"Have you had anything to eat?" Annie asked both Jack and Myra.

"Eat?" Myra snickered. "I have no appetite."

"I know that's where you go when you're upset—nourishment deprivation land. Not this time, my friend." Annie looked in Jack's direction. "And you, sir?"

Jack smiled. "I suppose I'm visiting Myra in nourishment deprivation land."

"Well, I'm closing down the park. The two of you are not going to fall apart from lack of food. And that's all there is to it." Annie turned on her heel and marched back to the living room. "We need to get some food delivered, ASAP," Annie barked. "And I don't suppose you've eaten anything either, Mr. Charles Martin?"

"I'll have you know, Ms. Smarty Pants, I fixed a wonderful basket of sandwiches and salads for our drive up here."

"And how many hours ago was that?" Annie tapped her watch.

Charles checked his, as well. "Going on seven hours or so."

"Need I say more?" Annie picked up the phone and hit the blue button.

"This is Edmond," came the immediate reply. "How can I help you?"

"Hello, Edmond. This is Annie de Silva. Could you recommend a takeaway restaurant where we can order some food?"

"Takeaway? Do you mean takeout or delivery?"

"Yes, sorry. My partner is from the UK. He uses that term. Someplace that delivers good food."

"Of course. There is a French bistro that many of the doctors and administrators use. The food is quite good. There should be a menu in one of the side table drawers. You will also find dinnerware and flatware in the kitchen drawers."

Annie walked over to one of the end tables and discovered several menus. "Fantastic. Thanks, Edmond."

Annie opened the menu. Very French. She dialed the number and gave them several orders for coq au vin, beef bourguignon, pommes frites, and string beans. She'd set up a buffet on the kitchen counter, and everyone could fix themselves a dish. She rummaged through the cabinets and pulled out the necessary dinnerware, napkins, and glasses. She snapped her fingers. She forgot to order beverages. A nice glass of wine with dinner would take off the rough edges that accumulated throughout the day. She phoned the restaurant again and asked if they could deliver a bottle of Bordeaux. The person on the other end of the line was a bit hesitant. "One moment." He put her on hold.

A different voice got back on the line. "Countess de Silva?"

"Yes. Who am I speaking with?" Annie gave the phone an odd look.

"I am Jean-Paul, owner of the bistro. We are not allowed to sell alcohol outside of our premises, but that doesn't preclude me from *giving* you a bottle."

Annie got the hint. "I'll be sure to include a good tip."

"Merci," Jean-Paul answered. "Lovely doing business with you."

Fergus and Charles split the list of Sisters and sent texts to all of them:

Whomever is available meet at the farm: tomorrow at 4:00.

A barrage of answers came back in a jiffy. Alexis, Yoko, and Isabelle were available. Kathryn was two days away. Maggie already had her marching orders, so she knew where to go and when.

It was almost 10:00 P.M. when the food was delivered.

"This smells delicious. I'm sure we can coax Myra into

eating something," Annie said as she set it on the counter and began to fix a plate for Myra. Charles picked up a dish, plated food for Jack, and set it on the table.

Annie brought the food into Nikki's room. She knew Myra wouldn't want to leave her side. "Jack, there's a plate for you on the table in the living room." She set Myra's plate on the portable adjustable table. "You need to eat."

Myra looked up at her. Her face was pale and drawn. "If you say so."

"I do, and I don't want to see one scrap left over." Annie moved to the other side of the room and sat on the small sofa. "Get busy." She motioned for Myra to start eating.

In the living room, Charles, Fergus, and Jack began discussing the perplexity of the breach as they ate their food. "I really don't understand it. I'm so careful." Jack was shaking his head. "This is all one huge nightmare."

"We will sort it out, old boy. Just give us some time. Meanwhile, we continue our vigil, praying for Nikki's speedy recovery." Charles poured a glass of wine for everyone. "Hold that thought." Charles went into Nikki's room and handed Myra a glass of wine.

It dawned on Myra that Annie wasn't eating. "Excuse me, but where is *your* plate?"

"It's on the kitchen counter," Annie replied.

"Well, you cannot have a glass of wine unless you have something to eat. Don't you dare give her the glass." She raised an eyebrow at Charles.

"All right, all right. But I expect a clean plate when I return." Annie took the glass from Charles's hand.

When she entered the living room, she overheard Jack berating himself for everything that happened that day.

"It should have been me." He dropped his head in his hands, elbows on the table, and began to sob. It was the first time since the incident that he let his emotions flow. Up until that point, it was all he could do to deal with everything that was happening and what needed to happen next.

Charles put his hand on Jack's shoulder. "It shouldn't have been anybody, and we are going to find that dodgy SOB."

Fergus was in accord. "Nikki is in the best of hands. Now it's up to us to find who did this to her."

"But the breach?" Jack blew his nose on a paper napkin. "That came from *my* computer. That has to be my fault somehow."

"Not necessarily. Hackers are getting more sophisticated every minute of every day." Annie leaned against the counter, picking at the pommes frites and waving one like a baton. "The frustrating part is waiting until tomorrow to see what Libby can find out."

"She said she'll keep digging for a few more hours, so perhaps she'll have more information in the morning," Charles said. "I'm going to check on Myra." He got up and went into the other room.

Annie looked at Fergus. "This is quite the crap-a-rama. I believe it's all tied together. The hack and the bomb. It can't be a coincidence."

"I agree." Fergus turned to Jack. "When was the last time you got a threat from someone?"

"It's been a while, but let's just say there were several, many years ago."

"Any of your convicted felons threaten you?" Fergus asked.

"Not to my face."

"What was the nature of the threats?"

" 'Send so-and-so to jail and you'll be sorry.' Nothing ever specific, and I have to say, it was over ten years ago."

"Anyone due for release?" Fergus asked.

"I'm sure there are plenty, but they're scattered all over the federal prison system."

"They should be easy enough to find," Fergus added.

"But not until we can be sure we are secure," Annie chimed in. "Surely someone you know could find out?" she asked Jack.

"I suppose. My head is spinning." Jack got up and rummaged around in another drawer. He found a pen and a pad. "Let's start making a list. Two things have to happen simultaneously. Getting the forensics from the bomb and getting a list of parolees from my previous cases. We know it's still going to take a few days for us to get any of that information."

"Meanwhile, Libby can see if she can find the leak. That may lead us to the person who did this to Nikki," Annie said.

"Provided they *are* connected," Fergus added.

Annie put her hands on her hips. "They are. I know it, and Myra agrees with me. How many times is it going to take for you boneheads to appreciate women's intuition?"

Fergus covered his head with his hands, expecting to be rapt on. "I give! You're right. We're imbeciles." His comment helped break the somber mood a bit.

Annie gave a big sigh. "We need to be more positive. I know it's hard with Nikki lying in the next room, but we have to keep up the positive energy."

Jack was the next one to speak. "Annie's right. We can't be maudlin." He began to take a few more notes. "Let's say we find out who hacked the computer. What's our next step?"

"Find out where the creep is, for one. Unfortunately, he could be anywhere," Annie answered.

"Right, but let's say he's in the States. Should we get Avery to try to track him?" Jack asked.

"We shouldn't get ahead of ourselves, as alluring as it may be." Fergus winked at Annie.

"Depending on where the person or persons are, we will have to plan our strategy accordingly. Which is what we normally do under all the circumstances," Annie stated.

"I know you're right. I'm just trying to busy myself." Jack tossed the pen on top of the pad.

"You'll be busy soon enough." Charles patted him on the shoulder.

The sound of voices was heard coming from the main hall of the hospital; then, a short rap sounded on the door. It was Dr. Jarmon, with a portable machine and a technician. "How is everyone doing?"

A round of "Good, fine, thanks," was the response.

"I'm going to run another scan," Dr. Jarmon explained before he led the way for the tech and the portable scanner. As he entered Nikki's room, Myra stood. "Hello, Mrs. Rutledge. I'm going to do a few more tests. Would you mind stepping in the other room?"

"No, of course not." She turned and went into the living room area.

Annie sidled up to her and linked her arm through Myra's. "Come," she said, "we're working on a plan."

The four others explained their tentative plans to Myra, who nodded silently. Her mood seemed to float in and out of melancholy.

"Are you sure you are up for this?" Annie asked.

"Yes. I'm just anxious about what the doctor is going to say," Myra replied.

Charles patted her hand and motioned that someone should start talking. Fergus took the lead, going through the details planned for the next day. Myra seemed lucid, but remained distracted.

Several minutes later, Dr. Jarmon emerged from the bed-room. "Her brain functions seem to be normal. Some of the swelling subsided."

"Does that mean you won't have to perform surgery?" Charles asked, before Myra had a chance.

"Possibly not, but I can't be certain right now. Another test in the morning should give us a better idea." He looked at the clock on the wall. "It's after eleven o'clock. You should think about getting some rest. She is in good hands."

"What if she wakes up?" Myra pleaded, clutching her pearls.

Dr. Jarmon smiled softly. "In that case, we'll certainly call you."

Charles put his hands on Myra's shoulders, knowing it wasn't likely that Nikki would wake up in a few hours. "He's right, love. Let's head back to the hotel, get a hot bath, and some rest."

Jack decided to stay at the hospital. The Tides Inn had Jack and Nikki's belongings delivered earlier, so he had a change of clothes and could shower in the suite.

"You all right, ole chap?" Charles asked Jack, wanting to be sure.

"I'm good. Thanks for everything." Jack gave all of them a hug.

"Come." Annie grabbed her tote and Myra's shoulder bag. As they walked toward the elevator, Annie whipped open her bag to give Myra a peek. "I brought these, so we can stomp and dance when Nikki comes around."

Myra chuckled. "You and those rhinestone cowboy boots. Are you ever going to part with them?"

"When I give up my tiara." Annie elbowed Myra, who seemed to have calmed down a bit. Perhaps it was just phys-ical and mental exhaustion.

The two men followed, saying good night to the staff as they exited the floor. Charles muttered to Fergus, "The next thing is to plug the leak. Once we know we can operate securely, we hunt down the scoundrel."

The next morning, Fergus would be on a helicopter to Virginia to meet with Libby and the Sisters.

All of it was a waiting game now—which was a game none of them liked to play.

Chapter Twenty

Outside Las Vegas

Eric slipped the duffel bag over his shoulder and got in the rental car. It was a Toyota Corolla. Very nondescript. Just the opposite of the flashy life he had become fond of. But it was temporary. Soon, he would be anonymously enjoying the architecture of the colonial historical town and the mountains of a non-extradition country in South America. He planned on staying there for several months and then finding something in Guayaquil, where the action was.

The drive to the Best Western took just under three hours. He checked in under the name Masters. Bennie would check in as Flint. As Eric approached the small front desk, he noticed a sign that read:

ROOMS WILL NOT BE RENTED TO INDIVIDUALS WHO RESIDE WITHIN A 25 MILE RADIUS OF HOTEL.

He snickered. He had to ask. "What's this all about?"

The desk clerk looked up at him. "Are you serious?"

"I've never seen a sign like that before."

"Keeps the riffraff out." He gave Eric a sour look.

Eric chuckled to himself. *If you only knew.* "I reserved a room on the second floor. Name is Masters."

The clerk asked him a series of questions, including his license plate number, before sliding the key across the desk. "Pool is closed."

"Good thing I didn't come for the amenities." Eric took the key, went back to his car, and drove around to the side of the building. It bothered him that they asked for the license plate of the car. Even though it was a rental, it had California plates. It could be traced back to the rental agency, but the name on the rental agreement was Gregory Masters.

Bennie was now Mike Flint. Darius was Jim O'Hara, and Leroy was now Larry Kratman. Eric figured it would be easier for Leroy to remember his new alias if it was similar to his real name.

Eric checked for security cameras. There was only one, in the front. Perfect. He sent a text to Bennie, telling him to park on the side of the building and then walk to the main entrance to check in. No sense in the cameras getting both of their vehicles on tape. He wondered how long they kept the security footage or if they recorded over it every twenty-four hours. It didn't matter much. In a few days, he would be on his way south.

About an hour later, Eric's cell phone buzzed. It was Bennie. He was in his room down the hall. Eric sent a text for Bennie to come to his room, where they would do their dark web surfing. Eric pulled out his OWE—Opportunistic Wireless Encryption device. It created a private network that others in the hotel would not have access to. A few minutes later, there was a knock on the door. Eric peered through the peephole before he opened the door.

"Hey, man." Eric stood to the side to let Bennie in. He checked the hallway. The place seemed deserted. "Huh. Deserted in the desert, a play on words."

"So what's on tap this time?" Bennie asked.

"Leroy is heading to the Caymans today. We'll wait for the

confirmation to go through. By the end of the week, everyone should have new bank accounts set up. The transfer will
come from a shell company."

Bennie sat in the chair next to a small table. "So who are
we looking for today?"

"Another one of Darius's 'enemies.' " Eric used air quotes.

"What's up with him, anyway?"

"He wants to confront the people who put him behind
bars."

"But won't that land him in the slammer again?" Bennie
asked.

"Not our problem. We made a deal." Eric paused. "And
I'm not sure why or how we got involved with him."

"Probably because he was like Velcro. We couldn't get
away from him. And as big a guy as I am, I didn't want to get
on his bad side."

"I know what you mean," Eric said. "There's something
not right with him." He turned to his laptop and fired it up.
"Let's get to work so we can move on. There are just two
more he wants us to find."

"Thank goodness. I don't like this cyber sleuthing." Bennie had flashbacks about the events surrounding his arrest,
and the Internet was the mother lode. "What's going to happen next?"

"We give Darius the info, he gets his new identity, puts
Leroy on a plane. Waits another day and brings Leroy back
to wherever he found him. Then I transfer the money into
everyone's new bank accounts."

"It can't happen fast enough. I feel like time is running out."

"Take it easy. We'll be done and out of here tomorrow,
then we'll be on our way to parts unknown. Sayonara. So
long. Happy trails."

Chapter Twenty-one

Pinewood

Maggie's nerves were more jangled than usual. She gnawed at her nails until there was no more cuticle left for her to chew. Her freckled face was beginning to perspire. She had been sitting in traffic for almost half an hour and hadn't moved an inch. She kept spinning the knob on her radio, hoping to get some traffic information. She finally called the newspaper where she worked. "Hey—it's Maggie. Anyone hear anything about the Beltway? I haven't moved in forever!" Maggie was nervous about meeting the jet and the helicopter on time.

"Oh, and hello to you, too," Gary, one of the editors, jokingly snapped back. "Where are you, exactly?"

"The 495 near Springfield," Maggie huffed. She thought she had given herself plenty of time.

"Hang on." Gary yelled across the cubicles, "Anyone hear of any accidents or construction on the 495? Near Springfield?"

Maggie heard mumbling in the back, but none of it sounded promising. Gary got back on the line. "Multi-car accident. Don't you have a radio in that hunk of junk you drive?"

"Actually, I'm in one of Annie's vehicles, and it's like navigating an airline instrument panel. I'm afraid to touch anything."

"Sorry, can't help you there, either. Good luck." With that, Gary hung up. Sometimes people in the office were a little envious of Maggie's relationship with Annie. Some thought it was "too chummy." If only they knew. But actually, it was a good thing they *didn't* know.

Maggie hurriedly punched several buttons on the GPS. "Dang. Why didn't I check before I left? Because I thought I knew where I was going. I didn't know I'd end up in a cluster-jam!" she yelled at herself. She hit a button that spoke to her.

"How can I help you?"

Maggie was startled. "Are you a real person or is this a computer-generated thing?" Maggie was suspicious of the strange voice.

"I'm real. You hit the driver's assist button. Do you need assistance? EMS? Are you all right?"

"Yes, but I'm in a huge traffic jam, and I need to get to Manassas Airport in less time than I have now."

"We'll get you there as quickly and as safely as possible. I see from the coordinates you are near the Springfield exit. Get off there, and I'll guide you the rest of the way. Sound good?" The woman's voice was reassuring.

"That would be swell. Thanks so much." Maggie breathed a small sigh of relief. It was as if their world was caught in a wildfire, and the Sisterhood was scrambling to put out the flames. She knew she shouldn't have brought that bag of donuts in Annie's car, but she needed something to calm her. She'd worry about all the powdered sugar later. For now, she had to get to Fergus and Libby. The woman continued to give Maggie directions away from the traffic.

"You should be there in fifteen minutes," the woman said.

"Thank you, thank you, thank you." Maggie began to see familiar landmarks. "I'm good to go. Thanks again."

Maggie pulled onto the service road that led to the airport. She parked in Annie's reserved spot and hopped out. Fergus was in the waiting area. Maggie ran up to him and threw her arms around his chest. "Oh, my gosh! What is going on?" She was almost in tears.

"Nikki is stable. Her brain functions seem okay. They're running more tests this morning. We should know something soon."

"How's Myra? Annie? Charles? Jack?" Maggie rattled off everyone's name in a nano-second.

"Everyone's a little weary but okay. Jack is taking this really hard. And now, with the computer hack, he's gutted. Blames himself for everything."

"Oh, man, that stinks. He can't possibly think any of this was his fault," Maggie exclaimed.

"The best thing we can do is get to the bottom of it, but we're still missing several pieces to this big puzzle."

Maggie spotted Annie's Gulfstream taxi in. "Let's get this show on the road." She and Fergus went onto the tarmac to greet Libby. Maggie gave her a big wave. Libby smiled and headed in their direction.

"Libby?" Maggie asked. It was only sort of a question. After all, who else would be coming off of Annie's plane?

"Yes. Libby Gannon." She held out her hand.

"I'm Maggie, and this is Fergus."

They all shook hands. "Nice to meet you. I must say this is quite an excellent way to travel. I don't know if I can fly commercial again." Libby giggled.

"Trust me—it's hard." Maggie laughed. "Follow me."

Fergus grabbed Libby's bag, and the three walked to Annie's vehicle. Fergus opened the doors for the women, and he put one leg in near the driver's seat. "Ugh. You are a short one, aren't you?"

"Don't mind him. He has a British sense of humor." Maggie smiled. "He'll find something to tease you about before you leave."

Fergus looked in the rearview mirror and nodded at Libby.

The ride to the farm was just under an hour. They chatted about ordinary things.

"What does one do in the summer in Missouri?" Maggie asked.

"Lake of the Ozarks. Stay away from grockles." Libby replied.

Fergus burst out laughing at her use of the British slang for tourists. "You get them too, do ya?"

"It's the *only* thing to do in Missouri," Libby said flatly. "I work most of the time, and when I'm not lost in cyberspace, I'm gardening or volunteering."

"Lovely," Fergus said. "You sound like you'll fit in with our crew."

"Speaking of crew, Charles said you'd explain what that means," Libby said.

Fergus gave Maggie a side look as if to ask, *How much do I tell her?*

Maggie's eyes got wide, and she pursed her lips as if to say, *I have no idea.*

Fergus began. "We are part of a very elite—and anonymous—group. We help people when the system fails. Speaking of systems, we have a highly sophisticated technological system that seems to be breached. As you know. As you proved."

"If it's of any comfort, I didn't look into any files. I only did what we call an exterior track. See who's been going in and out of your VPN." Libby pulled out a small paper notebook.

Maggie looked over her shoulder. "Paper?"

"Oh, yes. It's probably the safest way to preserve anything."

"Isn't that ironic?" Fergus smirked.

"Yes, it is. That's how the Taliban was able to get away with as much as they did. It was a lot of handwritten instructions, personally delivered."

"Well, that's what won the war. Couriers," Fergus added.

"Which war?" Maggie asked.

"Blimey. You know. World War Two."

"Well, there've been plenty others since." Maggie folded her arms.

"Agreed." Fergus nodded and continued. "We meet in a special room in the basement of the farm. That's where you'll meet the others today."

"Sounds intriguing," Libby mused.

"Oh, you just wait!" Maggie replied.

Fergus went on to explain how the farm was once an outpost for the Underground Railroad, and there were still a few tunnels that were in good and proper shape. "Myra made sure of it. She wanted to preserve it, but not make a tourist, or grockle, attraction out of it." Fergus snickered.

Fergus gave Libby a brief description of the key players, known as "the Sisters." First up was Alexis Thorne, a stunning African American woman who was set up by her partners to take the blame for fraud. After a year in jail, with the help of the Sisters, she got her law degree and now worked at Nikki's all-woman firm.

Yoko Akia was a florist, but her real talent was martial

arts. Fergus left out the part about Yoko being able to kill someone without leaving a trace. He didn't want to scare the bejeezus out of their new guest.

"I'm sure you know about Izzie," he went on. "Isabelle 'Izzie' Flanders was also a victim of injustice. One of her colleagues framed her, and Izzie was charged with drunk driving and vehicular homicide. She lost her business and her fiancé. It took time, but she rebuilt what she had lost and married Abner, your school chum.

"Kathryn Lucas was the first one Myra helped. She drives an eighteen-wheeler. During a cross-country trip, Kathryn was raped by a few weekend motorcycle blokes while her husband helplessly watched as he sat in his wheelchair. He eventually passed away, but Kathryn keeps driving."

Maggie chimed in. "You don't want to know what happened to those motorcycle jerks."

Fergus shot her a look.

Libby remained silent. She was getting the idea.

"Annie and Myra have been chums since they were kids." Fergus was rounding out the basics. "Myra's family owns a rather large candy company, and Annie is a stupendous resource. She's a countess, but she is quite low-key in that department."

"Except when she wears her tiara," Maggie added.

"And rhinestone boots." Fergus smiled and shook his head. "They are a pair of characters. Will put their life on the line for any of us, as we all would do for each other, but Annie and Myra have a very special bond."

Fergus continued to tell the sad story about Myra's daughter Barbara, who was killed by a hit-and-run driver who had diplomatic immunity. "She was in awful shape. And I do mean awful. Charles was beside himself. Myra wouldn't eat. She wouldn't speak, but one day she snapped out of her trance.

Charles and I go way back professionally. We've been the best mates since. And Bob's your uncle." Fergus ended the explanation with a typical British phrase used when you've finished listing or explaining something.

"Do you know anything more about Nikki's condition? How this happened?" Libby asked.

"Nikki is stable. Breathing on her own. There was some swelling in her brain, but that's subsided a bit. We'll know more later," Fergus replied.

"Do you know about what happened to me?" Libby asked.

Fergus wasn't sure how much Maggie knew, so he let Libby explain.

A couple of years ago, Libby had been in an accident in New York City. She fell backwards down the steps of a brownstone. She was in a coma for six weeks. When she regained consciousness, she had no memory of what happened that night. All she knew was her boyfriend disappeared before the ambulance arrived. She was terrified because she didn't know what exactly had transpired and thought whoever was responsible would come after her and finish her off. With the help of a gaming friend, she moved to a remote part of Missouri, used the alias Ellie Bowman, and set up shop on a dead-end street, where she sequestered herself in her house. She could not, would not, step foot outside. After doing her own cyber sleuthing by hacking into the NYPD street camera database, she discovered it was her boyfriend who'd pushed her. It finally came to a head, and he was now in jail.

"Wow, that's some story," Maggie said. "By the way, Fergus forgot to mention that I'm a reporter. I work for Annie's newspaper."

"Sorry, Mags. I thought she knew," Fergus apologized.

Libby had been taking copious notes. She wanted to be

sure she had all the right players. She flipped the pages. "Will everyone be at the farm later?"

"Charles, Myra, and Annie are still at the hospital," Fergus explained. "Kathryn is heading from the West Coast, but she will phone in, as will Charles. I'm not sure how involved Myra will be. But ever since she formed this tidy group, she has shown resilience in the worst of circumstances."

By then, they were pulling into the long driveway of the farm. "This is beautiful." Libby nodded at the trees and landscaping.

"Yoko and Izzie like to practice here. Izzie has a strong interest in architectural landscaping, and Yoko is a horticulturist extraordinaire," Maggie said.

Fergus drove to the back of the farmhouse, where everyone typically entered through the kitchen. Maggie handed a bag of dog treats she pulled from the glove box to Fergus. He never entered the house without a batch in his pocket. "Right-o, Maggie. Glad you thought of it."

"I can't take the credit. Annie reminded me."

Lady and her pups were yapping and whining as the three entered the house. Fergus squatted down to scratch their ears and offer them a chewy. He looked up at Libby. "You're a dog person, I hear?"

"Yes. I have a black lab named Buddy. Charles offered to let me bring him, but under the circumstances, I thought it might be too much for him. Me, as well . . . all of us."

"Next time," Fergus offered.

"I hope the next time will be under more favorable circumstances," Libby said.

"Let's get you settled." Fergus led the way to the guest room on the opposite side of the house. "You'll have lots of privacy here."

"Thank you. I'm sure we'll be rather busy for the next

couple of days." Libby smiled and petted Lady, who had followed them into the room.

"We'll be in the kitchen," Maggie said.

Fergus poked his thumb at Maggie. "She's *always* in the kitchen."

Maggie gave him an elbow in return.

When they entered the kitchen, Maggie moaned, "Who is going to cook for us?"

"What? You think I'm just the bottle washer?" Fergus looked insulted.

"No, but I don't think I've ever seen you with a spatula in your hand."

"Well, we'll just see about that." Fergus rummaged around in the refrigerator, then on to the freezer, and then in the pantry. He found enough ingredients to make shepherd's pie, and a phone call to Charles would also be on the menu. Fergus had about an hour before everyone would arrive, so he got busy in the kitchen.

Just before 4:00, there came the sound of cars on the gravel driveway. Lady and her pooches stood at attention by the kitchen door. One by one, they greeted the women as if it were a reception line. However, this time, it wasn't the usual jovial fist bumps and high fives among the Sisters. It was tearful hugs.

"Now, now. We promised we would stay positive. Nikki's condition is stable. Think good thoughts," Fergus advised them.

"Well, at least something smells good." Alexis took a big whiff. She held out her hand to Libby. "I'm Alexis."

"Nice to meet you," Libby said.

"Libby! Wow! How long has it been?" Izzie blurted. They had only met that one time, but Abner occasionally gushed about how smart Libby was and how they had friendly hacking competitions. In the beginning, it got on Izzie's nerves. But then she realized it was professional idolizing. Izzie was learning hacking as a hobby. Sort of. Truth be told, she was an excellent hacker, but this was beyond her scope. Someone had broken into *their* system.

"Since the class reunion a few years ago?" Libby couldn't remember, either.

Fergus wiped his hands and removed the frilly apron he found in the pantry. "Let's all have a seat at the table and run through a few things."

Maggie brought a pitcher of water with fresh lemons and glasses to the table.

Fergus dialed Charles's cell and placed the phone in the middle of the group. "We're here, mate. How's Nikki? Annie? Myra?"

"There's been no change, so that's the good news–bad news. Myra and Annie are sitting on the divan in Nikki's room. Annie procured a set of speakers so she can play some soothing music in the background. The doctor thought it might be helpful. Jack is here with me."

The women called salutations into the phone, including Kathryn, who was somewhere west of the Mississippi and also on the phone.

Fergus started. "I gave Libby a rundown of our group—nothing specific, but she's a smart egg. I think she's got the gist of it." He looked up at Libby and smiled.

Jack spoke next. "I've asked a former colleague to look into my old case files and find out if any inmates have recently been released. I can't think of any other reason why someone would want to blow up my car. And me. We still don't have the forensics from the blast. It's going to take several more days. But, as we discussed earlier, there has to be a connection between the bomb and the hacking."

Libby spoke up. "Hacking you is one way of disrupting your life, but bombing is one way of ending it. Most hackers are either looking for personal information or bent on disrupting things. Think about it—why would someone want to bring down a power grid? Clearly, they're not stealing anything. Chaos and disruption. When you have chaos coupled with fear, they feed into each other. That's their purpose. Distraction, disturbance, disorder. Divide and conquer."

Alexis leaned back into her chair. "I never thought about it that way."

"It's not always about money or industrial espionage," Libby continued. "That's why I tell people to be mindful of everything electronic. They usually say, 'I have nothing for them to steal.' But if your computer goes down, you are out of luck until it gets up and running again. Chaos in your life. Imagine multiplying that times hundreds of thousands, often millions, of people."

"Libby is so right. I've been working on an article on this very subject," said Maggie. " 'Think you're safe? Think again.' This is scary stuff. And we are living in scary times. Everything from fear of being physically harmed, electronically harmed, financially harmed, and emotionally harmed. People have anxiety up the wazoo." Maggie dumped a bag of candy bars on the table. "Stress relief." She laughed.

Libby chimed in. "Based on what I could find out, Jack's system was hacked via a dozen different IP servers. It's done all the time. They bounce from country to country. And it's very prevalent on the dark web. It appears someone wanted to find Jack Emery. Now, as far as I could tell, it doesn't appear that they breached his bank accounts, but they did hit his contact list. I can't tell how far or deep they went until I can check all of your individual computers. That's why you spotted those glitches, Charles. It was your system responding to an outsider. Almost like an alarm, even though it isn't set up that way. Sometimes artificial intelligence is helpful, and it appears you have some of that in your workings."

Charles's voice came through the phone. "I very much appreciate you taking the time to come. Let's hope it's an easy fix."

All eyes went around the kitchen table, each of them making a face. Yoko looked horrified, Izzie looked skeptical, and Maggie looked hopeful. With her red curly hair and freckled face, it was hard to tell when she wasn't. Fergus had his usual stoic face. Always the neutralizer.

"I have a question," Yoko said. "Libby said it was obvious someone was looking for Jack. Aren't there privacy laws to protect people who work for the judicial system?"

Jack spoke up. "Yes. But those are for law-abiding citizens. Criminals don't care what means they use. Let's face it—laws don't pertain to the lawless."

Grumbles of agreement circled the room.

"I'm going to push my contact at the CSI lab to see if we can get even a smidgen of information," Jack added.

"Brilliant," Fergus said. "We'll take Libby to the war room and see what she can find."

"Good enough. Let's check in again in two hours," Charles said.

"Roger that." Fergus disconnected the call.

Izzie took the lead. "You are about to enter a very sacred and secret space," she said to Libby. "This is where we do our brainstorming and much of our research and communication. We revere Lady Liberty, as she stands proudly in our midst. You should know that we always salute her when we enter and exit the room."

Libby nodded. Everyone rose from the table and followed Fergus to the back of the kitchen. As they descended the stairs, Libby remained silent, taking in the very old, very worn steps carved from stone. It truly felt clandestine.

When they reached the bottom, they entered a room that resembled the set from the show *NCIS*. Everyone, including Libby, saluted the statue of Lady Liberty. Libby scanned the room. "This is very impressive." She thought it would be super tech, but she was not expecting this. There was a multitude of supersized monitors, large digital touch screens that could display anything from maps to satellite photos, security feeds, and a bank of digital audio and visual recording devices. It was awesome, even to someone well-versed in technology like Libby. She had been in rooms like this hundreds of times. Even some private homes had extensive security, but this? This was extraordinary. "Wow."

"Where do you want to start?" Fergus asked.

"Let's start with the server and the routers." Libby turned to the other women. "Then I'll check your laptops for any malware, spyware, ransomware."

"Sounds good." Fergus brought her to a side room, where the external input and output electronics were housed.

Libby opened her kit bag and started to plug one device into another. "This is going to take a while." She looked up at Fergus.

"Yes. Right. I'll leave you to it then." He went back into the main room.

"What can we do in the meantime?" Maggie asked. None of them enjoyed waiting.

"Let me make a few calls. We may have to resort to pen and paper," Fergus said with a snicker.

Maggie stuck out her tongue. "See? You always laugh at me. Now look at us."

Fergus looked up the number of a colleague who worked as a consultant for Interpol. He thought he might help expedite by getting the list of recently released prisoners in the US. Many countries had reciprocity, but it usually involved persons who had known terrorist connections. Still, it was worth a try. Having once been the head of Scotland Yard, Fergus probably had more back doors at his disposal than most government leaders. He checked his watch. It would be after 10:00 P.M. in London, but when it came to a mission or any emergency, all hands were on deck.

After several rings, a voice answered. "Fergus? You old fart. What in blazes are you doing phoning me at such a late hour?"

"Did I wake you, Clarence?" Fergus knew his old pal usually burned the midnight oil.

"Are you a few sandwiches short of a picnic, old man?" Clarence asked mockingly.

"Not any more than you are one biscuit short of a packet!" Fergus laughed.

"What can I do for you, mate?" Clarence asked.

"One of my people was involved in an accident. Myra's daughter, Nikki. The car exploded just before she got into it."

"Is she all right?"

"In a coma, but stable."

"How can I help you with this?" Clarence queried.

"It was Jack's car. We believe it was meant for him." Fergus paused. "We're trying to figure out who would have done this. The thing is, Jack's computer was hacked we believe a few days earlier. It could be a wild coincidence, or it may be connected. I'm betting on there being a connection. One of the things we want to find out is who has been recently released from prison. Cases that Jack won when he was a federal prosecutor."

"And you want me to check Interpol?" Clarence already knew the answer to his question.

"I do realize it's a long shot, but it's our only idea right now. We're waiting for the results from forensics as to what caused the explosion. They suspect it was an IED."

"Did Jack have any cases that involved a bomber?"

"I can't answer that, but it's a good question."

"How soon do you need this? Besides right now?" Clarence chuckled.

"Don't laugh. Depending on what our IT person digs up, we may be using a fax machine or carrier pigeons. We don't know how bad this breach is, but we need the info ASAP."

"I'll see what I can come up with. It may take me a day or more."

"Thanks, mate. I owe you."

"Single malt, please." With that, Clarence signed off.

Fergus next phoned Jack and asked if he could remember any of his cases involving a bombing. Jack recalled there were at least three, most of them over fifteen years ago. He couldn't remember any of the names, but having that information was a good start. Once they got Jack's case history, they would be able to compare the lists and focus on locating those individuals first. Fergus felt some relief knowing they were doing something. He wasn't sure if any of it would be fruitful, but it was something.

The Sisters were fidgeting in their seats. Fergus thought it was probably a good time to have some chow. He went to check on Libby. "We're going to have a bit of dinner. Please join us."

Libby hesitated. "I'd rather keep working. I'm in the flow."

"Right. I'll fix a plate for you." Fergus nodded and went back to the war room. He summoned the three women, all of whom saluted, and then headed up the stairs.

The aroma from the shepherd's pies permeated the air. "If this tastes as good as it smells, Charles is going to have some kind of competition." Maggie chuckled.

Yoko and Izzie grabbed plates and flatware and set the table for the four of them. "I feel bad leaving Libby downstairs," Izzie said.

"She's in 'the flow'," Fergus said. "I'll fix her a plate." He scooped a large portion of the warm, aromatic chopped beef and vegetables covered with mashed potatoes into a bowl.

Maggie didn't even wait until she sat down before she sampled Fergus's attempt at cooking. "Yummy!"

"Please sit down and eat like a person," Yoko chided her.

"Yes, ma'am." Maggie climbed onto one of the wooden chairs surrounding the old farm table.

Fergus brought the dish to Libby. She had a smile on her face when he entered the room. "I trust that's because of the delicious aroma emanating from this bowl," he said.

Libby laughed. "That, too. So far, I haven't been able to find anything that's gone past the third firewall. It appears whoever did this was good, but not great. They hacked Jack's computer for sure and got access to his contact list, but as far as I can tell, nothing was hijacked from your system."

"Does that mean that all of us aren't at risk?"

"That I can't say right now. I'll have to do a manual check of their computers. 'Get under the hood,' as we say. Fragments can be very tricky and are almost indecipherable. Just like that little glitch Charles saw out of the corner of his eye. But if the same holds true for what I found here, I can do a sweep and clean them up."

"You are as good as Abner said." Fergus smiled. He set the bowl on a small portable table next to the console. "Anything else I can get you?"

"Thanks, I'm fine." Libby turned to the wafting food. "Mmm . . . I think I'll give that a try right now."

"I'll leave you to it. Give a shout if you need anything."

"Will do." Libby shoved a few forkfuls into her mouth and then returned to what she was working on.

Fergus climbed the stairs and announced to the women that it looked like the system was safe, but Libby would do a deep scan on all of their devices.

Yoko called Kathryn to tell her to bring her laptop, tablet, and all of her phones to the farm when she got back. "I've got a bit of a problem," Kathryn said. "I'm having some trouble with the engine, and I need to get it checked before I go any farther."

"Where are you now?"

"Outside Amarillo."

"Okay. Keep in touch. Good luck." Yoko ended the call, then relayed Kathryn's truck issue to everyone.

"She knows not to use anything electronic, correct?" Maggie asked.

"Yes. She's on that group text Charles sent."

After the women finished their food, they washed the dishes and made sure the kitchen was spotless. Except for the lingering smell of a hearty meal, there was no sign anyone had cooked or eaten there. Fergus looked around. "Splendid."

About an hour later, Libby came up the stairs. "The good news is that the system is safe. I ran a deep scan on everything and installed another firewall. Even *I* would have a hard time breaking into your system now." She chuckled.

"Is there bad news?" Maggie asked.

"Not really. I just need a little more time to trace where the originator of the search for Jack took place. As I mentioned to Fergus, whoever did this was good. I'm not so sure they intended to breach the system. But it came from Jack's contact list, so I have to work backwards. They may have used a dozen different IP addresses."

"How long do you think it will take?" Maggie asked, as if she were doing an interview.

"Hard to say. A couple of hours. Maybe less."

"So you think you'll know by tonight?"

Izzie came to Libby's aid. "Give the woman some room to breathe, Maggie."

"Sorry. It's been a bit stressful for all of us," Maggie apologized.

"No problem," Libby said. "I just want to freshen up a bit." Lady followed Libby into the guest room.

Maggie leaned in toward the other women. "I like her. She's a dog person." They shared their first high fives in a while. Maggie let out a hoot. One of the pups echoed her. "Thank goodness for Abner."

Izzie looked a bit crestfallen.

Yoko jumped in, taking Izzie's hand. "You are one of the best hackers ever. I don't know what we would have done without you for all those missions."

"Thanks. I know. But you know how it feels when you can't help. You feel helpless," Izzie explained.

"Well, you're not, and neither are we," Maggie said. "We are going to find those creeps." She stood up. "Whatever it takes!"

Another couple of hoots and a holler rang through the kitchen. "That's the best sound I've heard in a couple of days," Fergus said, and gave them a round of applause. The dogs thought it was an invitation for a treat.

Fergus checked the time. It was getting late. "Now that we know our system is safe, how about we grab a snack and turn in for the night? Libby still has work to do, and she probably needs a bit of a rest."

"If you don't mind, I'd rather start the tracking with a fresh head. Izzie, would you be able to help me in the morning?" Libby asked.

Izzie perked up. "Sure! What time do you want to start?"

"How early is early for you?"

"As early as you want," Izzie responded.

"I'd suggest you all stay here tonight so you don't have to drive home and back," Fergus offered.

"Pajama party?" Maggie hooted.

Fergus gave a wry smile. "No parties, but there is plenty of room for all of you here. I'm sure Myra and Charles won't mind."

"I have to get back to my house. I have a meeting with a bride-to-be first thing. But I'm available after noon," Yoko said.

"So Libby, Izzie, Alexis, and I will stay here," Maggie stated. "Now, what about that snack, Fergus?"

He let out a guffaw. It was a relief to know one of the issues was no longer an issue. "Let me see what I can rustle up in the kitchen."

"Charles better watch out. You might outdo him," Maggie joked.

"Hardly." Fergus smiled. "But before I do that, I'll call Charles and let him know how much progress Libby made today." Fergus went into the other room and used the landline.

Charles answered with a question. "I trust you have some good news to share?" Charles, Myra, Annie, and Jack had spent the day watching and waiting, hoping the tide would turn.

"I do indeed." Fergus felt as if some of the weight had been lifted. Not all of it, but an important change, nonetheless. "Libby found no breach in our system. Just some fragments from Jack's contact list. She added another firewall, so we should be good to go. Tomorrow morning, she and Izzie will work on tracing backwards to see where the breach to Jack's computer occurred."

"That is splendid news." Charles let out a big sigh of relief.

"Any updates with Nikki?" Fergus was almost afraid to ask.

"She's still stable, but no change yet. The doctor said it can happen suddenly or gradually. But we could use some good news on our end, as well."

"I'm taking Libby's news as a good sign," Fergus announced.

"Since when did you become a sign-keeper?" Charles scoffed.

"Since it seems appropriate." Fergus laughed back. "And tell Myra I said so."

"I certainly will. It looks like we're going to head back to the hotel and try to get some rest. Myra wants to stay, but I've convinced her that if she doesn't take care of herself, she'll end up in a hospital bed, too, and I wouldn't be able to handle it."

"Guilt trip?"

"You know the saying—'whatever it takes'." Charles chuckled.

"Right-o. By the way, Maggie and Izzie are going to spend the night, so they can get an early jump on the tracking."

"Brilliant," Charles said. "I'll share all of this with Myra, Annie, and Jack. He's going to continue to stay here at the hospital. The Tides Inn arranged for their things to be delivered, so he has a change of clothes and such."

"Sounds like we are moving in the right direction, mate." There was an uplifting sound to his voice.

"Indeed. Talk in the morning."

"Cheers." Fergus hung up the phone and began another hunt for food. There was a good-sized piece of roast beef, some cheddar cheese, and horseradish sauce in the fridge. Some rye bread in the pantry. Sandwiches were now on the menu. He prepared six of them, knowing Maggie would eat two, and Yoko had already said good night and left.

Several minutes later, he brought a tray out to the living room, where everyone had congregated during Fergus's call to Charles. "Nikki is stable, Myra is exhausted, and come to think of it, I haven't spoken to Annie. She'll have my hide."

He set the sandwich tray on the coffee table and hurried back into the kitchen.

The women sat on the floor and passed plates around.

Libby was the first to speak after chomping down. "I didn't realize how hungry I was."

"I'm always hungry," Maggie said. She was already eyeing the extra sandwich.

Chapter Twenty-two

Leroy's Big Adventure

Leroy was shuffling back and forth in the motel room. "Can you please sit down?" Darius was checking the time to see how much longer he'd have to put up with the bungler. *He better not bungle this.*

"I'm excited. And nervous." Leroy paused. "And nervous."

"You said that already."

"See? How much longer before we leave for the airport?"

"Another hour."

"I'm starting to sweat."

"Oh, cripes. Did you put on deodorant?"

"Yes, and talcum powder."

"Don't you know that stuff gives you cancer?"

"I thought it only gave cancer to women."

Darius shook his head. "Whatever keeps you dry."

Leroy felt under his armpits. "I have to change my shirt."

"Well, you can't wear the same one two days in a row. That would look suspicious."

Leroy took off his shirt and turned on the cheap blow-dryer that was one of the "amenities" of the motel. He aimed the nozzle at the armpits of the shirt and decided he might as well dry his own armpits. After a few minutes, he proudly walked out of the bathroom. "Problem solved."

"I hope it doesn't stink." Darius lit another cigarette.

"Hey, man, do you have to do that in here? I don't want to be getting all cigarette stinko. I have enough problems with my pits."

Darius stood and went outside on the sidewalk. His phone buzzed in his pocket. It was a text from Eric and Bennie. They had located his former dimwit lawyer, Daniel Stein. He stomped out the cigarette and went back inside to write down the information. He sent back a reply:

Thanks. Heading to airport in half an hour.

"What's that?" Leroy asked as Darius folded the paper.

"It's none of your business, that's what." Darius could not wait to unload Leroy at the airport. "Come on, let's get going."

Leroy gleefully grabbed his new luggage and practically skipped out the door. They got in the rental car and drove to the airport. Upon arrival, Darius was tempted to drop Leroy off and bolt, but he knew better than to leave him to his own devices. He wanted to be absolutely certain Leroy got on that plane. He looked for the signs for short-term parking and started to grumble. "Do any of these dang airports have signs that make sense? Leroy, keep an eye out for a sign for parking." Leroy gave him a quick salute. "And stop doing that salute thing. I'm not your captain."

"Sorry, boss." Leroy craned his neck, trying to read the multitude of signs pointing to different terminals, airlines, heliports, and cargo areas. "Hey! There's one. Short-term parking. Right?"

"Right." Darius shook his head. He must have said "short-term" three times.

Leroy stuck his arm out the window, eagerly pointing to a sign. "There!"

Darius cut in front of a taxi, bringing a mountain of expletives his way. Someone was pulling out of a spot, and Darius hurried his way in, getting too close for comfort to the exiting vehicle. That maneuver got him a dirty look and the middle finger.

"Gee, Darius. You seem to be in some kind of mood." Leroy almost didn't say it, but he was getting even more nervous by the minute.

"Yeah, what of it?"

"Nothin' really. I thought you'd be in a good mood. We're going to have the money soon."

"Right." At that moment, the only thing on Darius's mind was making the parts for his next two endeavors. Each would be different from the rest. He didn't want to create a "signature" someone could follow.

He figured it would take him twenty-four hours to drive back to Texas. Plus waiting overnight for Leroy. That was two days, plus or minus, depending on whether or not he drove through the night. Once he took care of the lawyer and then the ex, he guessed he'd be out of the country in about five or six days, if everything went according to his plan.

The two got out of the vehicle and walked toward the terminal doors. "We have to go pick up the package at the DHL counter." They spent another few minutes unraveling the information that was in front of them, above them, around them. The counter was several yards away. "Remember, your name is Larry Kratman. For now and for always," Darius said.

"Got it."

The two men approached the counter. Darius spoke. "Good morning. I'm here to pick up a package. Name is Jim O'Hara."

Darius didn't like the name had Eric picked for him, but it was what he had to deal with.

"Do you have some identification, Mr. O'Hara?" the clerk asked.

"That's the problem. My business partner and I were traveling, and we lost our wallets. A friend sent our passports here. If you'll open the package, you'll see everything is in order."

The representative gave him a questioning look. "Sir, we are not allowed to open customers' packages."

"How about if I open it in front of you?" Darius smiled. He finally found some charm in his personality.

"I don't know if that's allowed, either," the woman replied.

"But then you will be able to see our ID," Leroy chimed in, with a big grin.

Darius wanted to punch him. Instead, he said, "My colleague has a good point."

The woman looked around for some backup, but she was the only one at the counter, and a line was forming behind the two men standing in front of her. She handed them the package, thinking she could always call security if something fishy was going on.

Darius tore the top off of the envelope. The contents were exactly as Eric had promised. Darius handed the envelope, ticket, passport, and license to Leroy. "Here you go, Larry."

"Yep, that's me. Larry Kratman, see?" He flipped the passport open for the clerk to see.

Darius did the same. "Jim O'Hara."

"Thank you, gentlemen." The clerk turned to the next people in line.

Darius elbowed Leroy to move away from the crowd so they could check the rest of the contents of the envelope.

There was a coffee kiosk with high-top tables a few feet away. "Go get us some coffee," Darius ordered Leroy. "I'll wait here."

Leroy got in line to place the order. He kept opening and closing his passport. He was giddy. Then he spotted Darius giving him the stink eye. Leroy, aka Larry, snapped the passport shut and shoved it in his pocket. He kept feeling for it every other minute. He was definitely antsy.

Darius went through the envelope pouch. Round-trip ticket to George Town/Owen Roberts Airport, Grand Cayman Island. Hotel reservation for The Hideaway. Letter of introduction for the bank. Darius was a bit put out that Eric hadn't asked him to make the trip. Leroy could be a numbnut at times. Darius could have pulled it off, no sweat. But Darius had an imposing appearance. His rugged look would seem a bit out of place, although a lot of rich Texans hid their money in the Caymans. Darius shrugged it off. Soon, he'd be done with what needed to be done and on his way to a new life.

Leroy returned with two cups of coffee and a handful of sugar packets. "I forgot how much you take." He put six on the table.

"I don't use sugar."

Leroy shrugged.

"Everything is here. Let's run through it again."

Leroy went down the list he had memorized: the name of the hotel, name of the bank and the bank manager.

"Good. Remember—say as little as possible," Darius warned.

"Got it." Leroy gathered everything and put it in his wheeled overnight bag. Around fifteen minutes later, they walked to the monitors to check the gate. Leroy had an hour before his flight took off, but the line going through security was lengthy, as usual.

"Remember, you have to change planes in Miami," Darius said.

"Don't worry, boss. I'll manage. Bye for now." Leroy was getting tired of Darius treating him like a moron. Granted, he wasn't the best-educated person, having only completed the fifth grade. But he had a small measure of common sense. It was just that sometimes his mouth would engage before his brain had a chance to process information. People just needed to show a little more patience, that's all.

Leroy got into the queue and slowly made his way to the security guard who would be checking his ticket and passport. Leroy made a very good attempt at acting casual. He nodded at the guard. "Good morning."

The man scrutinized the photo, then Leroy, and let him pass to the next area, where he had to put his bag on the conveyor belt. He looked around and noticed people were taking off their shoes and putting them in plastic bins. It had been years since he boarded a plane, but he'd never actually flown in one. When he was a kid, he went to an air show. He got a tour of a cargo plane. He had seen lots of movies and TV shows with people at the airport, but he didn't recall ever seeing people take off their shoes. Noticing Leroy's confusion, the guy standing behind him in line handed Leroy a bin. "Put them in here."

"Uh, sure." Leroy took the bin and slipped off his shoes. *Dang that Darius!* He knew he should have worn socks! Leroy was extremely self-conscious and turned to the man. "This is my first time," he said sheepishly. Then he remembered Darius telling him *no chitchatting*. But it was too late. The guy engaged him in conversation.

"Where you headed?"

"Uh, Miami first. Then the Cayman Islands."

"Wow. That's quite a trip for a first-timer!"

Leroy didn't know what to say. Then he got a flash of *The Price Is Right* and the commercials for Publishers Clearing House. "I won it on a game show."

"Do tell!" The man was now intrigued. "Which one?"

Leroy froze. "Uh, it was a radio contest."

"I thought you said it was a game show?" The guy wrinkled his brow.

"It was a game on a radio show." Leroy was proud at how quickly he pulled out that lie. He watched his shoes go into the tunnel as a man on the other side looked at a monitor.

"How did you win? I mean, did you have to be the someteenth caller or something? Or did you have to answer a question?"

"Lucky guess."

"What was the question?"

Leroy thought quickly about the radio station he usually listened to. They never had contests but, if they did, what would it be?

"They wanted to know what Patsy Cline's first hit was."

" 'Crazy,' right?" The man stated it as more of a statement than a question.

"It was actually 'I Fall to Pieces.' Then she was in a car wreck. After that, she recorded 'Crazy.' "

"Well, you must be some kind of country music fan."

"Just the classics."

They were coming up to the metal detectors. As soon as Leroy went through, the machine beeped. "Sir, can you step aside?" asked the agent.

Leroy looked around.

The security agent repeated, "Sir? Can you please step aside?"

Leroy's knees got wobbly. "Is something wrong?"

"Do you have any prosthetics?"

"Pros-whats?"

"Metal."

Leroy had to think a minute. "Yes. There's a rod in my leg."

"Sir, have you ever been through a metal detector before?"

"Yes." Leroy's stomach was churning. He was so excited about getting on a plane, he'd forgotten about the pin in his leg.

"Stand over here, please. Raise your arms." The guard passed a wand under and around Leroy's arms, then up and down his legs. It buzzed around his tibia. "Next time, be sure to mention it so you don't waste people's time."

"Yessiree. Sorry. I'm just excited about my trip."

The man who had been standing behind him chirped. "It's his first flight. Won it on a radio show."

The guard looked unimpressed but said, "Enjoy your trip."

The man kept closely behind Leroy as they got closer to the gate. "I'm going to Atlanta. Flight's in a half hour. Want to grab a drink?"

Leroy looked at the clock. It wasn't noon yet.

"Nah. But thanks. I want to get in line."

"They will call your row once it's ready to board. Come on. You got plenty of time. Have a Virgin Mary if you don't want any alcohol. Me? I'm a bit of a nervous nelly when I fly, so I need something to calm the nerves."

Leroy thought again about Darius's instructions regarding conversations: *Limit the chitchat.* "Thanks, anyway. I gotta get going. Nice meeting you. And thanks for the help." He nodded at his shoes.

"Hey, never got your name," the man called out.

"Leroy." Then he wanted to crawl in a hole. He kept repeating in his head, *Larry . . . Larry . . . Larry.* "Larry Leroy," he amended.

"Nice meeting you, Larry Leroy." The guy did a double wave. One to the bartender at a nearby bar and the other to Larry Leroy.

Leroy hoped he would never run into him again. And he was more than happy Darius wasn't around to hear all this. Darius may have killed him. For real.

There were no empty seats in the waiting area, so Leroy positioned himself against a wall. He kept looking at the monitor and scanning the group of people traveling to Miami and/or parts unknown. Unknown to him, at least. It was a mix of people dressed similarly to him, a slew of tourists with gobs of children, and the gratuitous crying baby. He figured everyone was thinking the same thing: *Please not next to that kid.*

The gate attendant spoke into a handheld microphone. "Good afternoon, passengers. We will begin boarding shortly. Rows twenty-eight through thirty-two, please get in the line marked Group One." She continued giving instructions as the passengers moved to their places. The first-class line had its own sign. Leroy mimicked the rest of the passengers, clutching their boarding passes and passports in hand.

"We'll now begin boarding our first-class and Golden Wings members. General boarding will follow."

Leroy watched as the gate attendant checked every person and scanned their boarding passes. Leroy walked right through. So far, so good.

He shimmied his way to his seat, placing his bag in the overhead compartment. Just like everyone else. He couldn't help but notice some people had really large bags and backpacks, taking up more room than they should. If nothing else, Leroy was a polite person. His mother taught him the basics.

He took his seat next to the window and fastened his seat belt. It felt like he was on his first trip to Disney. He watched the baggage handlers toss luggage onto a conveyor belt carrying the cargo to the underbelly of the plane. Just like in the movies. Leroy was enthralled. He was so taken with this new experience, he thought he might ditch the Winnebago idea and just fly around the world.

An older couple sat next to him in the center and aisle seats. They nodded a cordial hello. *No small talk.* It was harder than he thought. He wanted to share his enthusiasm with someone. It would have to wait until he got back. Maybe he'd keep one of those journals he heard people talking about. Like a diary for a grownup. Or maybe get a bunch of postcards and write stuff on them. Light years away from anything scholarly, he, at the very least, knew how to read and write. That's when his father decided he didn't need any more learnin'. He could work at the junkyard with his old man and his uncle. Turn scrap into recycling. They paid good money for it. Sure, the rig they had was dangerous. There was always a chance for the burner to blow, but Leroy had it down by the time he was fifteen. It wasn't a bad way to make a living. Kinda dirty, but he made enough to pay the rent on the garage, grab a few brews during the week, and play some pool. Life wasn't too bad. Unless you compared yourself to a whole lot of other people, which he didn't. God put him there, and he wasn't supposed to doubt anything. That was another thing his mother taught him: *Be polite and don't ask questions.*

The flight attendant welcomed the passengers and began the safety video and instructions. Leroy felt under his seat to be sure his life vest was under there. The people next to him gave him an odd look. "Just checking. You never know," Leroy said to them. He had a point.

The flight took off on time and was uneventful. Leroy, aka Larry, managed to keep to himself during the trip. As they taxied to the gate, the flight attendant announced gates for connecting flights. Leroy paid close attention. Disembarking was also uneventful. Things were running smoothly. He had forty-five minutes to make his connecting flight to the Caymans. The gate was a short walk down the concourse. It was the same routine as his first flight. Wait. Stand. Walk. Sit. Fly. Then came the surprise: paperwork. He had to fill out some kind of customs claim form. He had no idea how he should answer the question: *Are you here for business or vacation?* If he said "vacation," then wouldn't they question him at the bank? Would they even know? He started to sweat again. He had to put his head in the right place. He made up his mind. He was conducting business for his boss. Yep. That was his story, and he was sticking to it.

When he got off the plane, he got in line for a taxi and then gave the driver the address of the hotel. The taxi driver knew it well. Leroy asked if he could recommend a restaurant nearby. It had been nearly ten hours since he had something real to eat. Larry, *né* Leroy, handed the driver a twenty-dollar bill when he realized he did not have any Cayman currency. "Dang. I only have American dollars."

"American dollars are all right with me, sir. Most people take them here."

"Whew. Thanks." Leroy exited the taxi and entered the hotel. Once he was checked in and had entered his room, he realized it was actually a one-bedroom apartment. He looked around. He wouldn't mind living there. It wasn't luxurious. But what did Leroy know about luxury versus adequate? One thing he did know was that it was light years better than the rathole where they'd stayed in Irvington. The one outside the airport in Washington wasn't much better. This *was* luxury in comparison. He sent Darius a text, letting him know he arrived unscathed and would go to the bank first thing in the morning.

Darius relayed the message to Eric, who in turn notified Bennie. They were almost there.

Chapter Twenty-three

Philadelphia

It was only 6:00 A.M. when Myra crawled out of the king-size bed in their suite at the hotel. Charles stirred and reached behind him. He sat up. "Myra?"

No answer. He jumped up, pulled on a robe, and shuffled into the living area of the hotel room. Myra was sitting on a window seat, staring into space. "Are you all right?"

"Oh, Charles, I didn't mean to wake you. I just couldn't sleep."

"You haven't slept well in two days. That's not going to bode well for you if you keep it up."

"I know. I know. This has been such a disastrous week. I'm almost afraid to see what horrible thing is going to happen next."

Charles sat down and put his arm around her. "Listen to me. Nikki is going to be okay. Did you hear Libby's story about her incident? She's fit as a fiddle now. It gives us hope."

Myra rested her head on Charles's shoulder. "I hope you're right."

"Remember, we have to keep thinking positively. Things have made a good turn already. We are back in business, so to speak. Libby and Izzie are going to hunt down whoever got into Jack's computer. He's going to have to stay off of it until Libby can install a new firewall. Jack checked all of his accounts, and none of them were hacked. Makes you wonder why."

Myra's eyes went wide. "Because they were trying to locate him, that's why. It's all starting to fit together, just as we thought. Whoever did that to Jack, did this to Nikki." All of a sudden, Myra had a burst of energy. "We are going to find this person, and he is going to fry." She got up with renewed energy and stomped into the bathroom to run a bath. She called out over the loud running water, "Whoever did this is going to be sorry he was ever born."

"That's my girl!" Charles was beyond delighted to see Myra be Myra again. He phoned room service and ordered a continental breakfast with a side of bacon. A few croissants and some crispy fat should renew Myra's appetite.

Half an hour later, Myra was drying her hair as their food arrived. The young server placed the food and dinnerware on the dining room table. "May I get you anything else, sir?"

"That will be fine. Thank you," Charles said.

The young man gave a short bow and exited. Myra came from the bathroom exclaiming, "Do I smell bacon?"

"You do, indeed. Here. Sit. A little nourishment."

"Nourishment and bacon do not belong in the same sentence." Myra smiled as Charles pulled the chair out for her. "Oh, Charles, you are a love. I do feel like some of the cloud has lifted." Before she could take her first sip of coffee, the phone rang. She halted, cup in midair.

Charles went to the phone. "Good morning."

"Mr. Martin? Dr. Jarmon."

Charles steadied his nerves. "Yes, Doctor?" Myra was still frozen in position.

"I have some encouraging news."

"Do tell."

"The swelling has greatly subsided, so there is no need for surgery. At least, not at this moment."

"That is very good news. So what's the next course of action?" Charles asked.

"We wait. The neuroscience team will be here shortly and do some basic tests."

"Such as?" Charles asked. Myra had sidled up beside him at this point.

"Reaction to stimuli. Light, touch, audio. We'll measure brain activity as we proceed. Quite standard." The doctor paused. "Our priority last night was to make sure she was stable and that the swelling didn't increase. Now we can do rudimentary tests."

"How long will it take?"

"Less than an hour. They should be here shortly."

Charles checked his watch. It was just after 7:00 A.M. "What time should we plan on getting there?"

"As you know, the suite is available to your family twenty-four hours a day. You can come whenever you like."

"Is Jack with you?"

"He is sitting with Nikki. I'm at the nurse's station."

"Would you be so kind as to ask him to call us from the hospital phone?"

"Certainly."

"We'll be there within the hour."

"Fine. I'll speak with you after we get the test results." Dr. Jarmon ended the call.

Myra was clinging to Charles with one hand and her pearls with the other. "What? What?"

"The swelling has gone down. They are going to do tests to see how she reacts to stimuli. Myra, this is a good sign."

Myra's eyes welled up with tears. "I really do feel a cloud has been lifted."

"Come. Finish your breakfast. I'll see if Annie is up." Charles rang the phone in the suite next to theirs.

"Everything all right?" Annie's voice was high-pitched.

"The swelling went down. They'll be doing rudimentary stimuli tests this morning."

"That sounds promising. How is Myra doing?"

"She's enjoying a bit of bacon with her croissant."

"That sounds promising, too!" Annie was almost gushing. She was terribly worried about her friend. All of them, but especially Myra. She remembered the dark days after Barbara was killed.

"Here, I'll let you speak to her." Charles handed Myra the phone.

"Good morning." Myra sounded chippier than she had twelve hours before.

"Bacon?" Annie teased.

"Charles called it *nourishment*." Myra slapped his hand as he was about to take a piece from her plate.

"Whatever works. When are you going back to the hospital?"

"Within the hour. I know they won't have test results, but I think Jack can use some company."

"I'll be ready. Buzz me when you're about to leave."

"Will do." Myra hung up the phone and licked the bacon salt off her fingers.

Charles was smiling at her.

"What?" She pulled open her napkin.

"It's good to see you shine."

Half an hour later, she gave Annie the heads-up they were

leaving. The three walked briskly to the hospital and used their VIP passes to enter. They made their way to Nikki's room, where Jack was slumped in a chair, looking disheveled. Cooper was the sentry, sitting at attention with his head at Nikki's feet.

"My good man. You might want to think about cleaning up your act." Charles was half-joking. "You wouldn't want Nikki to wake up seeing you like this."

Jack looked dazed. "Huh? Oh, right. I guess I'm a little crusty."

"They're going to be doing tests soon, so why don't you get in the shower and put on some fresh clothes?" Charles nudged.

Jack stood and sighed. "Good idea." He kissed Myra on the cheek as he left the room.

Myra went to Nikki's side and took her hand. "It's going to be all right, darling. We are all here praying for you." Myra could have sworn Nikki squeezed her hand, but she knew involuntary muscle spasms were common with coma patients. Yet she clung to the thought that perhaps Nikki was coming around. Several minutes later, the neuro staff entered the suite, which meant everyone else had to vacate and wait in the living room. Annie turned the subject over to something they could focus on together.

"We need to get Jack's laptop checked by Libby."

Myra was the first to respond. "Charles, why don't you take it to the farm and work with Fergus and the girls? There isn't much you can do here."

Charles looked at Annie, who nodded in agreement. "Are you sure?" he asked.

"Yes, I'm sure. There's no reason for all of us to be sitting around. Maybe Libby and Izzie will find out who did this, and then we can take some action." Myra was certain it was the right thing for him to do.

"I'll arrange for the helicopter to take you to the farm. It can land in the back field," Annie offered.

"Right-o," Charles answered. "I'll let Fergus know I'll be heading back as soon as we get an ETA."

They waited for Jack, who emerged showered, clean-shaven, and dressed in fresh clothes.

"Jack, I'll be going to the farm sometime today. I'll take your computer with me," Charles said. "Fergus got in touch with Clarence, who is working the Interpol records to see if we can get a list of parolees from your cases sooner."

"I've been thinking a lot about this. It's been a while since I was a prosecutor. I really can't think of anyone who would pose a threat. Most of the cases were a team effort. We should probably get in touch with my former colleagues and warn them. Or, ask them if they've heard anything."

"Excellent idea," Annie said. "Who would be the best person to contact? Someone who would have access to those records."

"My former clerk, Rose Tanner. She still works there. She had a memory like a steel trap."

"Let's hope she's been taking vitamin supplements," Annie snorted.

Jack was about to open his laptop when Charles stopped him. "Give it here. We don't know who might be tracking you, physically or electronically."

Myra gasped. "Do you think someone is still stalking them?" She was getting riled up again.

"It's possible, but it appears their main objective was to commit bodily harm." Charles tried to keep Myra from going to a dark place again. "They're probably far from here right now."

Annie chimed in, "If they know what's good for them. But even so, we will find him, them, whoever, wherever. Meanwhile, let me call the chopper service." Annie pulled out her phone and hit the speed dial number for a helicopter service they used from time to time. Not only were they swift, but they were also discreet. She gave them the information, nodded, and said, "Thanks. He'll see you in forty-five." Annie turned to the others. "Chopper will pick you up in forty-five minutes. Flight time is about thirty minutes. You should be there by ten-thirty at the latest."

"Good. Perhaps we can get a good day's work in." Charles turned to Jack. "Do you have Rose's contact information anywhere else besides your laptop?"

"Don't laugh, but it's in that old Rolodex that's on my desk at the farm," Jack replied.

"So that antique just might come in handy," Charles joked. "I'll check in with Fergus and then take one of the carts to your place."

"Great."

"This is starting to sound like a plan." Annie rubbed her hands together. She had a twinkle in her eye.

Charles checked his watch. "I better crack on." He pulled Myra tenderly in his arms. "I don't want you to fret about anything. I know that's asking the impossible, but rest assured, everything we are dealing with is in the best of care and hands." Myra rested her head on his chest for a moment. Charles lifted her chin and gave her a loving kiss. He held her chin in his hand. "See this?"

"What?" Myra squinted at him.

"Your chin. Keep it up." Then he kissed her on each cheek. The four of them stood in a circle and held hands.

Myra said a short prayer:

> *"Thank you for this morning light*
> *That saved us from the darkened night.*
> *Blessings for our health and friends,*
> *For peace and love we ask, Amen."*

Before Charles was about to leave, he turned to Annie. "Let me know Nikki's test results, and take care of my girl, here."

"Will do. Take care of my bloke," Annie replied.

Charles put the computer in a messenger bag, slung it over his shoulder, and grabbed his jacket. He gave Jack one more pat on the back. "Hang tough."

Jack squeezed out a small smile. "Thanks, Charles."

Annie, Myra, and Jack sat back down in the living room, anxiously awaiting the test results. Jack was pacing, Myra was fidgeting with her pearls, and Annie was sitting on the window seat, swinging her legs back and forth. About half an hour later, Dr. Jarmon entered the room. He was smiling.

All three jumped at him. He put his hands up as if to fend them off. "There was brain activity when we tested the bottom of her feet, as well as a reflex response."

"What does that mean?" Jack asked.

"That means her brain acknowledged the stimuli."

"But what does that mean, exactly?" Myra chimed in.

"It means there is a cognitive process going on. Her brain is registering."

"Does that mean she's awake?" Annie asked.

"No, she is still unconscious," Dr. Jarmon explained. "But this is a good sign. I know you would like me to tell you when she'll wake up." He paused to select his words carefully. "I can't answer that. She may or may not regain consciousness."

Myra gasped. Annie held her steady.

"However, it's been my experience that with her vital signs, less swelling, and a response to stimuli, it is possible she will regain consciousness. But, again, I can't tell you when. Remember, your only job now is to stay positive. We, and Nikki, will do the rest."

Myra let out a big sigh. Jack finally sat down, and Annie

sent Charles and Fergus a text, telling them Nikki had passed the stimuli test. After a few moments of silence, Myra launched into business mode.

"As soon as Charles gets to the farm, Libby will check out Jack's laptop. Libby will try to trace the infiltration backwards with Izzie's help. Let's call this Phase One. Phase Two would be to get that list of parolees from Jack's cases. Phase Three is to notify anyone who was involved in those cases. See if there were any threats. Phase Four is to find him or them. Phase Five . . . well, imagine the best justice we can deal out."

Chapter Twenty-four

The Cayman Islands

Leroy jumped when the alarm went off next to him. He couldn't remember the last time he slept so well. It was 7:00 A.M. He was trying to remember if Grand Cayman was an hour ahead of Virginia, the same time, or an hour after. He sat up and scratched his head. In any case, the bank wouldn't be open for another two hours. He imagined what Darius might be doing. Leroy was getting more and more fearful of him. That thing with the bomb had rattled him. He hoped the woman would be all right. He hated the idea that he was part of Darius's vindictive plan. He wondered if Eric and Bennie knew about it. They didn't seem the type that would want to kill anybody. What was the point? Soon they would all be sitting pretty with a pile of cash. Why take chances? He scratched his head again, shuffled into the bathroom, and took a shower, shaved, and tidied up his hair. He pulled a pair of fresh trousers and a shirt from his bag. No socks. He was still a bit embarrassed about the shoe thing at the airport. He decided he would buy a pair of socks before he headed back to the States.

Leroy felt chipper and confident. He had gotten this far without incident. He even brought breath mints with him. Yes, he was good at following instructions. Satisfied he was appropriately dressed for a bank transaction, he went outside in search of a place for breakfast. The bank was only several blocks away from where he was staying.

As he walked along the sidewalk lined with polished shops, he marveled at how beautiful and clean everything was. It really was like Disneyland to him, a place he had never been. Truth of the matter, Leroy had never been anywhere. Except for the trip to the pen in Forrest City, Arkansas.

He spotted large cruise ships just offshore, waiting to dock. He finally understood what *paradise* meant. Maybe he'd stay here. He could be a busboy at one of the big hotel restaurants. As he continued to stroll down the street, he played out a number of fantasies. There was nothing back in Virginia for him. He jumped when a car horn blared at him as he stepped onto the street, breaking his spell. He'd forgotten they drove on the left side of the road. Leroy went back to his ruminating. What if he didn't go back for real? Did it matter? Then he thought about Darius. Would he care where Leroy ended up? Definitely not. He had his own plans. Plans that Leroy was glad he wouldn't be any part of.

There was a small café a few doors ahead. He stopped for a muffin and coffee. He had another hour to kill before the bank opened. He continued his leisurely walk and came upon a small square with a bench. People were starting to fill the streets. Again, he wondered what life would be like here. Before he knew it, the hour had whizzed by. He hustled his way to Cayman National Bank.

It smelled of money. Cool, clean air, with a hint of something. *Cash*. Leroy chuckled to himself.

He walked over to a reception desk and politely asked the woman if he could meet with the manager. She gave him an odd look. "Do you have an appointment?"

Leroy wasn't expecting the question. "Uh, no, sorry."

"May I ask to what this is in reference?" She had a singsong tone but a crisp accent.

Leroy pulled the envelope from his jacket inside pocket. "I have a letter of introduction from my employer requesting a transfer of funds." He had rehearsed that line a dozen times the night before.

"What is your name, sir?"

"Le—Larry Kratman." He almost blew it.

"I'm sorry. Did you say Lee Larry?"

"Uh, no. sorry. Larry Kratman. He doesn't know me. I'm here for my employer."

"And what is his name, sir?"

Leroy paused for a second. He didn't want to fumble this one. "Gregory Masters."

The woman picked up the phone and hit a button. She explained to the person on the other end that there was a man here at the behest of his employer. "Will do," she said before hanging up. "Please have a seat, Mr. Kratman. He will be with you shortly. He is finishing up with another client."

Leroy nodded. "Thank you."

Almost half an hour had passed, and the manager still hadn't come out. Leroy's palms were getting sweaty. He tried to act casual, slowly wiping his hands on the sides of his pants. Finally, he heard a door open. He gave his right hand one more swipe.

"Mr. Kratman?" an older gentleman asked.

"Yes, sir." Leroy extended his dry palm.

"Please come in." The manager motioned to his office. "Have a seat."

Leroy tried not to look around. He didn't want to gawk. His knee started bopping up and down. The man behind the desk read and reread the documents. He finally looked up. "Mr. Kratman, I trust you are aware that we need to authenticate this letter and signature."

Leroy froze for a moment. His eyes were blinking like a railroad sign meant to protect you from oncoming trains. He gulped. "Of course, sir."

"It should take about three days." The man rested his forearms on the desk. "Where can we reach you?"

Leroy was close to hyperventilation, but he held his cool. *Slowly*, he reminded himself. "I'm at The Hideaway. Three days, did you say?"

"That is correct. One of our associates will contact you and set up an appointment to finish the paperwork." He said it matter-of-factly.

"Yes, of course, sir." Leroy knew he was going to get an earful from Darius. Maybe he should contact Eric himself. No, that would enrage Darius even more. There was a communication chain. You didn't deviate from it.

The man waited for Leroy to get up and leave. But he didn't move.

"Is there something else?" the manager asked.

"Uh, no. No, sir. Thank you, sir." Leroy wasn't sure if he should extend his hand. But he did. It was the polite thing to do.

The man stood and shook Leroy's hand. "Enjoy your day."

"You, too, sir." Leroy's mind was racing. There was no way he was going to be able to enjoy his day. It wasn't his fault. Eric should have known. But maybe the procedures had changed while he was in jail. It didn't matter. No one was going to get their hands on any funds for at least three more days.

* * *

Leroy held the phone a foot away from his ear as Darius let loose a mouthful of expletives. He knew there was nothing he could say to stop the oral assault. Once the rant was over, Leroy attempted a question. "What should I do?"

That set off another barrage, ending with, "You wait, you idiot!"

"I know that, Darius." Leroy was getting tired of being Darius's verbal punching bag. "I meant what do I do while I'm waiting?"

"Lay low. There should be plenty of money on the debit card. Just don't go crazy."

As if Leroy would even think of overstepping. The only thing he planned on purchasing was a pair of swimming trunks. *And of course, a pair of socks. Oh, maybe I will go crazy and buy two pairs.*

Leroy took a good look around. It was small apartment. He checked the rate posted in a booklet on the desk. Only 137 dollars per day. Then he did the math on a piece of paper, slowly remembering his times tables. Whoa. It added up to over four grand a month. He had to rethink his plans. Maybe going back to Virginia wasn't so bad. Or anywhere. Back to the dreams of a Winnebago.

Eric did not take the news well, but at least he didn't go bonkers. Neither did Bennie. Three more days wouldn't matter much. But for Darius, it was another story. He was on a schedule, just in case they managed to trace the first bomb back to him. He knew it was a one-in-a-million long shot, but Murphy's Law seemed to prove true more times than he would have liked.

Eric went back to LA, and Bennie back to Las Vegas. Darius thought this could actually be a good time for the second stage of his plan. He could make the round trip to Texas in three days if he hauled butt. He had the addresses. Then he thought about flying back. That would save him a day and a half. He would rent a vehicle when he got to Texas. Change it up for another one after Amarillo. He nodded. Maybe things weren't so bad, after all.

Chapter Twenty-five

Pinewood

Libby was up at the crack of dawn. She familiarized herself with the grand farm kitchen. Lady and the pups were eyeing her up and down. They wanted to be fed. Fergus had said he would handle it, but it wasn't quite 6:00 a.m. yet. "Okay, pups. Let me see what I can do." Lady walked over to the cabinet where the food was kept. She raised her paw. Libby chuckled. "Smart girl."

The rest of the dogs lined up, waiting to be served. Once Libby got the dogs fed, she rummaged around, looking for something to make coffee with. She scanned the counter. There was a Mr. Coffee, with bins of Folgers lined up next to it. She hoped there was something a little stronger somewhere. If nothing else, she loved a good, strong cup of coffee in the morning. She needed it to start her brain engine. She thought about that for a minute. Did the caffeine help her thought process? Probably, but she didn't want to take any chances that morning. As she went through each cabinet, she came across a French press coffee maker in the pantry. Maybe that was a sign there was a darker, more pungent roast hiding somewhere on a shelf. Libby opened the fridge and saw a bag of Sumatra roast tucked in the back. *Eureka!*

As she dug deeper into the refrigerator, she pulled out a dozen eggs, sliced brioche bread, milk, butter, cream, and blueberries, and began to make French toast.

Maggie appeared in the kitchen, as if materialized out of thin air. She gave Libby a start.

"Sorry. I have a thing for food." Maggie peeked at the frying pan. "French toast?"

"I hope so," Libby said as she rinsed the berries, then pushed down the plunger of the French press.

Maggie got out the dishes and flatware and set the table. "Where did you learn to cook?"

"This isn't exactly cooking," Libby said.

"Are you kidding? As much as I love food, I cannot cook a thing. There is crime-scene tape in my kitchen."

Libby hooted. "Living sequestered for almost a year, I had to do something with my time besides work, so I learned a few dishes. Cooking for one is more challenging than you'd think."

"I know. That's why I'm not allowed in my kitchen." Maggie laughed as she poured two cups of coffee. "Smells delish!"

A few minutes later, Izzie wandered into the kitchen, Alexis trailing behind. "Oh, my. Something smells delicious," Izzie said.

"Libby is making French toast with blueberries. And check this out. Real coffee!" Maggie announced.

"Impressive. Charles has some competition in the kitchen." Izzie grabbed a mug from the cabinet and handed it to Maggie to fill.

The three women sat at the table and chatted with Libby as she gently turned the egg-soaked bread. Libby filled them in on the rest of her story—her coma, her seclusion, her cyber sleuthing, and her ultimate reemergence. She told them had it not been for the humanity of her neighbors, she might still be sequestered. "At first, when I watched the people from my upstairs window, I thought it was a little creepy of me. But it made me realize that everyone has their own issues, their dreams, desires, and hopes. Even when I was working and living in New York, my life was consumed with work and my dipstick boyfriend. It took a coma and a small town in Missouri for me to get a better understanding of human nature."

Maggie sipped her coffee in wonder. "You know, that would make a really good story."

"Really? I think it's kind of boring," Libby answered.

"Seriously. How you overcame an accident, beat the agoraphobia, and tracked down the truth. It's inspiring. Really, it is," Maggie added.

Libby stood with the spatula in midair. "I never thought of it that way. The one thing I feel badly about are the lies I told my mother and my best friend."

"But you were only protecting yourself." Alexis got up and helped plate the French toast, piling blueberries on each.

"I know, but still, I was living a lie." Libby placed another round of the buttery, egg-battered bread on another plate.

"Don't be so hard on yourself." Maggie slurped more coffee with one hand and clenched a fork with the other. "People do what they have to do in order to survive." She almost dug into the luscious pile before Izzie put it on the table.

"Easy, girl," Alexis cautioned.

"See? I'm doing what I need to do in order to survive." Maggie jutted out her chin.

Izzie looked at Libby. "I don't know where this girl puts it."

"Well, there's plenty more," Libby replied.

The dogs' ears perked up at the sound of gravel beneath a golf cart pulling up. Fergus bounded into the kitchen. "Something smells scrumptious. Is Charles back already?" Lady wouldn't let him get past her until he handed her and her pups a treat.

"Not only is Libby a computer whiz, but she's also pretty good in the kitchen, too," Izzie said.

"Splendid," Fergus said with a big grin. "Now I can retire from being substitute chef."

"Charles should be here soon, so you'll be off the hook," Maggie teased.

"Good thing. I only know how to make one thing."

"You made sandwiches!" Maggie said. "And shepherd's pie."

"Lucky break we had the ingredients," Fergus said.

Libby handed him a plate of her breakfast fixings and made one for herself. The quintet sat at the table and happily devoured the delicious meal.

"More coffee, anyone?" Alexis moved toward the French press.

Fergus asked for a refresh, but everyone else had had their fill of caffeine for the morning. As they finished up, everyone brought their plates to the sink. There was nothing left to scrape off. The only evidence that food had ever been on the dishes was a smear of syrup.

Fergus patted Libby on the back. "Well done."

The others gave a round of high fives. The room crackled with positive energy. Once the kitchen was once more immaculate, the women changed from their pajamas and reconvened in the kitchen half an hour later. Before they knew it, the unique sound of a helicopter was in the distance. Lady sat up and gave a woof.

"Must be Charles," Fergus noted. Several minutes later, Charles came through the kitchen door. Lady and her fur-family thumped their tails like the beating of several drums. He stopped to give each of them a scratch around the ears.

"Good morning, everyone." Charles was in a reasonably good mood, given the circumstances. "Smells like I missed something delicious."

Libby looked sheepish. "Oh, Charles, my apologies. I should have made some for you."

"No worries. I'm fine." Charles extended his hand. "You must be Libby."

"I am."

"Nice to meet you in person."

"Likewise." Libby smiled. "You have quite an operation here."

Charles jerked his fingers at the Sisters. "Them? A bunch of trouble, they are."

"So I've been warned." Libby winked at the Sisters. "And your setup downstairs is a wonderland for someone like me."

"We do our best to keep up. But clearly, we needed a bit more tightening of the screws."

"Oh, they're tightened. But it's just a matter of time when you'll have to install another firewall. The technology grows exponentially."

"It's like poison ivy. The more you scratch it, the more it spreads," Alexis said, causing a round of guffaws.

Charles smiled. "It's good to see everyone in an upbeat mood. The news about Nikki responding to stimuli seemed to turn the tide somehow."

"How is Myra doing?" Alexis asked.

"Better, but you know how she frets," Charles answered.

"And Annie?" Maggie asked about her boss.

"She's raring to go." Charles snickered.

"What about Jack?" Izzie asked.

"We had to push and point him to the shower, but he's coming around. Poor boy. He was in such a state of shock."

"We all were. Still are," Izzie added.

"Yes, and we will continue to pray for Nikki's speedy recovery. Meanwhile, we need to find this ne'er-do-well." Charles handed Jack's laptop to Libby.

"Great. Izzie and I will get started," Libby said.

"I have to buzz over to Nikki and Jack's to get his Rolodex," said Charles.

"That old thing?" Alexis snorted.

"Yes, that old thing. And with some luck, that old thing will give us a lead as to Jack's former cases."

"Isn't the FBI helping? His former colleagues? Anyone?" Maggie asked. "I thought they were looking into it."

"It's the government, my dear. As good as they are at some things, expediency isn't often a priority."

"But this is urgent. What if the guy tries it again?" Maggie protested.

"That's why we are gathered here. If anyone can figure this puzzle, it's us." Charles gave a thumbs-up. "Be right back." He walked briskly out the kitchen door, hopped into one of the carts, and sped off.

Izzie and Libby went down the stairs, saluted Lady Liberty, and set up a few modules. Alexis and Maggie waited for Charles to return, and Fergus gave Clarence another call. At least it would be early afternoon this time.

The phone rang twice on the other end. "Fergus, you old fart. Here you are again," Clarence bellowed.

"I think you're an older fart than I." Fergus returned the quip.

"I have a list of inmates who were released in the past six months." Clarence wanted to manage Fergus's expectations. "It's quite a long one, old chap."

"Doesn't surprise me. How long a list?"

"Several hundred, spread out over the entire US."

"Several hundred. Three? Four? Five?"

"Four hundred eighty-two, to be exact."

Fergus gave a whistle. "Well, let's hope Jack's former clerk can get us his case file, and we can cross-check them."

"Splendid idea," Clarence spoke again. "How do you want me to send the information?"

"Our system is up and running again. I'll send you a link, and you can upload it. Give me a couple of minutes," Fergus said.

"Right-o. Anything else I can do for you?" Clarence asked.

"Not at the moment." Fergus paused. "I can't thank you enough."

"Always a pleasure to help. Ta-ta," Clarence said, and then ended the call.

Fergus turned to the others. "Clarence got a list from Interpol of inmates released from federal prison over the past six months."

"How many are there?" Maggie asked.

"Almost five hundred," Fergus replied.

"Yikes! That's a lot," Maggie chirped.

"Considering over a half million are released across the country each year, that is a drop in the bucket," Alexis said. Moving into lawyer mode, she added, "Did you know that within three years, at least two-thirds will be rearrested?"

"That is shocking, but not surprising." Maggie sighed. "When I was on the city desk at the paper, I covered a lot of crime stories, and it was shocking to see so many repeat offenders."

Alexis gave a wry smile. "They keep people like me, Nikki, and Lizzie in business."

"Not *those* people!" Maggie protested.

"No, but many of their victims, unfortunately." Alexis sighed.

The sound of gravel being upturned got everyone's attention again. Charles made a mad dash into the house. "I found Rose Tanner's contact information. I'm going to give her a call right now."

Maggie updated him. "Fergus just went downstairs to retrieve the list Clarence is sending of released federal inmates."

"Splendid. Now we're getting somewhere. I'm going to call Rose now." Charles dialed the number on the worn card that had been sitting in the round plastic device, which held almost a hundred more just like it.

A woman's voice answered. "Hello, this is Rose Tanner."

"Hello, Rose. This is Charles Martin, Jack Emery's father-in-law."

"Hello, Charles. To what do I owe this call? Is everything all right?"

Charles didn't want to get into the entire scenario. He didn't want anyone to know any details of what happened. Better to keep mum and not reveal anything that wasn't necessary. He skipped the second question.

"Jack asked if you could help him out with a project he's working on."

"Sure. If I can," Rose answered.

"I know it's a long shot, but is there any way you can find out information on Jack's previous cases?"

"That depends. When were they?"

Charles thought a minute. They couldn't possibly search through all of Jack's previous cases. Then it dawned on him. "Several years ago. What we need to find out is who would be up for release this year."

"Hmmm. I'd have to run it through the database. And to be honest, some records don't update as quickly. It depends on parole hearings, etcetera."

"We'd just need anyone who could have been released within the past few months. And the names of the other lawyers on the team."

"Goodness. That could take all day, Charles."

Playing on her ego, Charles added, "Jack said if anyone can do it, Rose Tanner can."

Rose was truly flattered. "What a nice thing to say. All I can promise is I'll do my best."

"That's all we ask," Charles said smoothly.

"I wouldn't want to disappoint Jack. He is one of the finest people I've ever worked with. We really miss him."

"I will pass that along to him." Charles waited for Rose to say something further.

"Let me see what I can do. What is a good number to reach you at?" Rose asked.

Charles gave her both his cell and the kitchen phone number.

"I'll be in touch later."

"Thanks ever so much, Rose. We are truly grateful."

"Don't thank me yet," Rose said kindly. "Bye for now."

After saying goodbye, Charles made a fist-pump gesture. "She's on it."

Maggie and Alexis clapped their hands. The dogs gave an approving woof.

"Come, let's see what havoc we can wreak downstairs." Charles led the way, with Alexis and Maggie following. They gave the respectful salute and gathered around the large conference table, where Fergus was downloading the file from Clarence.

"Rose Tanner is going to check Jack's former cases of inmates who were eligible for parole this year," Charles said.

"Fantastic!" Fergus looked up from his computer. "If we can cross-reference her list and this one, we will be closer to our target."

Charles addressed Izzie and Libby. "Any luck?"

"Working backward from Jack's system, we found over a dozen IP addresses that bounced," Libby said. "As far as we can tell, it originated in a small town in Arizona, near the Nevada and California borders, about a week ago. Whoever did this used a pretty sophisticated encryption device so no one could access their information while they were surfing the web. The dark web, to be exact. But I'm slightly better than they are, and I located the Wi-Fi source. It's a small motel. I have the address, but I doubt they'll still be there."

"How so?" Charles asked.

"I was able to track *their* system. It appears they did this again in another small town, a few hundred miles north of the first one."

"You mean this person or people are on the move?" Charles queried.

"It appears that way," Libby said.

Charles frowned. "That's going to make it more difficult for us to find them, yes?"

"Only if they stop," Libby said. "The second search they did was two days ago. Nothing since."

"Okay. Let's go over what we know," Charles began. "A person or persons are moving from place to place, tracking people down. We believe it was someone from one of Jack's cases. What we're waiting for is the list from Rose, so we can cross-check it with the list from Clarence."

"Meanwhile, I'll see if I can get any more activity from my scanning," Libby offered.

"How do you do that, by the way?" Alexis asked.

"Be able to track someone?" Libby asked. "Electronics has its own, shall I say, fingerprints. It's quite fractional, meaning unless you have highly advanced equipment, you can't possibly follow it. But if you do—and most people do not—you can piece it together bit by bit. No pun intended."

"Kinda like how they can trace cell phone activity?" Maggie asked.

"Yes. In a way." Libby didn't want to get into all the technology that was involved.

"What about search engines like DuckDuckGo?" Alexis was equally enthralled.

"That's a false sense of security. If someone wants to find you and has the means, they will."

Everyone in the room either chuckled or murmured.

Libby looked perplexed. "What am I missing?"

Charles cleared his throat. "As you can see, we are in total agreement with you."

Libby squinted. "I still don't understand."

"We're looking for someone, and we're using all our means," Fergus said.

Maggie resisted the temptation to blurt out some of the people they'd unearthed over the course of their missions.

Libby thought there was more to that story but was not going to push the subject. She turned and went back to work, trolling for the original source.

Once the list from Clarence was downloaded, Fergus began to sort the information to see if he could glean anything useful. Interpol facilitated worldwide police cooperation, so there was the possibility of a nugget of helpful information. He sorted the list via the date of incarceration and omitted anyone who was jailed before Jack took his post. From there, he sorted it in order of the severity of the crimes, the most heinous at the top. Anything involving physical violence came first. There were a handful who were associated with drugs and firearms. The rest were involved in crimes such as money laundering, wire fraud, unauthorized release of sensitive information, unauthorized use of government property. The list went on, but nothing in particular stood out. They'd have to wait until they also got Rose's information. With some luck, they'd then be able to narrow it down.

Chapter Twenty-six

Texas

Darius drove to Reagan National Airport and bought a one-way, nonstop ticket to Oklahoma City. His final destination was Amarillo, but OKC Will Rogers airport was only a four-hour drive as opposed to the five hours from Dallas. He could fly from Dallas to Amarillo, but he'd be losing too many hours changing planes and in the air. He sprung for the extra two hundred dollars for the expediency of getting him closer to his goal. Once he finished, he'd drive to Austin to cross off another item on his list. Then he'd get another nonstop flight to Washington, where he would fetch Leroy. He was feeling better about how things were moving along. Leroy getting stuck in the Caymans had forced his own plans to move up on the timeline. That was fine with him. The sooner he moved on, the better. As long as the money came as promised.

He'd arranged for a rental car and planned on purchasing the items he needed from The Tech Shack and a local sporting goods store. Time was of the essence. He had to complete both jobs before Leroy returned, which meant he didn't have time to use the nifty 3D printer. He'd improvise.

After he landed, he picked up his rental car and asked where he could find the nearest large shopping plaza, or a big box store that carried everything.

He was told there was one "down the road a-piece," which meant it could be thirty miles away. In under an hour, he saw signs for the big national chain stores. It was a large shopping plaza. Perfect.

His first stop was at the tech store, where he bought a few 9-volt batteries. Then on to a sporting goods store, where he purchased three pounds of black powder. From there, he went to a gigantic home improvement store and bought a small hacksaw, a two-feet length of PVC pipe, steel wool, duct tape, and a box of finishing nails. There was a uniform supply store in the same shopping center. On one wall was a rack of deliveryman jumpsuits. He pulled out an extra-large and held it up. It would fit. He ought to know his jumpsuits; it had been his daily attire for fourteen years. He also purchased a matching cap and work gloves. From there, he went into the office supply center, where he picked up two corrugated boxes, a mailing label, and a pen.

The drive would be just under four hours. He decided to stop at a motel halfway, where he would construct his creation. Two hours after that, he would deliver the goods.

There was no one on the highway except a few eighteen-wheelers, who were whizzing past him at seventy-five miles per hour. If he could keep up this pace, his ex-lawyer would soon be orbiting the moon. At least bits and pieces of him, anyway. Darius rolled down the windows, turned on the radio, and found some heavy metal music. He screamed along with the music, and two hours later, he pulled into a small, nasty-looking roadside motel. They surely wouldn't have any surveillance cameras. He walked into the very small office and rang an old-fashioned service counter bell. The place smelled like stale cigarettes. He hadn't planned on spending the night, but he wasn't going to tell that to the scruffy-looking troll who ambled out of a back room and said, "Yeah?"

"I'd like a room. For the night," Darius specified.

"Fifty-five dollars. In advance."

Darius didn't even blink. He was on a quest. He dug out sixty dollars. "Keep the change."

The motel manager slid a ring with a red plastic tag and a key across the old, chipped Formica counter.

"Thanks." Darius turned to leave.

"Check out is eleven A.M."

Darius kept walking, giving him a backhanded wave. He moved his vehicle over in front of Room Three. He couldn't imagine anyone staying here. *Who could possibly be in rooms one and two?* he wondered. There really wasn't much around except a lot of tumbleweed.

He grabbed the shopping bags and entered the dusty, musty room and laid out all the pieces. He was very unwavering about using a different kind of device for each of his purposes. He would not have the typical "signature" most bomb-makers used. No, they would all be different. And judging from the last mishap, he had a better chance of achieving his goal with something different. It was surprising how easy it was to build a bomb. The difficult part was not blowing yourself up in the process. He learned that the hard way. At least he got much closer to his goal with this most recent bomb.

He coated the nails with the black powder and put the detonator inside one of the boxes. Then he wrapped the box with duct tape. He placed the smaller box inside the larger one, wrapped that with tape, as well, and scribbled the address on top to make it look legit.

Satisfied the mechanisms were in place, he carefully put the box in the trunk of his rental car. Timing was everything, and this time, the bomb would go off only when the person opened the package. He donned the delivery uniform, cleared out the bags and rubbish, and locked the door. Two hours to go.

It was around 5:00 P.M. when Darius arrived in a residential area of Amarillo. He parked his vehicle a few doors down from his ex-lawyer's house. He got out and removed the box. He set it down on the front porch, rang the bell, and walked briskly to safety.

As he got closer to his car, from the corner of his eye, he saw the front door of the house open. It was now just a matter of time. Darius would wait in his car until after the explosion, so he'd have the satisfaction of knowing it was a success. But the heat and humidity could do funny things to black powder. It could become unstable and detonate.

Which it did.

Before the lawyer could bring the box into the house, it exploded, piercing his body with nails. People started running out of their houses, screaming about calling the police. It was Darius's time to exit the scene. Too bad he wouldn't know if the bomb had actually killed his target or not. He'd have to watch the news to find out again.

Kathryn checked into a home suite hotel and called the Sisters via her cell phone. She couldn't use her laptop until it was checked out by Libby, which wouldn't be until she got back to Virginia. And she didn't know exactly when that would be. At the moment, there was nothing to report. Libby and Izzie were busy triangulating the source of the breach, Fergus was culling the list of parolees, and Charles was downloading a list of names from Rose Tanner, who came through within a couple of hours after her phone call with Charles. Things were moving. Slowly, but moving.

Kathryn let everyone know where she was and what her plans were. One of the guys at the repair shop offered to loan her a car so she could "see the sights," of which there was really only one. The Cadillac Ranch.

Kathryn read the brochure in her room. Since 1974, visitors would stop to view the ten Cadillacs buried nose-down in a field. They were moved in 1997 to a cow pasture and were now considered a genuine public art installation. Kathryn was tickled when she saw that unlike other public places, graffiti was encouraged. Now that was something she could get behind. She'd pick up a can of spray paint in the morning. Charles joked about bailing her out of jail for defacing public property, but Kathryn insisted it was "encouraged."

She flung herself onto the bed and picked up the remote for the TV. The local news made her bounce back up with some breaking news. A lawyer in Texas had been the victim of a homemade bomb. The news anchor went on to say it was left on his doorstep at approximately 5:00 P.M. and exploded, sending pieces of metal everywhere. The victim, Paul Scovil, a public attorney, had been rushed to BSA Hospital and was listed in critical condition. Anyone with information was asked to call 555-555-INFO.

Kathryn immediately phoned Charles.

"Kathryn?" Charles answered.

"Charles. Get this—a lawyer, Paul something, was taken to the hospital because of an explosion. A bomb left at his house. I didn't catch his last name. It went by too fast, but he's a public defender."

"Check the other networks and see if you can get a last name. We may be on to something here."

"Hang on." Kathryn quickly clicked to the next channel, where the anchor was relating the same story.

"Paul Scovil, a longtime public defender, was the victim of a bombing outside his home. As of now, there are no witnesses, and he remains in critical condition," the anchor intoned.

Kathryn was almost breathless. "The guy's name is Paul Scovil."

Charles shouted to the others. "Check the list from Rose for a Paul Scovil." He turned his attention back to Kathryn. "You sit tight."

"You mean I'll have to reschedule my outing to the Cadillac Ranch?"

"The what? Oh, never mind. Just sit tight." There was a new level of excitement in his voice.

Kathryn clicked through the stations, looking for more information, but all she got was the promise of "news at eleven."

Chapter Twenty-seven

Pinewood

Fergus was cross-checking the lists. He looked for any association between Jack and Paul Scovil. *Bingo*. There was only one: Scovil was the defendant's attorney in a trial Jack prosecuted in Texas fifteen years ago. *But why target both of them? Only the bomber could answer that for now.* It was a case involving an attempted bank robbery and the discharging of a deadly weapon. A bomb. Fergus was ecstatic. "Darius Lancaster. Served fourteen years in Forrest City, Arkansas. Current address is Fort Worth, Texas."

Libby chimed in. "There are two places we identified where the hack originated. Neither are in Texas."

"Maybe he's working with someone," Maggie suggested.

"I'll get Avery on this," Fergus said. "See if he can find any of Lancaster's inmate pals." Fergus immediately reached out to Avery Snowden, whose private investigative team was unsurpassed.

"We need to get a visual on this guy," Izzie spoke over Charles's shoulder. "I'll check the federal penal databases."

The room crackled with excitement. Now if only they could get good news about Nikki . . .

Charles phoned Myra to tell her they had a name. "Avery is going to track down any known acquaintances while he was in jail," he concluded.

Annie had her head pressed to Myra's ear so she could hear the conversation. Myra didn't want to put the call on speaker.

"Fab!" Annie said in a loud whisper.

"How is Nikki?" Charles changed the subject to something even more important.

"Something odd happened earlier," Myra said softly. "Cooper has been sitting at attention with his head at Nikki's feet since they brought her in, except for when we take him for walks and meals. Well, when I went in there a few minutes ago, one of Nikki's hands was on Cooper's head."

Wanting to believe this indicated a favorable state of affairs, Charles also knew the dog could have nuzzled his head under Nikki's hand. Still, he said, "Maybe that's a good sign, love."

"Oh, I know Cooper could have done it himself, but I choose to believe otherwise." Myra sighed.

"As you should." Charles smiled into the phone. At least Myra was sounding more like Myra. Her voice, though soft, was strong.

A soft woof came from Nikki's room. Annie took the phone as they dashed in to see what Cooper was talking about. "Charles, let us call you back in a jiff." Annie ended the call.

The two women rushed to Nikki's side. Jack jumped out of his chair. Nikki's eyes gave a slight flutter. It was as if she were trying to open them. Myra grabbed Annie's hand and whispered, "Call Dr. Jarmon."

It wasn't a twitch or a spasm. The two women were sure of it. Jack was nodding in agreement. Annie phoned the nurses' station, explaining what had happened and could they please find Dr. Jarmon.

It was an excruciating ten minutes before he arrived. "What's happened?" the doctor asked calmly.

"Her eyes moved." Myra could barely speak.

He pulled out a penlight, lifted Nikki's eyelids, and shined light back and forth. Nikki's eyes followed the light. Dr. Jarmon stepped back. "She's responsive."

Myra's voice cracked as she asked, "What does this mean, Doctor?"

"It appears she is in a semiconscious state now. Aware of her surroundings, but not yet able to interact." He pulled out his tablet and made some notes. "I'll run another scan shortly." He tapped out a few sentences. "I'll be back in about fifteen minutes." He had a smile on his face. Myra's knees went weak.

Annie helped Myra over to a chair. "See? Everything is working out fine."

"Not until Nikki's standing on her own two feet, and we get the piece of filth that did this to her." Myra stroked her pearls.

Annie handed her a tissue. "Well, of course. What I meant was things are moving in the right direction."

"Oh, I know. I'm just so wound up."

"Understandable."

Jack sat down next to Myra and put his arm around her. "Annie's right. Right as rain."

Myra gasped. This was not the first time, nor the second, she had heard that expression over the past few days. It was an omen. A good one.

Cooper went over to Myra and put his head on her lap. Annie said, "See, even he knows things are getting better. This is the first time he's moved from Nikki's side except for a quick walk or meal."

Myra's phone rang. It was still in Annie's hand. "Oh,

Charles!" Annie said, answering the call. "Nikki seems to be coming around. Slowly, but the doctor said he thinks she may be semiconscious as opposed to unconscious. They're going to do another round of tests. Here's Myra." She handed the phone over to her friend.

"That's wonderful news, love," Charles said gently. Myra could feel his smile coming through the phone.

"So let's get to work," Myra said happily.

"Not so fast, dear." Charles knew a lot of things had to be uncovered before they could make any kind of plan. But he was thrilled to see Myra rip-roaring and ready to go. "We need to find this guy. Then we can put a plan into action. According to what Libby and Izzie discovered, the leak started outside of Texas, in two different areas. Meanwhile, Kathryn is already in Texas, so perhaps she can do something on her end. Not sure exactly what, but it would be fortuitous if that creep is somewhere convenient." Charles paused. "Avery will look into any known associates. If the guy has accomplices, then we'll have to get each of them simultaneously, so as not to allow one to alert the other or others."

"Good point," Myra answered. "I'll let you get back to business. Annie and I will phone you as soon as we know more."

"Cheers, love."

As soon as Avery Snowden could come up with a list of known associates, he would put his people on them. He just didn't know yet exactly how many people that would be.

But first, he had to get some names.

Avery's reputation was well-known among law enforcement officials. He phoned the prison in Arkansas and spoke to the warden. He explained the reason for his call, informing him of the circumstances surrounding Jack and Nikki, and as they now believed, Paul Scovil, as well. The warden was more than happy to assist, as long as they promised not to send Darius back to his compound. The warden told Avery he'd call him back with names and known addresses.

Things were moving quickly. Finally. It was almost 8:00 P.M. "Time for a dinner break," Charles announced to the group at the farmhouse. "We've been at this all day. Now we wait to hear from Avery. Come on." Everyone got up, stretched, and went single file behind Charles, saluting Lady Liberty on their way out.

When they reached the top of the stairs, the aroma of roasted chicken filled the room. Of course, Maggie was the first one to burst out with, "Food! You have food!"

Charles chuckled. "Did you think I would not?"

"But when did you do this?" Alexis asked.

"Everyone needs to take a potty break now and again," Charles replied. He went over to the oven and pulled out the goodies, which included roasted potatoes and carrots. A baguette was keeping warm on top of the stove.

The women brought the dinnerware to the table, and Fergus made a salad. It wasn't until everyone was seated that they realized how exhausted and exhilarated they were at the same time. They held hands and said grace, Maggie ending with, "Let's eat!"

"Don't mind her. She loses control over food," Izzie said to Libby.

"I'm getting that impression. She sure had a lot of French toast this morning," Libby teased.

"French toast?" Charles queried.

"Yes, Libby is quite the cook," Izzie explained.

"Let's not forget about my sandwiches." Fergus feigned a growl.

"True, because they were sooo difficult to make," Maggie goaded him.

"You behave, young lady, or I'll have to speak to your boss," Fergus taunted back.

"You mean *your* boss?" Maggie mocked.

A burst of *whoa*s went around the table. Lady and her pups yapped in agreement.

Fergus exaggerated his British accent. "Well, I n'er said she weren't." Another burst of laughter filled the room.

Plates were passed, and food was piled on. The kitchen phone rang, and Charles jumped to get it. "Hello?" he said.

"Charles. Nikki is coming around. She moved a finger. I think she was pointing at Cooper." There was a quiver in Myra's voice.

"Good news, old girl. Oh, sorry, love. Hard habit to break."

"You can call me anything you want to tonight. I am over the moon about Nikki."

"So am I."

Myra could hear chatter in the background. "Go have your dinner before Maggie eats everything."

"Will do. Talk later." Charles hung up and returned to the table. As a joke, the women had hidden the food while he was away. "Not funny," Charles quipped.

Back at the hospital, Cooper gently nudged Nikki's arm, causing her to whimper. Jack turned sharply and went to Nikki's side. He took her hand and spoke softly. "Nikki, can you hear me?" He brought her hand up to his face and kissed it.

Nikki gave another whimper. Jack immediately pushed the call button and shouted to Myra and Annie. "Come quick!"

A minute later, a nurse barged into the room.

"Everything all right?" she asked.

"She made a sound. Twice." Jack's eyes were wide. "It was a whimper, but she did it twice."

"We'll get Dr. Jarmon here as soon as possible," the nurse said.

It was another torturing fifteen minutes before the doctor arrived. He took out his penlight and checked Nikki's eyes once again. They all followed the beam. As soon as he stopped, Nikki's eyes fluttered again. She tried to speak. "J . . . J . . . J . . . k."

"I'm right here, sweetheart." Jack squeezed her hand. She weakly squeezed back.

Myra was beside herself, sniffling and trying to hold back her tears. She slowly leaned in and whispered in Nikki's ear. "We're here, honey. Including Cooper."

Nikki gave a slight moan and drifted off. Myra turned to the doctor. "What should we do?"

"Let her rest. Since she's been out for a couple of days, now that she is regaining consciousness, her brain has a lot to process," the doctor remarked. "We'll do a full evaluation in a couple of hours." With that, he turned and left them once more.

Myra was trembling. Annie grabbed the throw from the sofa and put it over Myra's shoulders.

Jack remained motionless. It was if he thought he could will Nikki into coming around.

"I'm calling Charles." Myra went to her get her phone from the living room.

Charles answered hurriedly. "Yes?"

"Charles, Nikki has made some sounds and fluttered her eyes. Jack said he's sure she tried to squeeze his hand."

"Marvelous." Charles let out a sigh he had been holding in for days. "What's the prognosis now?"

"They're going to do a complete evaluation. I have to say this hospital and Dr. Jarmon have been extraordinary. I want to make a donation when all of this is over," Myra said. Annie nodded, indicating she would do the same.

"Splendid idea," Charles agreed.

Myra and Annie went back into the living room area to finish their conversation. Jack remained at Nikki's side with Cooper.

Charles gave Myra and Annie the latest rundown. Along with the list of the most recent known addresses of Darius Lancaster's inmate chums, Avery Snowden sent two of his top operatives, Eileen and Sasha.

When Charles conveyed the news about Nikki's progress to the others, the thunderous sounds of hoots, hollers, and high fives bounced off the walls. Lady and the other pooches barked happily at the top of the stairs.

Chapter Twenty-eight

The Hunt

Eileen, Avery Snowden's agent, was on her way to Los Angeles to track down Eric Barnett. According to his record, he seemed to be the one with the most resources, so they would start with him. Chances were, he had changed his name, so she'd check in with Theresa, the local forger, first. See if there were any new identities handed out recently.

Eileen had met Theresa in art school in Boston. Theresa had moved back to Los Angeles when her brother Julio went to jail. She had to help take care of her mother. So far, she was lucky she hadn't been caught using her artistic ability for anything involving the underworld. But mostly, her customers were women trying to get away from an abusive husband or boyfriend. She tried to stay away from hardened criminals, but sometimes money was tight, her mother's medical bills were through the roof, and she had to take a job she didn't like or want.

The women had stayed in touch, and whenever Eileen was in LA, they'd get together for a shot of tequila. They never discussed business. It was better that way, but now, Eileen needed information fast. No one knew what they were planning. It would be a one-and-done.

They met at a cantina in San Pedro. Eileen explained everything to Theresa, about the bombs and the four known associates and Nikki's coma. She further explained that they didn't know who set the bombs, but there was a connection among these men. At least, that was the theory they were working on. It seemed logical, as the four men had served time together at the same prison. The same one Theresa's brother also called home. In spite of all those *Star Trek* episodes, one couldn't be teleported from Virginia to Arizona. At least not yet.

Theresa was more than happy to oblige. Another sister harmed by an angry man. The man—or men—responsible had to be dealt with.

"A man was sent to me by my brother. That Julio will be the death of me yet. The man didn't give his name, but asked for four different identities. He gave me pictures and names for each of them." She gulped sheepishly. "And cash."

Eileen reached out and patted Theresa's hand. "No one is judging you. Sometimes a girl's gotta do what a girl's gotta do."

"I don't keep an electronic copy of anything. Only paper," Theresa said.

"Smart girl. Old school is a darn good educational method."

Theresa pulled out a small spiral notebook.

"You carry that with you?" Eileen was surprised.

"It's the only way I'll know exactly where it is at all times." Theresa gave a little shrug. "And if I ever have to bolt, I have some leverage with me. Should it become necessary."

"I get it." Eileen motioned for the waitress to bring them another round and an order of chimichangas. "This is the *best* Mexican food."

"It's my Uncle Rico's place. The legal side of the family." Theresa laughed.

Eileen pulled out a similar spiral notebook and jotted down the names Theresa provided: Mike Flint, Jim O'Hara, Larry Kratman, and Gregory Masters. "Can you remember what their photos looked like?"

"Better than that." Theresa pulled out what looked like a flip-book. She thumbed through the pages of faces. They were black-and-white photographs of all of her former clients.

"I see your art classes weren't a total waste." Eileen immediately phoned Avery. "I have a visual and names."

"Your usual *par excellence*. Bravo." Avery tuned into the hidden camera on Eileen's phone for a live feed. She showed him each photo and the accompanying names. "Well done, Eileen."

"I'll track down Eric, aka Gregory. See what he's been up to."

"I'll convey all of this to Charles. Sasha is heading to Las Vegas to try to track down Benjamin Weber. She'll start with his last known address. I'll forward the pic to her."

"Sounds good." Eileen stopped the video feed and disconnected the call. She turned back to Theresa. "You have no idea how much this will help."

"I'm happy to do it. Makes me feel a bit less guilty."

"Like I said, no judgment."

They finished their food and drinks and then parted on the sidewalk outside the restaurant. "Thanks again, my friend." Eileen gave Theresa a big hug. "Stay out of trouble. Maybe become an art teacher or something."

Theresa shrugged. "You never know."

Later that evening, Eileen drove to Eric's last known address. It was a modest apartment building. His unit was on the second floor. She thought she saw some movement through the blinds. It was getting late; soon, she'd have to call it a night. But before she settled in, she did a once-around the building, looking for points of entry, exits, and surveillance cameras. There was only one camera at the front entrance. Satisfied she could get in and out of Eric's apartment quickly, Eileen pulled her car over to an inconspicuous spot and settled in. This was the worst part of her job. The waiting. *Wasn't that the worst part of most things?* she mused.

Hours later, her watch beeped. It was 5:00 A.M. She got out of the car and stretched. A few people were already jogging down the street. She dug into her backpack and pulled out a few extra-large moist towelettes and wiped the important parts. About an hour later, a man fitting Eric's description came out of the building and got into a small sedan.

Eileen fastened her tool belt, which contained lock-picking tools and surveillance bugs. She'd be in and out of there in eight minutes. Her only concern was if he returned immediately. She'd deal with that, if it should happen. It was an easy escape over the balcony.

She entered the apartment through the rear patio. She listened by the door for any sounds. Nothing. She picked the lock faster than most people could with a key. Eileen was always amazed at how little people thought about their personal safety unless they were in a big city. Crime happened everywhere.

She quickly walked the distance of the first floor and then took the stairs at the far end. She stuck three audio-recording devices in the usual places: living room, kitchen, bedroom. A quick check to see if they were registering, and then she was out like a flash. When she got to her car, she unwrapped a cold empanada from the night before and waited some more.

Two hours later, Eric returned, carrying a duffel bag. Eileen didn't see him leave with it, so he must have picked it up somewhere. She'd follow him the next time. She had to bug his apartment first, in case he was communicating with others. That phase was now complete, as she could hear him walking across the apartment via her planted devices. An hour went by, and still nothing, but then she heard the sound of a cell phone ringing.

"Yeah?" Eric answered.

Eileen could only hear Eric's side of the conversation, which went like this: "They said a few days. We just gotta wait." Eric sounded a bit exasperated. "I hadn't planned for Leroy to take a vacation in the Caymans. I was told there wouldn't be a delay when I opened that account at Cayman National. But who am I going to complain to? Problem is, I'll be running out of cash soon," Eric whined. "I'll let you know as soon as I know." Eric clicked off the call.

Eileen sent a copy of the recording to Avery. Avery, in turn, forwarded it to Charles. The Sisterhood now knew that Leroy was in the Cayman Islands and that Eric was in Los Angeles. Bennie was probably in Las Vegas, and Darius recently left a mark in Texas. They were narrowing it down.

Back in the war room, Libby had confirmed the new security measures and rebooted the system. It was go time! Yes, they were back in business. All their resources were once again at their fingertips.

Fergus checked the airline manifests for flights arriving from the US in the Caymans. He discovered a man going by the name of Larry Kratman had flown from D.C. the day before. It matched with one of the phony IDs Eileen had uncovered. Another piece of the puzzle was found.

Charles forwarded the photo of Darius's new appearance to Kathryn. "Chances are, Darius hasn't left the state. When do you think your truck will be ready?"

"They said late tomorrow, but I don't think I can be chasing this guy in my truck. I'll see if the guys at the garage will let me use the car for a few more days. It will be easier for me to get in and out of places."

"Good point," Charles said. He gave Kathryn the address the authorities had on file for Darius. It was in Abilene.

"Abilene? Geez, I don't think I can drive their car that far. Let me call them and find out when the truck will be ready. I'll rent something when I get there."

"I'll make a reservation for you and text you the information." Charles disconnected the phone.

Kathryn checked her watch and dialed the number of the mechanic's shop. She offered to pay him an extra 300 dollars if he could get her back on the road by midday. He didn't think it would be a problem. She figured she could be in Abilene by 5:00.

Darius rolled into the driveway of the small cottage he was renting. He had decided to get what he needed locally for his next target, and then clear out his place. He'd do the same disassembly and destruction of records as he did when the printer arrived. He wasn't going to leave an easy path of clues. He wasn't going to rush this one, either. With Leroy's extended stay in the Caribbean, there was nowhere for Darius to go until he had his money.

Sasha, Avery's other operative, was on the trail of Benjamin Weber. Last known address: Las Vegas.

He was almost too easy to find. He was staying in a low-budget motel. The guy had a routine like a clock, probably due to coaching and doing time. Sasha recorded his daily actions:

Out the door at 7:00AM
Walks around the block 2xs
Stops at Black Jack Diner for half-hour
Goes to casino
Gets $20 worth of chips
Plays slots

Leaves by noon
Walks back to motel
Nothing after that

Sasha figured he must sit at the same slot machine every
day. He got there early enough to beat the crowd. By the second day, Sasha knew he would be an easy mark for the Sisters.

Darius was still on the loose, but not for long. Not if they
had anything to do with it. Kathryn's unfortunate engine
trouble in Texas turned into a godsend, and now she was
within a few hours of tracking down what appeared to be the
mad bomber. It hadn't been confirmed that Darius was the
culprit, but it was a good guess. He was within reach of
the latest explosion. It was the car bomb in Virginia that
was a bit of a stretch, but there was no reason to think Darius was working alone, or that he couldn't have made a trip
halfway across the country. One of the known associates,
Leroy Crenshaw, lived in Virginia. Perhaps he'd served as
Darius's lookout. They'd find out at some point. The main
objective was to locate the four men and bring them all to
justice.

Kathryn pulled into the car-rental lot late in the afternoon.
When she arrived, she asked about a suitable place to park
her rig. The attendant suggested she pull behind the building,
which would be a perfect place to transfer Mr. Lancaster
once she got hold of him. She smiled to herself. *The guy has
no idea what's coming. Mess with one of the Sisters? You will
wish you were dead.*

The road where Darius resided was remote, so she needed
to be careful not to draw any attention. As she drove past his
place, she saw him bring out large trash bags and place them
in the back of his van. He went back in the cottage and
stayed inside for another hour.

Kathryn phoned Charles. "I have him in my sights."

"Good," Charles said. "Keep an eye on him. Maggie is flying down in Annie's plane. She should be in Abilene by midnight. She wants to have an exclusive on the story."

"What if he tries to bolt?" Kathryn asked.

"Dear girl, I trust you'll find a way to detain him." Charles chuckled.

"You got it," Kathryn said. "Do you have a plan?"

"Bring him back here," Charles answered.

"But if Maggie is doing a story, won't people want to know what happened to him?"

"We'll do as we always do, as will Maggie. Remember, *she* will be creating the story. Perhaps he will have been sent back to a high-security prison."

"That's not really going to happen, is it?" Kathryn asked.

"Don't be ridiculous. I said 'create' a story," Charles reassured her. "No one ever gets a do-over after we've taken care of them."

Kathryn let out a guffaw. "That's true. Just wanted to be sure. Where should I meet Maggie?"

"She's going to meet you at the hotel. You have until midnight to wrangle the target."

"I don't want to break down his door. He might have a gun. This is Texas, after all. I think it's required."

"If he leaves, follow him. Pretend you need help with the car. Play the damsel in distress."

"Who, me? You can't be serious," Kathryn balked.

"I know it's a stretch for you, but do your best." Charles chuckled. "Maybe you can tempt him to your hotel room."

"I repeat: Who, me?" Kathryn was very far removed from flirting.

"I know you can do it," Charles said. "Keep us posted."

Chapter Twenty-nine

Philadelphia

Nikki's suite was a flurry of activity. She was moving her fingers and attempting to smile.

Dr. Jarmon took Myra, Jack, and Annie into the other room. "She is going to need physical and occupational therapy. Perhaps speech therapy, but we won't know that for a couple of days. We'll start her with very simple movements. It could take weeks before she can stand on her own, but her vital signs look very good, and her oxygen saturation levels are in the low to normal range. But that is to be expected."

"Do you think she'll have a full recovery?" Myra asked as she fiddled with her pearls.

"Her prognosis is good, but it will depend on her perseverance," the doctor replied.

Myra and Annie tried not to laugh.

Jack grinned. "You don't know Nikki. She is one tough cookie. Perseverance is only one of her many attributes."

"We'll have her stay here for a few more days and then transfer her to a rehabilitation center," Dr. Jamon added.

"But Doctor, we have the resources to provide what she needs at home," Myra protested.

"I understand, but it's to her advantage to be in a facility where there is staff and everything else she needs."

Myra was about to protest once more, but Annie held her back. "She'll be all right. I know you want to be a helicopter mother right now."

Dr. Jarmon continued to convince Myra this was the best course of action for Nikki. "It's also good psychologically. It can be a great motivator to move forward."

"What do you mean?" Myra asked.

"To get out and go home." The doctor smiled. "We can transfer her to a facility near your home. That way, you can visit and start to plan for her return to her house when she's ready."

Annie chimed in. "That sounds like a reasonable plan. You'll help me arrange for the medevac? As you know, a regular chopper isn't equipped for patient transport."

"Certainly. I'll even accompany her," Dr. Jarmon offered.

"That is wonderful of you." Myra reached out and squeezed his hand.

"It will be a pleasure. I am thrilled she is rebounding so well and so quickly."

"Nikki can be stubborn. I keep teasing her that her head is made of concrete." Jack chortled.

Annie gave him a backslap across the arm. "Don't talk about our girl like that!"

"I'm kidding," Jack argued.

"I know." Annie winked. "I just felt like smacking something."

"Well, thanks." Jack frowned.

After the doctor departed, Myra received a call from Charles, as Annie listened in. After Myra provided an update on Nikki's condition, Charles delved in. "We have eyes on Eric Barnett. He's gone out twice and has come back with a duffel bag each time, but he left his apartment empty-handed. He may be getting ready to clear out."

"We'll need to distract him until we can round everyone up at the same time," Myra said. "Give me a few minutes. I'll think of something. Call you right back."

Annie turned to Myra. "My dear, dear friend. I have an idea, but I don't want you to feel as if I am abandoning you."

"What are you talking about?" Myra winced.

"Eric Barnett has an unhealthy love of money."

"And?"

"And, I think he might be interested in an older, *extremely* wealthy woman."

"Oh, I see what you're saying." Myra was getting excited. "You are going to lure him with your money."

"*Exactamente!*" Annie proffered in a French accent.

"Maybe you can make use of that tiara," Myra teased.

"Don't tempt me." Annie giggled. "I'll have the jet do a turnaround after they drop off Maggie." She pursed her lips. "I need to get some better clothes. I'll have to order something quick. I hope the hotel has a personal shopper available. I'll check the concierge first. I doubt if Mr. Money Grubber would be impressed by someone who dresses like a hillbilly in rhinestone cowboy boots."

"You can't ditch the boots!" Myra protested. "They're your trademark."

"White jeans, white blouse, hat, and costume jewelry should be enough to impress." Annie wrote down her list.

"If he's a money guy, he will have heard of you," Jack added.

"True, but looking the part makes it more alluring. I'll call Charles and Fergus and let them know I'm pretending to be available to another man." Annie giggled again.

Fergus answered Annie's call on the first ring. "What's up, old girl?"

"What's with you Brits and 'old girl'?" Annie barked.

"My bad." Fergus had forgotten about the previous

tongue-lashing he and Charles had gotten from Myra and Annie about how insensitive it was of them to use that kind of slang.

"Forgiven," Annie said. "I thought you should know I'm going to LA and throwing myself at a younger man. Can we do a conference call?"

"Sure thing. Say what?" Fergus had just absorbed Annie's previous sentence. "You're going to throw yourself at *what*?"

"Oh, Fergus, don't be dense. I'm going to lure our fund manager into a false sense of security and bring him to the farm."

"Right." Fergus called over the large conference table. "Fire it up, ladies." With that, several monitors lit up. Charles pinged Kathryn to dial into the call on her cell. Her computer hadn't been cleared, so she was still relying on her cell.

Libby leaned back into her chair and smiled. "Impressive, for sure."

"Thanks to you," Izzie said, along with a murmur of agreement from those assembled.

This was the first meeting they'd had with everyone present, except for Yoko, who was still working with Bridezilla.

Charles took the lead. He went over the notes Avery had sent from Eileen and Sasha, and recapped all of the information they'd gathered thus far:

- The locations of the nefarious quartet were verified.
- Kathryn had eyes on Darius. Maggie was on her way to meet her.
- Annie was going to Los Angeles to pick up Barnett. Eileen would keep a tail on them throughout. She'd signal if anything goes awry.
- Alexis would go to Las Vegas and disguise herself as a croupier at the casino. Sasha would have eyes on her.

- Annie's plane would drop Alexis in Vegas on the way to L.A.
- Leroy was on hold in the Caymans.

"Leroy will be stuck in Grand Cayman for a while," interjected Annie. "I made sure of it. I called the manager of Cayman National Bank, who is an old friend of the family's. I gave him a description of a man who will attempt to transfer funds. He had no problem confirming such a man had visited his office. He thought he seemed a bit out of place. I confirmed that he was indeed very out of place." Annie smiled with satisfaction. Her only disappointment was that Leroy's current location was the Caymans and not Purgatory. Now she had to hustle and pack a suitcase for Los Angeles.

After all of the Sisters had listened to the latest info and agreed to the various plans, they quickly signed off and ended the meeting. There was work to be done.

The plane would be back in four hours. Annie had contacted another pilot to take over, as surely her regular pilot would have surpassed his allowable flight miles for the day. She planned to board at Philadelphia National.

Myra decided to walk back to the hotel with Annie. She needed to freshen up. Maybe take a nap. The days and nights were blurring into each other. They walked arm in arm. "I wish I was going with you," Myra said wistfully.

"Me, too, but your job right now is helping Nikki get ready for reentry."

"This has been a crazy week." Myra sighed.

"I don't remember the last time there was this amount of chaos," Annie replied. When they got to the hotel, Annie ordered room service—tea and a basket of baked goods. "A little nourishment."

"Have I eaten anything lately?" Myra asked.

"Not really," Annie said as she pulled out a few things from her closet. "How's this?" It was a purple caftan dress. "Goes with the boots."

"Perfect." Myra smiled and yawned. She felt a weight had been lifted off her shoulders since Nikki had awakened.

"You should probably take a nap before you go back to the hospital."

"You know? I just might do that." Myra rested herself on the bed and stretched.

Annie went back to the closet to fetch a few more items. When she turned back, Myra was sound asleep. *Finally.* There was a knock on the door. It was room service. She silently pointed to the coffee table and signed the check. She was debating waking her friend when the house phone rang, jolting Myra upright. For a moment, she was disoriented. Annie put her hand on Myra's shoulder as she took the call.

"Yes, thank you," Annie said before she hung up. "That was the front desk. A package from Neiman Marcus arrived. I ordered a few things I know will fit."

"How do you manage to juggle so many things?" Myra rested against the pillows and covered her eyes with her arm.

"Because I can." Annie picked up a few of the hotel bath amenities and began to juggle them.

Myra burst out laughing. "I can't believe you can still do that."

"Practice, darling, practice." She set the items down and answered the door. A bellman handed over three shopping bags.

Myra sat up. "Let's see what you bought."

Annie opened the bags and took out a pair of white jeans, a white blouse, black slacks, a black tank top, and a kimono. "I already have a belt for the jeans. I'll have to wait until I get to LA to pick up a cowboy hat."

"And what about a head-wrap to go with the caftan?"

"Brilliant!" Annie shouted. "Might as well go full Hollywood."

Annie stopped packing and fixed the two of them a plate of cheese and croissants. "I want you to eat all of this."

"I didn't realize how hungry I was," Myra said as she gladly accepted the plate.

Within the hour, Annie finished packing, and Myra finished her plate. Myra phoned Jack to tell him she was going to take a nap and come back to the hospital in a couple of hours.

"That's fine, Myra. Cooper is good company. He plays a pretty good game of checkers."

"Oh, I know. He's beaten me on more than one occasion." Myra laughed. Jack wasn't kidding, as Cooper always traveled with a set of checkers in his gear. How he learned to play had always been a mystery.

"See you later." Jack hung up and went back to studying Cooper's technique. The dog would put his paw on the space where he wanted to move; then he would tap the checker he wanted to jump over. It was incredible. The dog possessed some very unusual talents.

Chapter Thirty

The Roundup

Annie left for the airport. Her plane would stop in Virginia and pick up Alexis before heading to Las Vegas. Along the way, Annie phoned an acquaintance in Las Vegas named Felicia Wainwright. Felicia's family owned several hotels and casinos in Sin City.

"Of course your associate can hone her skills at one of our tables," Felicia said after Annie had explained her request. Felicia gave Annie the name of the hotel and who Alexis should contact upon arrival. Felicia would also book a room for her.

Now it was up to Alexis to concoct a story to get Bennie to meet her at the casino. She would be sure to be at the diner when Bennie usually arrived. She'd chat him up about her new job.

By the time Annie's plane had stopped in Virginia, then Las Vegas, and finally arrived in Los Angeles, Annie had been up in the air for almost ten hours. Good thing the jet had sleeping accommodations.

Las Vegas

After the plane landed in Las Vegas, Alexis got in the town car that was waiting for her. It dropped her off at the hotel, where she checked in at the front desk before briefly meeting up with Sasha. Not having any other Sisters with her for backup, Sasha was willing to keep an eye out on Alexis's behalf. Plus, Bennie was a hulk of a man. It would take at least two of them to transport him. Sasha would keep her distance, but both knew if trouble ensued, there was coverage. It also made it easier for Alexis to move freely, with Sasha relaying information to Charles. Alexis wouldn't have to worry about sneaking off or hiding behind a palm tree or statue of Julius Caesar if she needed to make a call.

Once Alexis was safely in her hotel room, she enacted her transformation. She donned a dress that revealed at both the bottom and the top. There wasn't a whole lot of fabric anywhere; if she bent over too far, she could be arrested. Then again, she was in Vegas. Probably, no one would notice. Her hair and makeup was equally dramatic. Her eyelashes stood out like tarantulas, and the wig was long and black. The heels on her shoes made her very long legs look like sexy stilts clad in sheer stockings. Very sexy, but not *too* trashy.

The diner Bennie frequented was within walking distance of Alexis's hotel. Once outside, she checked her watch. Right on time. She spotted him a few feet from the entrance. He went inside. She picked up her pace and followed him in.

Sasha followed a block behind. She leaned against a nearby building and sent a text update to Charles:

A. made contact with the mark. At diner.

Bennie sat down at the counter. Alexis wiggled onto the stool next to him. He didn't notice. She had to start a conversation.

"Excuse me—could you hand me one of those napkins?"

"Sure." Bennie slid the metal dispenser toward her.

"Thank you kindly," Alexis cooed. Still nothing. "I'm sorry to bother you, but I'm new in town. This is my first time here. What would you recommend?" She waited.

"I usually get an omelet and a side of pancakes. I don't think I've ever ordered anything else. Sorry." He turned away from her.

The waitress came over and asked Alexis what she wanted. "I'll take the pancakes with two scrambled eggs, please, and a coffee," Alexis answered. She was not about to quit moving in on Bennie. "I'm starting at job at the Casa Bella Casino today," she told him.

"Good for you," he said, still looking straight ahead.

"I'm sorry if I'm bothering you. It's just that I'm a little nervous. They put me at a high stakes table."

Bennie finally spun his seat slightly in her direction. "Blackjack?"

"Uh-huh." Alexis subtly licked her lips. "I know sometimes when people are losing, they can get a bit testy."

"No one is going to hassle you. That place is fat with security. Plus cameras."

"You seem to know a lot about it." She was pouring it on thick.

"It's pretty much the same everywhere." He turned back to face front.

"Do you play blackjack?" she asked.

"Nah. Too rich and risky for my budget."

"Why don't you stop by my table?" Alexis said. "Maybe I can be your good luck charm."

Finally, Bennie did a ninety-degree turn on his stool. "Look. You seem like a nice person, but it's really not my game."

"My name is Geri." Alexis put out her hand. She was unflappable.

"Ben . . . but my friends call me Mike," he added hastily.

"Okay, Mike. Nice to meet you." Now she had him fully

engaged in conversation. "Do you live here, or are you just visiting?"

"I live here. For now." He turned front-forward again.

"Are you planning on leaving?" Alexis blew on her coffee.

"Yeah. Maybe." He obviously was not in the mood for small talk.

"I don't know where I'd go if I had to move."

"You'll figure something out." He motioned for the check.

"Too bad you have to rush off," Alexis said calmly, while her brain spun for a way to get him to stay. "I could use the company."

He seemed to relax a bit. It has been a long time since he'd had a conversation with a woman. What harm could it do to shoot the breeze for a little bit? Besides, he had nothing else to do.

Alexis chatted him up for another half hour as she daintily ate her breakfast. By the time her check came, Bennie seemed even more relaxed. Alexis had to go all-out at this point. "I get off at four o'clock. Want to meet for a drink?"

Bennie bit his lip. Then he reminded himself he still had nothing better to do. "Sure. Why not?"

They agreed to meet at one of the bars at the hotel. The next step would be to convince him to come up to her room. She'd slip him a mickey, zip-tie his legs and feet, then gag him with duct tape. He'd remain in the bathtub until she could get a ride to the farm. If Kathryn and Maggie could nab Darius, they could have their show on the road in the next twenty-four hours. Alexis knew she could keep Bennie safely sedated for at least a day.

Alexis reported to work at the blackjack table and put in her shift. When she was finished, she walked through the casino, then the hotel lobby and into the bar. Sasha watched from a few yards away. Alexis was a few minutes early, so she took a seat at a cocktail table away from other people. A waitress came over to take her order.

"I'll have a tonic with lime, please," Alexis said.

"Just tonic?" The waitress looked surprised.

"For now. Thanks." Alexis wanted to be sure she had all her wits about her.

A few minutes after 5:00, Bennie, aka Mike, wandered into the lounge. He was squinting to see if he could spot her.

Alexis gave him a little wave. She noticed he had changed his clothes from earlier that day. Maybe that was a good sign that this part of the mission would be easier than she originally thought. He had been nearly implacable during breakfast. He made his way over to the table. Sasha watched from two tables over. The waitress reappeared with Alexis's tonic and asked Bennie what he wanted to drink.

"Jack Daniels. On the rocks." He nodded at her and finally added, "Please."

Alexis thought he might be nervous, so began the conversation with typical questions without sounding like she was interrogating him. She decided to add a little dash of flirty and casually brush against his arm. She didn't want to scare him off, but time was ticking away.

"What do you do for a living?"

"Retired."

"How long have you lived here?"

"Too long."

"Do you have any kids?"

"Nope. Never married."

That explains a few things, Alexis thought.

After Bennie took a second sip of his drink, his shoulders relaxed. Alexis wondered how many more sips it would take before he was pliable. She glanced over at Sasha, who feigned interest in the piano player.

Alexis motioned for the waitress to bring her another tonic and Bennie another drink. "It's on me. I did pretty well with tips today. That's one of the perks about dealing at the high-end tables, although there are a ton of cheapskates, too."

Bennie tapped his finger on the table as if to agree. A few minutes later, and another Jack Daniels had been delivered to the table. If he didn't go for the invitation to go up to her room, Alexis would have to slip something into his drink. Then she and Sasha would have to lug him up to the room and pretend he was their drunk uncle. That would be a hassle.

They already had a removal plan—out the back in a laundry cart. Sasha made arrangements for a box truck rental with a mechanical liftgate. The women would put on janitorial uniforms and wheel the sucker out the door, down the freight elevator, and up the ramp of the truck. Once the package was ready, they would contact Kathryn and Maggie. If their schedule was in sync, they would set a rendezvous time and place.

Halfway through his second drink, Bennie was getting a little loose. Now it was his turn to lean into Alexis and ask questions. *When did you get here? Where are you from? Kids? Ever married?* It really didn't matter what she told him. All of it was a lie.

As Bennie was draining the last of his drink and sucking on the ice cubes, Alexis made her move. "So, Mike, what do you say we go up to my room? I bet the mini fridge has some of what you're drinking."

Bennie blinked several times. It has been decades since he had been with a woman. He wasn't a complete idiot. He was well aware this woman was way above his league. She was quite a looker. Then he had a frightening thought. *What if she was going to try to roll him?* He cleared his throat nervously. "Listen, I find you very attractive, but I'm not, uh, let's say, looking for a transaction."

Alexis faked mortification and surprise. "That's a bit insulting. I was just trying to be friendly."

"In this town, you can't tell the real folk from the fake ones."

Alexis gave him a quizzical look. "Look, I'm new in town. I'm a little lonely. I just wanted some company. And, by the way, I am not a hooker." She pretended to make a move to leave.

"Sorry. Like I said, this town is a bit strange." He motioned for the waitress to come over. "This round is on me."

It was beginning to look like Alexis was going to have to slip something in his drink sooner rather than later. She glanced at Sasha again and gave her a *no-go* look.

Now she had to figure out a way to distract him while she poured a large dose of Benadryl into his glass. She got up quickly. "I'll be right back. I want to change my order." She sashayed to the bar and told the waitress to make his a double and hers a ginger ale. "I'll get these," she said quickly, and picked up the glasses as soon as the bartender put them down. She carefully pulled the vial of Benadryl powder from her pocket and dumped the contents into the Tennessee whiskey. She plucked a stir stick from the bar and swirled his drink. All that whiskey should mask the bitterness of the powder. At least, she hoped it would. She shimmied into her seat and handed him the glass.

He threw all of it back in one shot. He winced. "Wow, that was a lot harsher than I expected."

They continued to chat until Bennie started to slur his words.

"Honey, you're sounding a little funny," Alexis cooed. "Come on. Let's take you up to my room. I promise, no funny business. You can leave your wallet with the bartender if it will make you feel safer."

He looked up at her, bleary-eyed. "N—n—no. I'll be all right." He tried to rest his elbow on the table, but it kept slipping, and he practically knocked his head on the table.

Alexis motioned for Sasha. "Come on, Uncle Mike. Let's take a little walk." Alexis and Sasha helped "Mike" to his feet, which were attached to his rubbery legs. Alexis nodded to the waitress and then nodded to the table. She had left her a hundred-dollar bill. That should cover their drinks and still leave enough for a decent tip.

Alexis and Sasha slung one of Bennie's arms over each of their shoulders as the three stumbled out of the bar. Thankfully, he was still coherent enough to shuffle his feet, but if asked what day it was, he might not be able to answer. The women shot "here we go again" looks to any onlookers.

"Our drunken uncle," Sasha whispered to a passerby. Alexis snorted. Ancestry.com would have a field day with that. A tall, beautiful African American woman; a fair-haired, wiry, athletic woman; and an old white dude. Now there's some family tree. Sasha snickered, as if she were reading Alexis's mind.

They made it upstairs and then into Alexis's room. When they got inside, Alexis and Sasha shoved Bennie onto the bed. To make sure he was totally out of it, Sasha put a cloth soaked in chloroform over his mouth. In seconds, he was out cold. Dead weight. He was a big boy and not easy to maneuver. Between Sasha and Alexis, he still had about eighty more pounds over them. They rolled him on his back and zip-tied his hands behind his back, and then his ankles. Duct tape went over his mouth. They hoisted him onto a chair and then shoved him into the waiting laundry cart. Sasha would keep dosing him with the chloroform when necessary. There was plenty of room for him to breathe, but not enough to move.

Alexis sent Charles a text:

BW—B&G.

Translation: Benjamin Weber—Bound and Gagged.

Texas

Maggie sent Kathryn a text, letting her know she'd arrived at the hotel. Kathryn told Maggie she was tailing Darius and was currently down the street from his house.

What's the plan? Maggie texted back.

Don't have one yet. Waiting for him to make a move.

What if he doesn't?

I'll knock on his door and tell him I'm having car trouble.

Once I get him outside I'll use one of Yoko's moves

The one where he passes out?

Yep. That one.

Good luck.

Thanks. Stay tuned.

Just a few minutes later, Darius's front door opened. He exited, carrying several large black trash bags, and stowed them in the back of his car. Kathryn wondered what he was hauling, which reminded her to get in touch with one of the local farmers. She'd need a trailer to transport Mr. Evil and his friends. She sent off a quick text to Maggie informing her the target was on the move with four large bags. Kathryn was going to tail him. She donned one of her baseball caps and started her engine. She'd have to be careful, since the roads had little traffic. Fifteen minutes later, Darius pulled into a strip mall and drove toward the back. She'd have to wait in the parking lot. Kathryn noted the name of the plaza. Less than five minutes later, he was back on the road.

Hanging far behind, Kathryn followed as Darius drove for another fifteen minutes before pulling into another plaza. He followed the same routine as before—drove to the back and a few minutes later was on the highway. Again, Kathryn noted the name and address.

She whipped her car into the same lane as Darius, getting behind a slower-moving vehicle. She didn't want to pass the crawling car, but she didn't want to lose Darius, either. Then the slowpoke ahead of her put on their turn signal and pulled onto a side street. Darius was almost half a mile ahead of her now. She kept her pace as he drove into a third parking lot. This time, it was a car dealership. She wondered if he was going to ditch his car. Instead, he maneuvered toward the back of the building. That's when it occurred to her: He must be dumping the bags. She didn't have time to check, so she sent Maggie a text, giving her all the locations.

Maggie bolted from the hotel and jumped in her car, thinking about the task at hand. Dumpster diving. Not her idea of a good time. She'd rather be on a stakeout, something that was already at the bottom of her list of fun things to do. Maggie checked in with Charles and gave him an update. She hoped she could get to the dumpsters quickly before anyone else had a chance to throw who-knows-what inside. She pulled up to the first dumpster, flipped the lid, and jacked herself up to look inside. Sure enough, the type of bag Kathryn described was at the bottom, which meant she would have to climb in to get it.

Maggie let out a loud moan and vaulted over the bin. The stench made her eyes water. The good news was there were only three bags. She pulled out a pocketknife and slit open the first one. Coffee cups, paper plates, and leftover pizza. Not likely his stuff. The second bag revealed broken pieces of plastic and something that could have been a printer, but it was too demolished to tell what it had been in a previous life. The third bag contained more of somebody's lunch. She surmised the bag of plastic pieces must belong to Darius. She flung it over the edge, pulled herself up, and bounded out. She threw the bag in the cargo area of the small SUV. On to the next. This time, she was a bit luckier, as the bag was at the top of the pile. She recognized it because it looked exactly like the one she'd just fished out—black with red drawstrings. All the others were in various shapes and sizes common for commercial operations. Sure enough, when she opened the bag, she found similar items inside: plastic parts, batteries, steel wool, all of it chopped into lots and lots of pieces.

When Maggie arrived at the last address, she noticed she was not alone in the rear parking lot. A guy was smoking a cigarette. She couldn't inconspicuously crawl into the dumpster without drawing attention to herself. She hoped he wasn't a chain-smoker. She sent Kathryn a text while she waited.

Kathryn was still tailing Darius. It appeared he was heading back to his house. A few miles down the highway, he stopped at a roadhouse. Maybe he was going to get something to eat. Kathryn got out of her car and managed a sneaky glance inside. She kept her head down, pretending she was looking for someone. With a quick scan, she scoped out the rickety old place with the mismatched tables and chairs. A long, dark bar took up the entire side of the room. There was hardly anyone in there. It would be too risky to try to lure him. It was better if she followed him home and faked a car problem. She ditched the place before anyone could notice or say anything. She quickly returned to her vehicle and sent Charles an update: Kathryn was shadowing Darius, and Maggie was collecting trash.

Los Angeles

Once Annie's plane landed, she walked over to the Elite Car Rental counter to pick up the Rosso Corsa Ferrari 296 GTB. She was all in with their slogan, *Defining Fun to Drive*. Annie was a speed demon, but she had rare occasion to be behind the wheel. Even though the golf carts at the farm were supercharged, they wouldn't go past forty miles per hour, no matter how hard she stomped on the accelerator. She chuckled, thinking about how Myra would cling to the siderails as Annie tore up the gravel back home. Annie would have rented a Maserati, considered the fastest in their class, but she preferred the lines of the Ferrari. It was a hot-looking car, and she needed to be hot-looking to catch the eye of Eric Barnett, aka Gregory Masters. Not that her money wouldn't be an aphrodisiac, but she needed him to notice her right away.

The clock was ticking. They had to coordinate all their efforts, and fast.

Annie received an update from Charles informing everyone that BW was B&G, and sedated. Thanks to her connection at the bank in Grand Cayman, Annie knew the money wasn't going to be transferred any time soon. Granted, her associate never divulged the name or the amount. That was sacrosanct. But that didn't preclude him from confirming what Annie suggested. That meant Leroy wasn't going anywhere. He had to stay and make sure the transfer went through.

Annie phoned Eileen as she sped out onto the freeway. The car was a dream; slick and responsive. All she had to do was push a button on the steering wheel and say, "Phone Eileen" and the call was made. Hands-free.

"I'm pulling onto the 405. Where is he now?" Annie asked.

"Jogging," Eileen answered.

"Where?"

"Santa Monica. He drove here."

"How long has he been at it?"

"Under an hour. Wait—he's stopping for a smoothie."

"I'll pull into a shopping mall and wait for you to call me back. No sense in my driving across the city if he's going to up and leave."

"Good idea."

"Maybe I'll do a little shopping in Beverly Hills." Annie laughed. She would much prefer to be dressed in a pair of baggy flannel pants and a long-sleeve T-shirt. She would always dress appropriately for any occasion, but her predilection was casual and comfy. And, of course, her rhinestone cowboy boots. She'd had them for ages, and they were well broken-in. Fergus would tease her about hiding them, but he knew better than to make any attempt at separating her from those gawdy clodhoppers.

Annie pulled off the freeway at Wilshire Boulevard and

pulled into the parking area of a large office building. If she were anywhere else, her car would have been noticeable, but she was at the crossroads of Beverly Hills, Hollywood, and Santa Monica. Red Ferraris were a dime a dozen.

While she was waiting, she sent Myra a text:

How's Nikki?

Myra texted immediately back:

Coming along. Recognizes us. Still trouble talking.

How are you?

Much better Jack is doing better too.

When can Nikki go to rehab?

In a few days, we hope. Fingers crossed.

Let me know what I can do.

You're the best. Miss you.

Miss you too.

The text exchange was interrupted by Eileen's call: "Subject is on the move again. Looks like he's heading home."

"Dang. We have to get him out of the house, into my car and, onto the plane," Annie said.

"Okay. I'll keep an eye on him. With any luck, he'll go out for dinner. He doesn't seem like the Gordon Ramsay type. Can't picture this pretty boy in a kitchen."

"Keep me posted. I'd rather not drive this fine piece of machinery in his neighborhood. It might be a bit noticeable."

"He doesn't live in a hovel, but you are correct. It's a modest part of LA."

Annie sat in the parking lot, trying to decide what to do. She might as well check into her hotel until she got further word from Eileen. She motored to The Beverly Hills Hotel. When she pulled in, she told the valet she would only be a few minutes and to please keep the car out front. A twenty-dollar bill got her a nod. The bellman helped her with her bag. "Would you mind leaving it here for now?" she asked.

He gave her an odd look. "I may need to get something a

little later, and I won't have time to go back to my room."
Another twenty dollars got her another nod.

She then hightailed it to the front desk, waving and saying
hello to some of the staff, who recognized her. She didn't
know if she was coming or going. At the desk, as she checked
in, she asked for two keycards in case she had to give one to
Eileen. Now if that jerk Eric Bennett/Gregory Masters would
just sit still in a public place, the rest would be a piece of
cake.

Texas

Kathryn followed Darius back to his house. She gave the
address to Maggie so they could meet. Kathryn was a big,
strong woman, but it might take two of them to shove the
guy into the trunk. Even if he was out cold.

Maggie brought Kathryn up to date regarding the mysterious trash bags. "Looks like printer parts. Lots of bits of plastic. Batteries, steel wool. Shredded paper, too."

"I'll haul it back with the vermin. I'm waiting to hear back
from Bud Greenleaf. He has some produce he wants me to
bring back East. Cabbage, mostly."

"Ew. That's gonna be one heck of an odoriferous jour-
ney," Maggie exclaimed.

"He's pulling into the driveway now," Kathryn noted.

"So what's the plan?"

"You park your car a few houses down. I'll put on my
flashers and open the hood. I'll walk up to his door, ring the
bell, and ask for assistance. I'll pretend I locked my keys and
my cell in the car and ask him if I can use the phone."

"And then you'll call me instead."

"Yep. I'll have a fake business card in my hand. You will
tell me it's going to be at least two to three hours. I play
damsel and ask him if maybe he could take a look."

"You. Damsel. That's a show I'd pay to see."

"You won't have to, Ms. Smartass. You'll be a couple hundred feet away. I thought you were covering this as a story. Get with the plot!" Kathryn taunted.

"I'm hungry," Maggie whined.

"Oh, for crying out loud. Do you have a tapeworm or something?"

"I can't help it if I have a voracious appetite," Maggie grumbled.

"I don't know where you put it, girl." Kathryn shook her head. "How far are you?"

"Coming around the block." Maggie turned on her blinker, indicating she was pulling over.

"Okay. Lights, camera, action!" Kathryn popped the hood and put on her emergency flashers. She purposely left her backpack in sight. She'd say that's where her phone was. Her keys would be in her pocket, but he wouldn't know that. She casually walked up the sidewalk, looking in all directions. There was no one in sight.

Kathryn rang the doorbell. She could hear music playing in the background. Some kind of angry heavy metal, with a guy screaming words that were indecipherable. *Who listens to this?* Dumb question. She was about to take down a member of their audience.

She rang again, then heard footsteps. A man's voice boomed, "Yeah? Who is it?"

"Uh, hi. My name is Patricia. My car broke down across the street, and I locked my bag in the car with my phone."

The door opened but only a crack. A rugged six-feet-something guy with an odd shade of gray hair peeked through. "What do you need?"

"I think I might need a jump, but I'm not sure. May I use your phone?"

He opened the door slowly. The woman looked harmless

enough to Darius. She was wearing a denim shirt and jeans. Tall-ish, but not threatening. Or so he thought.

"Yeah. Let me get it." He walked over to the cigarette-charred coffee table and handed her his burner phone without thinking. When she started to dial, it hit him. Too late. He couldn't stop her without making a scene. Heck. It was only one call. He'd delete the number after she was done. Not that it mattered.

Kathryn punched in the number of Maggie's burner phone. "Hello, Roadside Assistance. How may I assist you?" Maggie played the part in case he was close enough to hear.

"Hello. This is Patricia Sullivan. My car died. Just stopped running. Lights went out, and then I stupidly left my phone in the car."

"What is the address?" Maggie chirped.

Kathryn looked up at Darius. "Address?"

He hesitated, then decided to give her his neighbor's address, where the car was actually parked.

Kathryn repeated it to Maggie.

"One moment please. Let me see who's available." Maggie put Kathryn on hold for an annoyingly long time. She wanted to seem authentic. "Hello, Ms. Sullivan?"

"Yes?"

"I'm sorry, but we won't have anyone available for at least two, maybe three hours."

"Two or three hours?" Kathryn gave Darius a wide-eyed look. "Are you sure there is no one else available?"

"Ms. Sullivan, if there was, I'd send them. Now you be safe and get back in your car."

"I told you I locked my keys in my car."

"Some late-model cars can be opened via satellite. Did you know that?" Maggie was being annoying on purpose.

"Yes, and unfortunately, my car doesn't have that luxury."

"I understand, Ms. Sullivan. I wish I could help you. Better sit tight wherever you are. Have a good evening and thank you for calling Roadside Assistance."

Kathryn quickly deleted the number before she handed the phone back to Darius. She feigned frustration. "Can you believe this? Just my luck. My kid has his first baseball game tonight, and I'm gonna miss it."

Darius had a flash of humanity. "Let me take a look at it. Lights went off, you say?"

"Yep. Then I turned the wheel so I could get out of the way."

The two of them went around to the front of the car. Darius leaned in and tinkered with the battery cable. As soon as Maggie's car was directly behind them, Kathryn performed a move known in martial arts as a sleeper hold. It compressed the carotid artery, restricting blood flow to the brain and causing the person to pass out for a short period of time. Kathryn inflicted the sleeper hold on Darius without a hitch. It allowed just enough time for Maggie and Kathryn to bind him with duct tape, wrapping it around his head and mouth, arms and legs, and torso. He looked like a silver mummy. Kathryn popped the trunk and dragged him to the back of the car.

Kathryn took his upper body, and Maggie grabbed his legs. Kathryn counted, "One, two, three!" Then they lifted, heaved him in, and slammed the trunk shut.

"Now where to?" Maggie was breathing heavily.

"I'll be right back," Kathryn said.

"Where are you going?" Maggie shouted after Kathryn as she ran back inside the house.

Less than a minute later, Kathryn scurried toward the cars, carrying Darius's cell phone. "This just might come in handy."

"Genius," Maggie said in awe.

"I have my moments." Kathryn laughed. "Come on. We need to get this guy planted in the land of cruciferous vegetables. Along with the cabbage, there will be cauliflower, kale, bok choy, brussels sprouts, and broccoli."

"A most gaseous combination even when it's not eaten." Maggie giggled.

"Follow me." Kathryn hopped in and pulled away. If anyone came looking for Darius Lancaster or Jim O'Hara, he would be MIA. Forever. And most likely, no one would care.

Kathryn knew she didn't have a lot of time before Darius came around and would start flailing in the trunk. She had to get to the farm quickly. Even though it closed an hour earlier, Kathryn told the owner she would pick up the freight, no problem. He'd agreed to leave the clipboard on the fence so she could sign out the merchandise. They had done business together many times, so this was almost routine. It wasn't always easy to judge arrival times, so they'd make arrangements in advance.

They got to the farm twenty minutes later. Kathryn could hear faint rumblings coming from the trunk. She'd have to do another sleeper hold; otherwise, it would be like wrestling cattle to get him inside.

Kathryn opened the trunk. Darius made some mumbling sounds. "Save your breath. You stay still while we move you, or it's nighty-night for you. Trust me—you don't want to hear me sing a lullaby."

They could see the panic in his eyes. Maggie thought the Sisters, Charles, and Fergus would like to see a photo of Darius's pure terror. It was rather hideous. But satisfying. She snapped a pic on her cell phone and texted it to Charles.

When Charles brought the photo up on the screens for everyone to see, a roar of applause, fist bumps, and howls filled the room. Charles said, "One of the other blokes is unconscious, so he still has no idea what's happened to him."

"Wait until he wakes up," Fergus said with pleasure.

Though Darius had nodded to indicate he would cooperate, his fight-or-flight instinct kicked in. Since he couldn't flee, he began the fight of his life, trying to twist his body away from the two women. No luck there. Kathryn put her arm around his neck again. "You are being a very bad boy." *Bonk!* He was out cold. Again. Kathryn unhooked the lift-gate and pushed the button. The battery-operated hydraulic cylinders brought the gate to the level of the trunk of the car. Maggie jumped in the trailer and found a space between the pallets. "It isn't perfect, but it will have to do!"

They dragged Darius by his ankles and shoved him onto the liftgate. Another push of the button, and he was now a Cabbage Patch Felon.

Kathryn lowered the gate and locked the back of the truck with a padlock. "Let's get rid of this tin can and get my rig."

"I'll go to the hotel and pick up our stuff and meet you back at the rental lot."

"Good plan." Kathryn gave Maggie a high five. It felt good.

Kathryn sent a message to Charles: **DL B&G. In veg truck.**

Charles wasn't sure what that meant. **Veg truck?** he texted back.

Amid the green leafy kind. Heading to Vegas. ETA Noon tomorrow.

Splendid.

After sending his text to Kathryn, Charles conveyed the information to the rest of the group. Kathryn would transport Felon Number One to Vegas, where she would then pick up Felon Number Two. If all went according to plan, Annie would deliver Felon Number Three to Kathryn via her plane. She'd have to play the part of a cougar until the plane landed. She didn't want to mess up the fine upholstery with some slobbering, unconscious dolt. Once the plane landed in Vegas, they would sedate him and pack him into the veggie truck for a road trip with the others.

Los Angeles

Annie was getting impatient, but there wasn't much she could do about it. She phoned Myra. "Hello, my friend. How are things?"

Myra chuckled. "Are you bored? We just texted each other an hour ago."

"You're right. I'm bored. And antsy. I'm sitting in this gorgeous automobile with no one to show it off to."

"I hope you have your PBA cards with you. What did you rent? Ferrari or Maserati?"

"Ferrari. It's spectacular."

"And I'm betting it's red," Myra said.

"You know me too well," Annie replied. "Hang on. Eileen is sending me a text." She paused. "Oh, goody. He's leaving the house. In an Uber. Interesting. We're prayin' he goes to dinner somewhere, so I can make an entrance."

"You make an entrance no matter where you are, my friend," Myra teased.

"Gotta run. Talk later. Ciao!" Annie said as she slammed the accelerator of the lavish automobile. She peeled out of the parking lot. She still had no idea where she was heading, but if Eric was leaving his house, she decided to drive in that direction.

Eric had decided if he had to hang out in LA a few more days, he would make the most of it. There was nothing he could do until that money transfer went through. He hadn't heard from anyone so decided to call Bennie. No answer. Odd. Then he dialed Darius. Straight to voice mail. Very odd. Then on to Leroy. He hoped Leroy had the sense to bring the charger for the phone with him. After the first ring, a jumpy Leroy answered.

"Yes, boss?" Leroy's voice was shaking.

"I don't suppose you have any word on the letter?" Eric knew the answer to the question, but he had to ask anyway.

"Sorry, boss. I can't get an answer from anyone. I walked into the bank today, but the receptionist told me that they would call me when they had the information. So I turned around and left. I didn't want to seem desperate. Even if we are." Leroy was trying to calm himself.

"Okay—well, thanks for trying."

"Sure, boss, but I'm running out of cash."

"How much is left on your debit card?"

"I'm not sure."

"Well, how much did you spend?"

"Maybe a hundred and eighty dollars, getting clothes for the trip."

"What else?"

"Just some food." Leroy didn't want to tell him about the two pair of socks he bought for the plane ride home. Not that they cost a lot. It was just embarrassing. *Who leaves home without socks?* He should have never listened to Darius. It suddenly dawned on Leroy how much more relaxed he was without Darius around. Perhaps it was also the tropical air. Whatever it was, he felt like he could breathe a little easier.

"Next time you go to an ATM, check the balance."

"Right. Good idea. I didn't think of doing that. Darius was always in charge of things."

"Well, you're on your own now, Leroy. I'm counting on you." Eric tried to sound kind. He understood how intimidating Darius could be. Heck, that's how he finagled his way into their little group. "By the way, have you spoken to Darius lately? I just tried to call him, and his phone went to voice mail. Kinda strange."

"I haven't talked to him since last night."

"Did he say anything? Like he was on the move or something?"

"Nope. Just said he had to finish up some business, but he didn't say where."

Eric was worried he had a loose cannon on his hands. Every time he spoke to Darius, he seemed more incendiary. "I didn't leave a message. So if he calls you, you tell him to call me."

"Right, boss. Sorry I'm not doing a great job for you." Leroy felt responsible for his inability to perform the task at hand.

"Not your fault, Leroy. Take it easy. Go sit in the sun for a couple of hours. There is absolutely nothing any of us can do until the letter gets authenticated. I just don't know what's taking so long. No one has gotten in touch with me yet."

"Maybe you should call the bank?" Leroy suggested.

"That's a possibility, although they're not going to take my word for it over the phone. They're going to want proof of my signature." Eric sighed in frustration. "This has never happened before. I guess it's because of the new tax laws." He was thinking out loud now about how odd the situation had become. They had his signature on file. It matched the signature on the letter. The letter was written on fine linen with embossed initials. It was real, so to speak, even if it was in Gregory Masters's name. "All right, Leroy. Hang tight."

"Thanks, boss." Leroy hung up and put on a pair of swimming trunks he'd bought at a local store. He thought he better start writing down everything he purchased. He was no algebra whiz, but he could do simple math.

Eric unzipped one of the duffel bags and counted out the cash. $50k. He counted the rest. He still had just under 200 grand if he needed to get out of the country. But why should he? He wasn't on the run from anyone anymore. As far as the government was concerned, they seized all his assets years ago. But he was still careful and a little paranoid. One never knew who was watching. After all, he was accessing funds that he wasn't legally entitled to.

When he first arrived back in Los Angeles, he spent some of the money on clothing. He couldn't look like a bum while walking around the streets of Tinseltown.

He'd checked a few men's magazines to see what the latest trends were. He'd made an attempt to fit in. He'd purchased a gray blazer with pockets, a checkered shirt, a dotted tie, and distressed jeans. He'd also bought his normal look of button-down shirts, chino pants, a set of workout clothes, a pair of Peter Millar Hyperlight sneakers, and Ferragamo loafers. They said you could tell a lot about a person by their shoes. It was just enough to get him through a week or so. He didn't want to use up any more of his cash. Leroy's extended stay would run a couple thousand more than he had planned.

Eric pulled out a thousand dollars and decided to take himself out to dinner. It had been years since he was at The Ivy. He had altered his appearance enough that the odds were good he wouldn't be recognized by anyone. He called to see if they could fit him in. He could be there in an hour. He looked through his sparse wardrobe and pulled the hipster outfit together. It actually looked good on him. "Back in the saddle," he said to himself.

Then he thought about the car he was renting. Bland. Unimpressive. It wouldn't look cool for him to pull up to the restaurant in an ordinary-looking vehicle. He decided to call an Uber. Then he could also have a few extra cocktails without worrying about driving. The night was starting to come together. They had made strict rules about how and when to use the phones, but he figured one Uber app wouldn't matter.

He was going to ditch the phone the next day, anyway. He punched in his address and got a reply. A driver would be there in twenty minutes.

Eileen watched Eric leave the apartment building and get into the Uber, which is when she called Annie. They were now heading East on the I-10.

"Where are you now?" Eileen asked Annie over the phone.

"Just pulled onto Wilshire and South Beverly Glen."

"Sit tight until I can get you more coordinates."

"You want me to sit tight in a Ferrari?" Annie whooped.

"Good point." Eileen kept her eyes on the Uber. "Now they're getting off at South Robertson and then merging north."

Annie drove around the block instead of parking. She decided it was quicker to catch up with them if she was in motion.

"They're slowing down. Looks like he's stopping at The Ivy," Eileen reported.

"The Ivy? He is quite the audacious man." Annie knew about Eric Barnett's scam and his cohorts' criminal records. "Let the games begin." Annie ended the call with Eileen and then phoned the restaurant. As with anywhere Annie went, people were happy to hear from her.

"Countess! So nice to hear from you. Will you be dining with us soon?" asked the host.

"How about in fifteen minutes?" Annie asked.

"Absolutely! We'll see you shortly."

Annie zoomed around the block again and made her way to 113 North Robinson Boulevard in less than five minutes. The roar of the Ferrari turned a head or two as Eileen watched from a block away. Not one but two valets ran to the car to assist Annie.

"Welcome to the Ivy, Countess. Nice to see you again."

"Thank you, Roy. Nice to be back. It's been a while." The other valet hopped ahead of her to get the door.

As predicted, Annie made a grand entrance. "Peter! How good to see you!" They exchanged a kiss on each cheek. Annie's eyes darted around the dining room. Just ahead of her, a man wearing a gray blazer was being seated alone. She spotted a table nearby. "May I sit there?" She pointed.

"Of course. I thought you'd want your regular table, but your wish is my command!" If the host was any more effusive, she was going to gag.

Eric couldn't help but notice the very attractive, vivacious woman who sauntered in. He guessed her to be about ten, maybe fifteen years older than he, but she was quite the looker in her slim white jeans, white shirt, decorative belt buckle, and boots. *Those boots. Only she could rock those*, he thought. *And she was monied.* He was pretty sure she was the one who pulled up behind him in the red Ferrari. She looked the type who would drive one. She ordered a gimlet, something the place was known for. As she sipped her cocktail, her eyes locked on Eric. She gave a sly smile and put down her drink. He smiled back.

Annie picked up the menu and pretended to be interested. When the waiter came over to take her order, she decided on fried chicken. She knew it would be messy, but it was easy to flirt with that kind of food. Something you could have some fun with. Maybe spill a little chutney on her shirt, make a fuss. She'd play it by ear. She knew he noticed her. Who didn't?

As she continued to sip her cocktail, she kept looking in Eric's direction. He smiled again. She raised her glass in his direction. He raised his in return. When the waiter came back, she asked him to tell the man at the nearby table that she would like to buy him a drink. The waiter bowed and moved toward Eric. He leaned in and whispered, "The lady would like to buy you a drink." He discreetly motioned in her direction.

"Tell her that would be a lovely gesture, but I insist on buying *her* a drink," Eric replied.

"Very well, sir." The waiter made another short bow and went back to Annie.

She responded with, "Tell him if he wants to buy me a drink, he has to sit with me."

"Yes, Countess." The waiter went back to Eric's table and relayed the message. Eric leaned past the waiter and looked at Annie and nodded. He folded his napkin, stood, and walked over to her table.

"Good evening. I don't believe we've met." Eric was the perfect gentleman. He put out his hand. "Gregory Masters."

"Annie Ryland de Silva." She purposely left out the "Countess" part. She'd let the waiter drop that one. "Please sit." She gestured to the chair the waiter was pulling out. "I think we may have met at an art opening in Milan." Annie knew that wasn't true, but she had to pad the banter.

"No, I don't believe so, but I am delighted we are meeting tonight." Eric was his ever-charming self.

The waiter returned with a new place setting for Eric. He turned to Annie. "Would the Countess care for another gimlet?"

"How many times must I tell you to call me Annie?" She, too, was a bit over-the-top.

"Yes, of course, Countess. I mean Annie." He cleared his throat. "Another cocktail?"

"I think I'll have a beer with dinner. Stella Artois? Seems to be a better fit with fried chicken. Don't you think, Gregory?"

"Absolutely!" he replied with way too much vigor.

Annie thought he may have figured it out by now. She was

one of the richest women in the world. And she was known to be very charitable. Maybe Eric could benefit from her generosity. He rested his elbow on the table and propped his head on his fist. "So what brings you to The Ivy tonight, Contessa? Or is it Countess?"

Slam. Dunk.

"As I said to the waiter, it's Annie. I'm here for a quick business trip."

"Oh? What kind of business?" Eric leaned in closer. Now he was being a bit bold.

She gave him a sly grin. "Monkey business."

Leaning in even closer, Eric said, "Do tell." He was practically breathing down her neck. He hadn't been this close to so much money in years, and even then, it wasn't anywhere near to what this woman was worth.

The waiter brought the beer and a frosted glass. "The only way to drink beer." Annie made a curlicue on the frosted glass. "I'm having a little party tomorrow night in Vegas. I'm here to pick up a few friends."

"And how does one get to become a friend?" Eric was almost nauseating. He couldn't help himself. When it came to money, he had no shame. None. Zero. Zilch. Nada. *Non. Niente. Affatto.*

"It's a fundraiser. The entry fee is five thousand dollars." Eric tried not to choke, but thought it might be worth his while to get in on this shindig.

"That shouldn't be a problem. I don't have that much on me now, but I can certainly make a cash contribution." He was really pressing his luck, but you couldn't change a leopard's spots. He was addicted to the thrill of getting as much as he could without breaking a sweat. He figured if he ingratiated himself to the Countess, maybe he could make some further financial connections. Up until that point, all he cared about was getting out of the country, but the opportunity to hobnob with the uber-wealthy was a temptation he could not resist.

He rationalized away the threat of running into anyone from his past. Those who could afford the loss from his scam had long retired. The others were too poor to be traveling in Countess de Silva's circle. This was an opening for something bigger than a flat in Ecuador.

They chatted about film, books, and music—which were their favorites, and all the other various and sundry topics one covers with a total stranger via small talk. As the evening was winding down, Annie gave Eric her card. "Wheels up at nine A.M. sharp," she said. "Burbank Airport. Be there no later than eight-fifteen." She gently patted him on the arm and got up. He stood also.

"Let me get the check," he offered as he waved down the waiter.

"It's already taken care of." Annie ran her finger under the collar of his blazer.

"That is most kind of you." Eric blushed.

"I was the one who invited you to my table, remember?" She batted her eyes at him, even as her stomach was turning.

"I'll walk you to the door." Eric was half-hoping she'd invite him to her hotel, but it was not the time to rush things.

The slick, shiny sports car was idling in front of the restaurant.

"Nice wheels," Eric said.

Annie whisked past him and got in the car. "See you tomorrow. Don't be late."

"How many days should I pack for?" he shouted after her.

"As many as you'd like." The car rocketed away, as if Mario Andretti were behind the wheel.

Eric stood there with the biggest grin on his face. He couldn't remember the last time he felt this elated. Maybe Countess Annie could help him dislodge his money from the Cayman Bank. He'd tell her his tale of woe. The waiting.

How frustrating it was. *Blah . . . blah . . . blah.* He figured once he gave her the 5,000 dollars for the charity party, they'd be chums.

Annie could barely contain her delight. She phoned Eileen and told her to continue to watch Mr. Moneybags. As of right now, he would be meeting them at the airport tomorrow morning. "He thinks he's going to a fundraiser party."

"Annie, you are amazing."

"And get this—he's going to give me five thousand dollars. Cash." She was giddy.

"He's *what*? Why?"

"I told him it was a fundraiser, and the ticket was five thousand dollars. He obviously wants to impress me, so he offered to pay in cash. I couldn't say no, now, could I?"

"Excellent point. So I'll stay on him until he gets to the airport."

"Then you can fly back with us," Annie said.

"Great. I'll let Avery know and bring him up to date."

"I'll do the same with Fergus and the rest." Annie ended the call and drove to the hotel. The valet greeted her and retrieved her bag, handing it to the bellman.

"Thanks. I'll be leaving around seven o'clock tomorrow morning," Annie said.

"You got it. Have a good night."

"Thanks. You, too." Annie was practically skipping her way to the elevator. She couldn't wait to tell everyone what had transpired. That Eric, aka Gregory Masters, was a master of none. So predictable.

She handed the bellman a tip and said, "I'll take that. No sense in you rolling it when I can." She smiled. "Good night." She was in a huge hurry to get to her room.

The minute she entered, she saw a bouquet of flowers on the coffee table with a note that read: *Wishing you luck. Miss you. Myra.*

It was 11:00 P.M. in Los Angeles, which meant it was 2:00

A.M. in Philadelphia. She didn't want to disturb anyone, so she sent a text: **If u r up, call me. Exciting updates.**

She knew Fergus would be awake. He was a night owl whenever there was a mission at hand. Most of them were. You never knew when someone needed updates or assistance. Annie's phone rang almost immediately, and she quickly answered.

"Annie! Good to hear your voice," a wide-awake Fergus said. "Everything good?"

"Just dandy. How is Nikki?"

"Making excellent progress every day. They're going to release her to a rehab center near the farm. Well, relatively near. About twenty minutes."

"That's wonderful news."

"And what's yours?" Fergus asked.

"I convinced Mr. Eric Barnett, aka Gregory Masters, to accompany me to Las Vegas tomorrow, where I am hosting a fundraiser."

"Brilliant!" Fergus roared. "You didn't kiss him, did you?"

"Hardly. I barely shook hands with him. He was enamored by my money, darling."

"And how did he come to know about your financial means?"

"The waiter called me 'Countess.' He asked, and I casually blew it off. He's a money guy, so he knew exactly who I was after the countess comment. Plus the red Ferrari. Well, you know me."

"And those blasted cowboy boots!" Fergus chuckled. "They're a blessing and a curse."

"Aren't you the funny man," Annie teased back.

"Give me the rundown," Fergus said, then took copious notes as Annie spoke.

"He's meeting me at the plane tomorrow morning. Get

this—he's giving me five thousand dollars to attend! Such an arse."

"You are something else. How did you manage that trick?"

"I told him it was a fundraiser, and the tickets were five thousand dollars. He offered to pay me in cash. I couldn't possibly say no to money for one of our favorite charities. I think the money should go to the hospital where Nikki is."

"Superb idea."

They went over the notes from Maggie and Kathryn. They had the human burrito in the back of the trailer containing very gaseous vegetables. They'd haul the trailer to Vegas and meet up with Annie, Eileen, Sasha, and Alexis. Alexis and Sasha would deliver Bennie the Calzone. He was too rotund, and they needed a better food-related euphemism for him. Once they landed, they would subdue Eric, turn him into another wrapped bundle, and put him in the trailer with the other two. Maggie would ride back with Kathryn, and the rest would take Annie's plane. It wasn't ideal, but it was the safest way to transport the criminals. Once the truck arrived in Virginia, they'd move the men to the farm, where they could ferment in a different kind of prison.

They still hadn't come up with a plan for Leroy, but they had almost two days to figure it out.

Eric couldn't believe his luck. He was going to a fundraiser in Las Vegas with one of the richest and most powerful women in the world. With his new identity, he could hobnob with the elite. Mix and mingle. He went through his meager wardrobe, cursing himself for not buying a few more things. There would be no time in the morning. It would just have to do. He could always pick up something at one of the high-end shops at the hotel. That's when he realized the Countess hadn't said which hotel they were going to stay at. He shrugged. They'd work out all those details on the flight. A flight on her private jet. He was beyond excited. He looked in the mirror and said, "Welcome back to the world of the well-heeled." He checked his hair. The color was good, and the length was much longer than his past, pre-prison look. Not scroungy but with a bit of flair. The five-o'clock shadow on his face made him look cool. He could pass for Eurotrash. Perfect for Vegas and a rich party.

He hadn't gotten into any specifics about his employment with Annie. He told her he was an entrepreneur working on some digital coin futures. Sounded like a lot of bull, but she seemed interested and enthralled. He'd work on a more detailed dossier for himself before he boarded the plane.

He packed carefully, knowing he had limited items. He was still kicking himself for not buying that beautiful Italian leather jacket, but it cost 3,000 dollars. He consoled himself with the thought that the money was going to a good cause. His.

The following morning, he called an Uber again. He didn't want to show up at the airport with something less than a luxury car.

Kathryn was hotfooting it across the interstate. If the roads remained clear, they would make it to Vegas in plenty of time to meet Annie's cargo. Maggie took a sniff at her shirt. They had been on the road all night. "Cripes. I stink. How do you live like this?"

"First off, if you hadn't bought those Italian submarine sandwiches, the cab wouldn't smell like a delicatessen. Talk about stink? That provolone is going to linger in here for weeks. Second, they have showers at a lot of the truck stops. Sometimes I even get a motel room, but time's a wastin', girl."

"Hey, don't mock good provolone."

"Then stop complaining about smelling like it." She motioned behind the seat. "There are some large towelettes. Give yourself a wipe."

Maggie made a snarly face. "Okay. Fine." She reached back and picked up a box labeled DUDE. "Seriously?" She shrugged, pulled one out of the dispenser, and proceeded to give herself a trucker's shower.

"I wonder how our passengers are doing," Kathryn said as she made a wide turn onto US 93 North.

Maggie started to laugh. "Well, I'm sure they don't smell any better than I do."

"Just two more hours to go before we pick up the other creeps."

"Do you think they'll be all right back there for another long haul?"

"Do you really care?" Kathryn shrugged. Having been through hell and back, she had no patience or sympathy for men like the ones in the back of the trailer, or the one they were going to pick up in Las Vegas. Even though the Sisters dished out some of the most appalling justice, it was still never enough to satisfy Kathryn. Having been raped by three men while her husband was forced to watch from his wheelchair had been horrific. Then, after her husband died, well, something died inside her, too. She blamed the rapists for his untimely death. She was grateful for the friendships and sisterhood, but nothing could bring back the love of her life. *Cynical* wouldn't come close to describing Kathryn. Bitter? Maybe, a little. Perhaps that was what drove her mentally and physically.

Maggie sent Annie a text: *ETA 11:00.*

Annie texted back immediately: *OK!*

Annie was at the Burbank terminal, at the private jet hangar. And there were plenty of them—corporate jets, private jets, single engines, and classic props. Annie went inside the waiting area and took a seat. She was wearing a vintage Chanel red and gold silk tunic-length jacket with matching pants. A Hermès Birkin tote was on her arm, Versace sunglasses on her head, and her signature boots on her feet.

Eileen was the first to arrive. "I appreciate the lift back East."

"You're part of the team. I know you work for Avery, but we all work together."

"Thanks. Sometimes I just think of myself as a private investigator with extra skills."

"Very important skills, my dear." Annie stood. She spotted Mr. Charm coming in. His smile would make the Cheshire Cat blush. Annie stayed cool. "Gregory! So glad you decided to join us."

"How could I miss a fundraiser with you?" He acted as if they were long-lost friends. He went to kiss her on the cheek. She obliged. Had to make him feel welcome. Unsuspecting.

"Gregory, this is one of my friends and associates, Eileen."

Gregory and Eileen shook hands, and then Annie hooked her arm through his. "Shall we?" She motioned toward the waiting Gulfstream jet.

"Is it just the three of us?" he asked casually.

"For now." Annie smiled. "Have you had breakfast?"

"Well, no, I haven't." Eric smiled back.

"Good. We'll have the steward fix us some brunch."

The three of them climbed the short staircase that led to the posh airplane. Eric resisted the temptation to whistle. A long sofa that converted into a bed was on one side. There was a big-screen TV and four oversized lounge chairs. A folding table pulled down from one of the walls. A person could live comfortably in such a space.

Once they got settled, Annie asked Paul, the flight attendant, to fix them a little brunch. Mimosas to start. Annie excused herself to speak to the pilot. A few minutes later, she returned and gave Eileen a covert look.

The duration of the flight was about ninety minutes, counting taxiing on the runway and waiting for air traffic control's instructions. Everyone was in a jovial mood. Just for different reasons. Eric talked about the new monetary systems and how they were eventually going to replace normal financial transactions. Bitcoin was a perfect example. He touted the new forms of virtual art and how people were making millions off it. Annie shared her opinion that it was all fake. "You can't own air!" she hooted. "I'd rather buy a pet rock."

The atmosphere inside the cabin was buoyant. Eric was in a partying mood and gladly accepted the nonstop champagne. A few bumps of turbulence set them off with a few "whoopsie daisies." Eric showed no sense of concern. He was having the best time in years.

A few more bumps in the air, and the oxygen masks dropped down. The pilot got on the audio system. "Not to worry, folks. The oxygen is responding to the change in cabin pressure. Please leave your masks on until we make our final approach."

Annie calmly pulled hers over her face. She helped Eric with his. He was still giggling. Annie wasn't sure if it was the twilight gas being fed into his mask, or the champagne, or both. Regardless, he would be in la-la land in less than a minute, then bound, gagged, and folded into a steamer trunk. Once they had finished preparing him for the cross-country trip, he resembled a human pretzel.

As they touched down, Annie could see Kathryn's rig on the far end of the tarmac. Timing was everything. Still buckled in, Annie used the intercom phone and asked the attendant to call ahead for an electric luggage cart to transport the trunk to the awaiting rig.

* * *

Maggie pointed out the window. "There's Annie's rig."

"*This* is a rig," Kathryn corrected her.

"True, but that is Annie's kind of rig. Mine, too, if I had my druthers."

"Stop pouting. You want to fly back? I can handle this on my own."

"I couldn't, wouldn't let you do that. Not that you can't take care of yourself, but we have to take care of each other."

Kathryn gave Maggie a warm smile. "I think I might be starting to like you."

Maggie did a double take and then burst out laughing. "Sorry about the provolone."

When the plane arrived at the hangar, everything was in place. A baggage handler was waiting to unload the cargo from the plane and bring it to the awaiting truck. Alexis and Sasha had arrived half an hour earlier and delivered the laundry cart stuffed with Bennie the Calzone. He was now stashed with the rest of the produce.

Annie and Eileen got into an electric passenger transport and followed the baggage cart to the perimeter. As tempting as it was, Annie was careful not to exceed the speed limit on the tarmac. Kathryn and Maggie were standing outside the cab, waiting and waving.

Annie brought the transport to a stop and jumped out. "Woo-hoo! We made it!" She wrapped her arms around them, then stopped abruptly. "Whoa. What is that smell?" Annie gagged.

Kathryn jerked her thumb at Maggie. "The cheese monger."

Annie roared. "Glad I'm not going to be in that cab for the next thirty-six hours!"

"Ha. Ha. Very funny," Maggie said, smirking.

Kathryn lowered the liftgate, and the baggage handler slid the trunk on to the truck. Annie gave him a very nice tip and a big smile. They waited for the man to depart before resuming their conversation.

"But speaking of food, you're going to have to feed them," Annie said with a nod toward the rig.

"Only with a straw," Kathryn said solemnly. She folded her arms. "We have smoothies. Don't worry; we'll deliver them alive. Maybe not in the best shape, but they'll still be breathing."

"You know Myra can't wait to get her hands on these monsters," Annie said. "They're going to be moving Nikki to a rehab center, so Myra is rip-roaring and ready to go."

"Aren't we all!" Alexis chimed in.

"Love the hair, by the way." Annie stroked Alexis's long black wig.

"Thanks. I think it makes me look like a drag queen." Everyone hooted at her remark.

"Are the two of you going to be okay with the precious cargo?" Annie asked.

Kathryn gave Annie a sideways glance. "We'll be fine. Worst case is they'll faint at the smell of Maggie."

"Oh, come on! I used a wipe!" Maggie pouted.

"We better get moving," Kathryn suggested. "We have many miles to go. We'll do about eighteen hours today, and then the other eighteen the next, unless I can get Maggie to drive," Kathryn joked.

"Not a good idea," Maggie said. "You know I'm a horrible driver with four wheels."

"Alrighty!" Annie exclaimed. "Let's roll!" She held her nose mockingly and hugged Maggie, then Kathryn.

Maggie pulled Darius's phone from her pocket and handed it to Annie. "A little parting gift."

"*Molto bene*! The only one missing is Leroy, but we know where he is." Annie slipped the phone into her tote bag along with Bennie's and Eric's.

Alexis, Eileen, Sasha, and Annie got back into the transport, and Annie drove to the jet, which was being refueled. The four of them would fly east together. Eileen and Sasha would go back to doing their normal work for Avery, and Annie and Alexis would help get the accommodations ready for the arriving guests.

Chapter Thirty-one

Philadelphia

Nikki was progressing slowly but surely. Her voice was still raspy from the oxygen tube that had been up her nose. But her eyes were bright, and she could manage a smile. She recognized everyone and acknowledged the flowers and who sent them. She would nod when Myra read the cards aloud. Her long-term memory seemed to be intact, but the short-term was still a blur. She couldn't recall anything from the morning of the explosion.

Dr. Jarmon explained it was very common for trauma patients to have short-term memory loss, whether it was the minutes, hours, or a day or two that preceded the incident. Usually that memory would come back with time and therapy. He explained the mind forgets what pain feels like until it's healed. He half-joked when he added, "Otherwise, women would never have a second child." Myra nodded in agreement. She could understand why someone would want to black out a horrible recollection. She comforted herself with the idea that maybe it wasn't such a bad thing if Nikki didn't remember that particular morning, as long as it didn't return to her as a nightmare. She'd remind herself to discuss that with Libby if Libby was amenable to recalling her own experience.

Jack and Myra made arrangements for Nikki at the Longview Rehab Center, twenty miles from the farm. The center agreed to allow Cooper to serve as Nikki's therapy dog during her recuperation. It was difficult to convince both Myra and Jack that it wasn't necessary for them to camp out at the rehab center. The head of physical and occupational therapy explained that Nikki would be put on a routine, and she would progress faster with fewer distractions. They could visit every day, but only when she wasn't in therapy. She also needed to rest between sessions. Rehabilitation could be grueling, but it was necessary to achieve the most optimum results. Too often, people stopped before their bodies were fully recovered and could experience setbacks or fail to achieve the best outcome.

Myra went back to the hotel to pack. It finally struck her how exhausted she was. She wanted to lie down on the bed and sleep for a week. But there were still many things to do. Many. She shoved her clothes into the suitcase willy-nilly, sitting on top of it to get it to close. Done. She called the bellman and asked for him to fetch her bag and a taxi. Even though the hospital was a few short blocks, she didn't think she had the strength to lug her suitcase that far. Even if it *was* on wheels.

Jack pulled his personal belongings together to prepare for the medevac trip. Nikki's suitcase was still intact from when it was delivered from The Tides Inn.

Jack took a look around. He had been so distraught during the past few days, he had hardly noticed the suite was filled with flowers and balloons sent by friends and clients. Myra kept track of who sent what in a notebook and would send thank-you cards once Nikki was settled.

Jack asked the nurses to send the balloons to the pediatric unit and distribute the dozens of bouquets amongst themselves. Once things got back to a more even keel, he'd have gifts sent to the staff with a personal note for each of them. The care and compassion they provided to Nikki, Myra, and to him had been extraordinary.

When he returned to the hospital room, they were transferring Nikki to a gurney for her trip. She wouldn't be allowed to stand or walk until she reached the rehab center. She was too weak and wobbly.

Jack grabbed her hand. "Ready?"

"So very ready," Nikki whispered.

Myra squeezed Nikki's hand.

"Ouch, Mom," Nikki rasped. Myra looked horrified. "Just kidding." Nikki squeezed back. Cooper gave a soft woof and followed the procession down the hall. People waved and offered well wishes, many patting Cooper as he passed by.

An ambulance was waiting to bring them to the other building, where the helipad was located. Myra phoned Charles and gave him the rundown. The medevac helicopter would bring Nikki directly to the rehab center, accompanied by Dr. Jarmon. Jack and Myra would follow in a separate chopper, and Charles would meet up with them upon arrival.

Over the past few days, Charles had kept Myra in the loop about their pursuits, but not with every detail. She had enough on her mind, but now she was on a mission and wanted to know every little detail, dirty or otherwise. He filled her in on the stuffed cargo in the back of Kathryn's rig, surrounded by stinking vegetation. Myra laughed so hard, she had tears rolling down her face. This time it was good tears.

"Charles, do we still have those stun guns?" she asked.

"Of course. We haven't used them in a while. I'll check that they are in working order."

"And the room with the eight-foot video screens?"

"Of course, love." Charles did not want to imagine the fury Myra would let loose on these yanks. It made him shudder. "What do you have in mind?"

"A few things. I've been taking notes during Nikki's stay in the hospital."

Charles rolled his eyes at Fergus. Again, he shuddered.

"I have to go. They buckled Nikki in and are taking off. Our chopper is coming in a minute. See you soon." Myra put her phone in her pocket and linked arms with Jack. "Well, this has been one helluva week, eh?"

"Was it only a week?" Jack asked. "It felt like a lifetime."

"Fortunately, we have many more years ahead of us. I can't say that for the four fellows we are about to educate. Speaking of, there is still one that needs to be reined in." Myra pulled her phone out again and sent a text to Annie:

What about the guy in CI?

Annie texted back:

We have the others' phones. Will text him to come back to the states. Ask Yoko to pick him up at airport. Will text details.

At the same time, Myra was sending a text to Yoko:

How are things with Bridezilla?

Yoko texted back:

I think she's happy. Today. Tomorrow is another story.

We need to get #4 here. Can you pick him up at airport tomorrow?

What time?

Flights arrive at 6:00 PM.

No prob. Send details.

Myra then sent a text to Annie:

Use Darius phone. Tell Leroy to return to US Flight leaves at 3:00 PM. Look for Asian woman with sign.

Got it. Will do. C U soon. Miss you!

Ditto.

Annie sent off the requested text to Leroy using Darius's phone:

Problems with letter. Return to US 3:00 flight leaves tomorrow. Asian woman with sign will meet you at arriving passenger doors.

Leroy jumped when his phone beeped. It had been over a day and a half since he'd heard from anyone. He read and reread the text. *Asian woman? Who was that?* He sent a text in return:

Asian woman? Who?

The answer came back swiftly:

Don't ask questions. Just get on the plane and follow instructions.

Leroy was more confused than ever. Who was this Asian woman? How come no one ever told him about her? Where did she come from? Why wasn't Darius picking him up? What did Eric have to say about all this?

He sent another text:

Are you sure?

Annie had anticipated some pushback, so she pushed harder, texting:

Just do it.

She practically punched the message into the phone.

Leroy texted back:

Got it.

He was still confused, but he wasn't going to piss off Darius.

Chapter Thirty-two

On the Road

Kathryn pulled the rig into a large truck stop, making sure they were parked far away from the other vehicles. It was nightfall, and several other rigs were also pulling in. She made sure the back of the trailer was facing the opposite direction of the rest of the vehicles. It was time to give the cargo their smoothies. She hopped out of the cab, and Maggie did the same.

"I'll go get the protein shakes; you keep a lookout for any busybodies," Kathryn instructed.

Maggie positioned herself so she'd have a full view of the parking area. Kathryn went into the diner and ordered three Greenies for their prisoners, along with three bacon, egg, and cheese sandwiches for her and Maggie. She knew Maggie could eat two. As she waited, she recognized a couple of regular long-haulers and nodded at them. It was funny how you could make acquaintances driving across the country. There was an understood respect for one another. It was not an easy life, nor was it a safe one. In addition to their phones and GPS, most of them still used CB radios. Often it was the fastest way to communicate the presence of danger, troopers, and drifters. When her order was ready, Kathryn waved at the two guys sitting at the counter. They pointed east as if it were a question. She nodded. They gave her a short salute.

When she returned to the truck, she handed Maggie the bag of sandwiches. "Leave one for me."

"Ha." Maggie put the food in the cab and went to the back to give Kathryn a hand.

Kathryn dropped the lift and glided it up to be level with the truck bed. She lifted the tailgate. The fumes from the produce mixed with excrement was putrid. "Geez. I forgot about how rank piss and turds can stink when wrapped in a bundle."

Maggie could smell the stench from where she stood. "It smells toxic. Can they die from that?"

"If only." Kathryn pulled the bandana that was around her neck up and over her mouth and nose. Maggie handed her two of the protein drinks and a flashlight. Kathryn swept the light across the pallets of veggies. The three men were crumpled in between. She shined the light in the bulky one's face. His lids were heavy. *Must be dehydrated*, she thought. She swung the flashlight toward the not-so-pretty-boy. His eyes shot open like a bullet.

"Easy, dude. I'm not going to hurt you. Not just yet, anyway." She shoved a straw into the small hole they left open near his mouth. "Bon Appetit!" He sucked down the liquid quickly. "Good boy." She moved on to the bulky one and gave him a slight kick. His lids blinked like a traffic light. "Dinner." She repeated the same routine with him, inserting the straw in his mouth. He, too, gulped it down. Kathryn returned to where Maggie was standing and picked up the third drink.

"So far, they're still breathing," Kathryn said. She took the shake from Maggie and returned to the passengers. When she got close to Darius, he made a valiant attempt to kick her—but to no avail. He just made matters worse for himself. If that were even possible. Kathryn returned the favor and kicked him in the groin. The tape was so tight around his face that his lips protruded through the hole and got stuck. "Did that hurt, big boy?" He groaned in pain. "Now, are you going to behave and let me serve you dinner?"

She could see the agony in his eyes. "Here you go. Chef's specialty." Kathryn stuck the straw between his bloated lips. He finished off the smoothie in less than a minute.

Kathryn fixed the flashlight on each of their faces in turn. Satisfied they would make it another eight hours, she departed the disgusting smell. "Sorry we don't have turn-down service. Hope the accommodations aren't too crude for you. Nighty-night."

She lowered the liftgate and hopped off, then fastened it to the back. "I may have to pay for that load of vegetables. I'm not comfortable with the idea that they would end up on someone's table after traveling with the stinko brothers."

"I'm sure Annie will take care of any issues," Maggie said. "What was that noise I heard?"

"That douche tried to kick me, so I kicked back. He must be delirious to think he could do anything while hog-tied and taped."

"Like I said, that smell is toxic. Maybe it's affecting his brain."

Kathryn chuckled. "Well, his balls aren't feeling too good right now."

They got back into the cab, reclined the seat a little, and dug into their gooey egg sandwiches. "Mmm . . . this is really good." Maggie smacked her lips.

"I'm telling you, they have some great comfort food at these places. One of my faves is their Thanksgiving sandwich."

"Ooh, do tell." Maggie took another big bite.

"Turkey, cranberry sauce, and stuffing, on rye bread."

"Do they serve it all year?" Maggie was thoroughly enjoying her meal.

"They do."

"Oh, can I go get one?"

"I just gave you two sandwiches!"

"For later." Maggie gave Kathryn a puppy-dog look.

"Sure. Fine. Let me finish this, and I'll go back inside."

They ate in silence for a few minutes before Maggie said, "I wonder what Myra has in mind for these dirtbags."

"I can't even imagine. Doing this to one of us? And Myra's daughter, no less?" Kathryn shook her head. "We're going to see some kind of nasty."

Maggie giggled. "I can hardly wait."

Kathryn wiped her mouth and hands with a towelette. "Anything else you want?"

"How about an order of fries with brown gravy?"

"That's not going to taste good cold."

"What do you mean?"

"Oh, you're not going to save it for later?" Kathryn made it more of a statement than a question.

"Uh, no."

"I swear you have more than one stomach." Kathryn hopped out of the cab and went back into the diner. The two other truckers were still sitting at the counter. She smiled at them, then said, "Traveling with a friend. She eats like a horse."

The two men laughed. "If you need anything, just give a holler. You got our call letters, right?" one of them said.

"I might need for you to make a few food deliveries," Kathryn joked. She took the sandwich and fries and paid the waitress. The guys gave her a thumbs-up.

Kathryn thought about the days when she and her husband drove cross-country together. He was the love of her life. She tried a few times to establish other relationships, but to no avail. However, she took comfort knowing there were other drivers on the road who had her back.

She went around to the passenger side of the rig and handed Maggie the sandwich and the fries dripping with gravy.

"Woo-hoo! It's been ages since I've had this!" Maggie exclaimed.

Kathryn shook her head. That Maggie girl sure could eat, and she was barely 100 pounds. Kathryn got back behind the wheel and pulled out of the parking lot. They kept moving across the country. Kathryn was looking forward to a hot bath and one of Charles's sumptuous meals. Over the years, Charles had honed his culinary skills, and it had become a new tradition—after each mission, he would prepare something lavish and delicious.

As if Maggie were reading her mind, she said, "I wonder what Charles is going to prepare for dinner when this is over."

Kathryn did a double take. "I hate when you do that."

"What do you mean?" Maggie asked innocently.

"Read my mind."

Maggie laughed. "I think it's called synchronicity or something like that."

"Yeah, and a whole lot of woo-woo. Give me one of those." She pointed to the fries. "I want to experience what this is all about."

"You mean to tell me after all these years of truck stops, you never had fries with gravy?" Maggie dug the plastic fork into the sloppy mess and handed it to Kathryn.

"Oh, wow. You're right. I had no idea!"

"Well, keep your mitts off, lady." Maggie polished it off in a few minutes. "Are we there yet?" she joked.

"Soon, but not soon enough. I really dread having to feed

those baboons again. I better let Charles and Fergus know to get out the hazmat suits."

"Ew, yeah. Remember when we had that nefarious fake doctor in the holding cell? They had to hose him down." Both laughed. "If those jerks in the back think this is hell, wait until Annie and Myra get their hands on them."

Chapter Thirty-three

Leroy

Leroy was a hot mess. He had been on his one last nerve ever since the bank wouldn't release the funds. It was too bad he couldn't enjoy his extended stay in the Cayman Islands. Unfortunately for him, this would be the last time he saw anything that resembled civilization. But he didn't know that yet.

He checked his duffel bag several times, not that there was much to pack. He checked and rechecked his ticket and his passport. He had the jitters. What was Darius going to do to him? Who was this Asian woman? Where were they going once he landed? Too many questions and no answers. He grabbed his gear and went to the front desk to check out. Luckily, there was still enough money on the debit card to cover the hotel. He counted his cash. Just barely enough to get to the airport.

When he arrived, he went through the same security procedures, but this time, he was wearing socks. He arrived at the gate and took a seat. He still had an hour before boarding. He sent a text to Darius:

At airport. Boarding soon. Will you be at airport?

Annie heard the buzz of one of the cell phones. It was the one they took from Darius's house. She saw the text and replied:

No. She will find you. Go to baggage claim.

Annie had read the prison records and various reports that Fergus and Charles had pulled together. Eric stole money, Bennie was a peeping tom, Darius had a penchant for explosions, and Leroy was a bit of a pudding head. Nothing indicated he had ever committed bodily harm to anyone. Just stupid moves. He was a bit of a patsy, in her estimation. They would carefully assess everyone's previous sins and deal out justice accordingly. Annie knew that Myra would want to handle Darius herself.

Leroy handed the gate attendant his boarding pass. His hands were shaking. He hadn't advanced to the fear of flying syndrome yet. He was shaking from fear of the unknown. He had no idea what was waiting for him at the other side of the flight.

He took his seat and buckled up. He thought he was going to hyperventilate.

"Fly much?" the person next to him asked.

"N-no," Leroy stammered.

The man sensed Leroy's trepidation. "Don't worry. Flying is safer than driving a car."

Not if you're with Darius, Leroy thought. "Huh. Yeah. So they say."

"Maybe you need a drink to calm you down," the man next to him advised.

"I don't have any cash with me," Leroy replied.

"They take credit cards."

"I lost mine." Leroy thought fast for a change.

"Well, that stinks. Let me buy you a drink when they come around."

"That's very nice of you." Leroy let out a big sigh.

"No problem. So what brought you to the Caymans? Vacation?"

Uh-oh. Here we go. Leroy remembered his orders not to chitchat so tried to keep his answer brief. "I was checking on a resort for my employer."

"Really? What does he do?"

"He's in finance."

"Really? What area?"

"Construction, mostly." Leroy had to think quick. Something he wasn't accustomed to doing.

"Commercial?"

"Yes. Commercial." Leroy prayed the man would stop with all the questions, so he decided to ask a few himself.

"What do you do, sir?" Leroy said, changing the subject.

"I'm retired."

Leroy was surprised. The man hardly looked like he was over fifty.

"What did you do before you retired?"

"Insurance. Pretty boring."

"Huh."

"Yeah, I was lucky. I bought stock in a company years ago, and it went through the roof. We cashed in and decided to enjoy ourselves."

"Wow. That's great." Leroy was always in awe of people who figured out ways to make money legitimately.

Once the plane leveled out to cruising altitude, the flight attendant came by to take drink orders.

"What'll you have?" the passenger next to Leroy asked.

"I usually drink beer."

"I think you need something stronger than that. You've been gripping the armrest since you got on board. Four Jack

Daniels, please," the man said to the flight attendant as he handed over his credit card. "Two for each of us." She passed along the mini bottles and plastic cups.

Leroy didn't think he could drink one, let alone two, but he wanted to be polite. "Thank you, sir. This is most kind of you."

"No problem. I used to be scared witless when I first started flying. This ought to calm you down a bit." The man guzzled his first glass in one fell swoop. He cracked open the second before Leroy swallowed his first sip. It burned his throat, but he was determined to finish it. Maybe not the second, but at least the first.

"Come on, man. Drink up!" the man urged.

"I like to sip mine." Leroy was getting uncomfortable.

"Suit yourself." He finished the next one the same way. Down the hatch. A few minutes later, the man was snoring like a chain saw.

Leroy was relieved. No more small talk. He could feel the alcohol warming his body, calming his shivering nerves. He pulled out the in-flight magazine and flipped through the pages. He couldn't take his mind off wondering what was in store for him. For all of them. He hadn't come back with a letter. The money hadn't been transferred. And now some strange woman was meeting him at the airport. For a fleeting moment, he thought he would slip past her and run, but then he realized he had no money. He wouldn't get far. He made up a few scenarios in his head, but none of them made sense. He finished off the whiskey and closed his eyes. *Why, oh why, did he always get himself into such sticky situations?*

Several hours later, the captain let the passengers know they were making their final approach and would be on the ground in approximately thirty minutes. Leroy couldn't check his phone yet, so he'd have to wait another half hour to see if there were any other messages from Darius, Eric, or

Bennie. When the plane landed and the captain gave them the all-clear for cell phone use, Leroy checked his phone. Nothing. He shrugged. Maybe this woman got the funds somehow. Maybe things were going to work out. Maybe.

After he exited the plane, he took the escalator to the baggage claim area. He looked around. Toward the back of the crowd, a meticulously dressed Asian woman with dark sunglasses held a sign that read: LARRY KRATMAN. For a minute, he forgot that was his new alias. Then he nodded and walked in her direction. She said nothing, just motioned for him to follow her. They walked toward a black SUV with darkened windows. She opened the rear passenger door and gestured for him to get in. She took the seat next to him. Another woman was driving, and she hit the childproof safety lock. Leroy wasn't going anywhere except for where they were taking him. Leroy didn't know if he should speak or not. He chose not. He figured it wouldn't matter what he said. The women remained quiet.

They had driven for approximately twenty minutes when Yoko used her famous sleeper hold on Leroy. Once he was knocked out, she placed duct tape over his mouth and a burlap bag over his head. She zip-tied his hands. She almost felt sorry for him. But not that much. He seemed less of a criminal and more like a tool. They reached the farm, and Yoko and Alexis brought their passenger to the rear entrance. He was the first to arrive. When the car came to a complete stop, he regained consciousness and started to squirm. Alexis unlocked the doors, and Fergus unbuckled Leroy's seat belt.

"Take it easy there, mate." Charles assisted Fergus in getting Leroy out of the car. "Steady now." They each grabbed an elbow and steered him. "Step up." Leroy obeyed. "Good boy. Now we're going down a flight of stairs. Take it easy. One at a time."

They guided him down the stone steps. Leroy could smell the old concrete and heard the sound of keys jangling. It was a familiar sound. Like prison.

Charles opened the cell and escorted Leroy inside. Once the door was locked, Charles helped Leroy onto a wooden bench. He began to explain. "You, sir, are in deep, deep, hot water."

Leroy tried to speak, but the tape only allowed for grunts and moans.

Charles continued. "We know you are associated with several other reprehensible men." Leroy was shaking his head violently. "This is what is going to happen. Your cohorts will be arriving soon, and we will decide what the best punishment is for all of you, individually and collectively. Am I making myself clear?"

Leroy nodded ferociously.

"Good. Now sit tight. Someone will be along momentarily to ask you a few questions. Understood?"

Again, Leroy nodded like a bobblehead. He wished they would remove the bag. He was getting claustrophobic. He started to whimper.

"There. There. It won't be long." Charles unlocked the door and exited.

Long before what? Leroy wondered.

Chapter Thirty-four

Pinewood

The farm was busy. Their first guest had been delivered. Initially, they didn't want Libby to be a witness to any of the forthcoming activities, but Izzie convinced the others that she had come this far with all of their innermost security secrets. As Izzie pointed out, Libby was very involved in the tracing and tracking down of these men. She should be given the option, if she wanted, to meet the creeps or not. They ultimately agreed she could stay, but they would spare her the gruesome details.

Myra and Jack arrived at the rehab center shortly after Nikki. Charles was waiting. He was happy to see Nikki had come a long way in a week. He explained to Myra he couldn't stay long, because they were expecting the first of the quartet to arrive.

A tingle of excitement went through her body. "Let the games begin," she said.

They were helping Nikki get settled while Dr. Jarmon went over her chart with the head nurse and director of physical therapy. All her limbs were functioning well. She needed to recuperate from the shock more than anything. Walking Cooper several times a day would do wonders for her.

Dr. Jarmon joined the rest of them and explained what Nikki's daily routine would be like. As of the moment, he estimated she could go home in eight to ten days.

Thankfully, the injury didn't do any permanent damage, and her recovery should go smoothly if she followed the protocol. And Nikki being Nikki, she was a stickler for protocol. She was determined to get strong and vertical posthaste.

Nikki joked and said it was her hat that had softened the blow. Jack quipped back with, "Maybe it's because you are a hardheaded woman!"

Myra felt something beyond relief, as if she had exhaled for the first time in over a week.

It was then time for Nikki's introduction to the physical therapist, followed by a session with the psychotherapist. Myra and Jack hugged and kissed her and promised to check on her later if she was up to it.

Jack and Myra shared a car service back to the farm. Jack headed to his house to swap out Nikki's vacation clothes for something more appropriate for physical therapy. Once inside, he placed the bag on the bench in the entryway and popped it open. *That hat*, he thought. He didn't know if anyone put it with their things when they sent them from the hotel. He hadn't looked in Nikki's suitcase the entire time she was in the hospital. When he thought about it, he remembered it had blown off her head before she hit the ground. Maybe he'd let her believe it really was the hat that saved her.

Myra was on pins and needles, anticipating the serious consequences of misconduct. But first, to be fair, she would interrogate each one of the culprits individually. She would know who was telling the truth or not. There were several methods to assure honesty.

The car let her off in front of the house. She didn't know what kind of shenanigans could be going on by the back door. She could hear Lady and her pups yelping in chorus, with Yoko, Alexis, Izzie, and Libby standing by. When she opened the door, she was greeted with cheers, tears, yaps, and squeals. After all the hugging and high fives, they introduced Myra to Libby.

Izzie spoke first. "Myra, meet Libby Gannon. She has been aces with everything."

Myra gave Libby a huge hug. "I don't know what we would have done without you. Charles has been gushing about your work."

Libby blushed. "It was kinda fun, honestly. A lot more interesting than all the beta testing I do."

Myra hooked her arm through Libby's. "Can I ask you to do one more thing for me? For us?"

"Absolutely. What?"

"Visit Nikki at the rehab center. I cannot tell you how encouraging your story was to me. To all of us. I think if she met someone who went through something similar, it would inspire her. Don't get me wrong, Nikki is a terrific self-motivator, but as you may have gathered, we work as a team."

"I would be more than happy to visit her." Libby smiled warmly.

Charles put his arm around Myra. "Come. Let's get you settled, so we can begin our operation." He walked her into their bedroom and turned on the shower. "Or would you prefer to put off the introduction until later?"

"Oh, no. I'll only be a few minutes." She kissed him on the cheek and then wrapped her arms around him. She let out another long breath. "Dorothy was right. There's no place like home."

Charles gave her a squeeze and patted her on the hiney. "Go. I'll fix you a cup of tea and a bite to eat."

Myra was true to her word. In less than fifteen minutes, she was in the kitchen, wearing a baggy pair of flannel pants and an equally baggy sweatshirt. The women were sitting around the table, chatting.

"So, tell me about our first visitor," Myra said after she took a sip of her tea.

Annie pulled out her tablet and read aloud. "Leroy Crenshaw. Thirty-eight-year-old white male. Unmarried. No children. Last known place of employment, Forrest City Correctional Facility. Prior to that, he worked as a mechanic in Tremont, Virginia. Prior arrest was for trespassing at Stillwell Art Center in Asheville, North Carolina."

"Wait! Did you say Stillwell Art Center? Ellie Stillwell's place?"

"Yes, the one and only."

"Funny. Last time I spoke to Ellie, she never mentioned a break-in. Her security is almost as tight as ours!" Myra seemed shocked.

"He and his friend, George Nelson, didn't actually break into the facility. They entered through the rear of Bodman's Restoration. Apparently, they were looking for some items that they salvaged. Mr. Nelson thought he may have sold something valuable and went back to check. They were discovered by Luna Bodman, where she held them at bay with a fire extinguisher."

Myra hooted. "That Luna. She is a pip. Doesn't surprise me in the least!"

Annie continued. "US Marshall Christopher Gaines came on the scene, and Crenshaw and Nelson were arrested."

Myra gave Annie a puzzled look. "That's what put him in federal prison?"

"No. Apparently, Leroy was not satisfied with his lot in life and decided to purchase a firearm."

"But he's a convicted felon."

"Correct. Now get this. He was too afraid to buy one on the black market. Too dangerous and too expensive, so he decided to do it the formal way and fill out an application, where he lied."

"You have got to be kidding." Myra blinked.

"Nope. It's all right here. He went to jail for falsifying his permit application. It's a federal offense."

"Any record of violence? Other felonies or misdemeanors?" Myra asked.

"Not that we could find. But here's something you'd appreciate. He saw a man throw a puppy out the window of his truck. Leroy rescued the dog and reported the guy. The guy was fined a thousand dollars, and Leroy adopted the dog."

"Where's the dog now?" Myra was almost afraid to ask.

"He's an elder companion. He resides at an assisted-living complex. He's good therapy for seniors." Annie went on to say, "Leroy made those arrangements before he went to jail. He was really concerned about the pooch."

"Well, I'll be darned," Myra said.

Charles chimed in. "Sounds like the bloke is a little more daft than evil."

Myra stroked her pearls. "Interesting. I wonder how he got involved with the other three."

"From what Avery told us, the warden said he was pals with Barnett, Lancaster, and Weber when he was in jail. He was never in trouble. Followed the rules."

"I suppose prison makes for strange bedfellows," Myra mused.

"In many ways." Fergus guffawed. Annie gave him a backhanded slap on the arm. "Ouch. Feisty, eh?"

"What about the rest of them?" Myra asked.

Annie gave her the rundown on Eric Barnett. "Hedge fund

fraud. The Department of Banking and Insurance believes he is hiding money somewhere. They were able to trace much of it with all of his exorbitant spending, but there is a big hole to the tune of five million dollars."

"The Cayman Islands," Fergus said.

"My thoughts exactly," Annie agreed. "That's my guess as to why Leroy was there."

Yoko produced an envelope. "We found this in his luggage. It's a copy of a letter to the Cayman National Bank, introducing him as Larry Kratman, and that he was in possession of a letter of intent from a Mr. Gregory Masters to transfer funds to Banco de Guayaquil."

"That checks out from my conversation with Mac at the bank," Annie said.

"We need to find out what was the rest of the plan. And why the bombs?" Myra asked. "It doesn't make any sense."

"Maybe if you have a chat with Leroy, he might be able to shed some light on things. I think he may be open to a conversation," Charles suggested.

"I shall." Myra got up and started walking toward the steps that led to the basement.

"Want company?" Annie asked.

"And if I said no?"

"I'd go with you anyway." Annie laughed. "I think Charles, Fergus, and I should all be in the room with him."

"Of course. I was teasing." Myra winked. "The rest of you lovelies wait here. Relax in the atrium. Pour yourselves a glass of something. We'll record everything and share with you later. Meanwhile, Izzie, can you check on Kathryn and Maggie?"

"Will do!" Izzie said.

Izzie, Yoko, Alexis, and Libby wandered into the atrium and admired Yoko's floral artistry. "It must be very relaxing to work with plants and flowers," Libby commented.

"It is," Yoko replied. "But you don't want to be around to plan anyone's event. Weddings, showers, bar mitzvahs, sweet-sixteen parties. A total nightmare. Now we also have gender-reveal parties, promposals, preschool graduations. It's madness."

"Wait, did you say 'promposal'?" Libby asked.

"Oh, it's the latest in how to spend your parents' money. You have to do something over the top to ask a girl to go to the prom. Rose petals in the shape of a heart covering the entire front yard. Limousines covered in carnations. That's where I draw the line. Looks too much like a funeral instead of the junior prom."

Libby started to giggle. "How many of those couples do you think make it past college?"

"College? Try high school!" Yoko added. "I can honestly say the world has gone completely mad about conspicuous consumption."

"Back up a minute. Preschool graduation?" Alexis's jaw dropped.

"Yep." Yoko pursed her lips. "I refuse to do those, as well."

"I blame social media," Alexis said. "The stuff that's put out there is corrupting our culture, our minds, our souls."

"Don't get me started," Izzie said as she typed a text to Maggie. It read simply:

ETA?

Maggie responded:

Under an hour. Get ready.

"Whoa. Listen up. Kathryn and Maggie will be here in less than an hour. I'll let Charles and Fergus know." Izzie hightailed it down the stairs.

Down in the basement, Myra spoke to Leroy at long last. Annie, Charles, and Fergus stood silently outside the cell, observing the interrogation. They would only intervene if needed.

"I'm going to take off the burlap bag. Nod your head if you understand," Myra said.

He nodded.

"Good. We are going to have a conversation, and you are going to tell me everything you know. Every detail no matter how minute. Do you understand?"

Again, a nod.

Myra lifted the bag from Leroy's face. A bright light was shining into his eyes, so he couldn't see her face or anything else in the room. "Don't try to scream. Believe me, no one can hear you," Myra said as she slowly removed the tape from his mouth. "Why were you in the Cayman Islands?"

Leroy was hyperventilating again. "I . . . I . . . was supposed to br-bring a l-letter to a b-b-bank. They were s-supposed to t-transfer the m-money."

"Who arranged for you to do this?"

Leroy's eyes went wide. As terrified as he was at the moment, he was still more terrified of what Darius would do to him. Then Eric. Then Bennie.

"Leroy, you need to tell me the truth. What you say will have a strong influence on what happens to you next. Do you understand what I'm saying?" Myra's voice was calm and even.

"Eric," Leroy blurted. "Eric Barnett. It's his money."

"I doubt that," Myra said knowingly.

"I mean, it was in his account."

"Yes, and do you know how it got there?" Myra asked.

"Something to do with fraud. He said it was an Internal Revenue thing."

"Well, he lied. Just like he lied to everyone he stole money from." Myra enlightened him. "He pretended to invest people's money and then told them their investments didn't work out. He stole over one hundred million dollars. Meanwhile, he stashed away over five million dollars for himself as insurance. Insurance he would have a pile of cash for when he got out of jail. He was willing to waste five years of his life behind bars to continue his lavish lifestyle."

Leroy simply blinked several times.

"Tell me how the rest of the gents fit into this gruesome foursome?"

"It started in the pen. Me, Bennie, and Eric kinda drifted toward each other. You know someone's gotta have your back, and you gotta have someone's, too."

"Go on. What about the money?"

"Eric promised each of us fifty K. I was going to be the messenger; Bennie would work out the details."

"What was Darius's role in all of this?" Myra pushed.

"Well, that's just it. He kinda glommed on to us. There was no shaking him. He's a scary dude." Leroy was shaking his head; the words were flowing much easier. They said confession was good for the soul. "None of us wanted to get into any kind of tangle with Darius, but Darius promised he'd have all our backs, except he was the one who we needed protection from."

"So you're saying he coerced you guys into letting him tag along, and he was going to get fifty thousand dollars?"

"Yep."

"And what was his contribution to this project?"

"Beats me. All's I know is he made me follow some people to Irvington. Then he met me there." Out of nowhere, he started to bawl. "I didn't know what he was planning. I swear! I thought he was just going to tag someone's car with a device. Like so he could follow them. I didn't ask any questions. You don't ask someone like Darius questions. Then when we were around the block, I heard the explosion. When we got back to the motel, he put the TV on, and the news said a woman was hurt in a car explosion." Leroy's chest was heaving as he tried to catch his breath. Then he wet himself. "I swear to God, I didn't know. I didn't know."

Myra gave him a few minutes to regain his composure before continuing. "Then what happened?"

"Darius got all pissed and started slamming things. He said it was supposed to be for some guy."

"Did he say his name?"

"No. All's he said was at least he'll suffer if she dies." Leroy was hysterical at this point. "I woulda never have done it. I swear! You've got to believe me."

Myra was pretty certain she did believe him, but she still wanted every last drop of information she could squeeze out of him. "And after the explosion? Where did you go?"

"Darius got a text from Eric to go to the airport. There'd be an envelope with debit cards, passports, licenses, a letter to the bank, and a ticket for me to go to the Cayman Islands. Eric and Bennie made all the arrangements. Then when I got there, they wouldn't do the transfer."

Annie nodded, encouraging him to go on.

"Then after a couple days, I got a text from Darius telling me to come back." He heaved another breath. "And here I am."

"What about the second bomb?"

"What second bomb?" Leroy looked genuinely confused.

"The one Darius left for his lawyer."

"I don't know what you're talking about. For real."

"So you didn't know Darius was planning on setting off another bomb? In Texas?"

Leroy's eyes went wide. "Texas? I seriously don't know anything about that. Honest to God."

"Okay, Leroy. We're going to leave you alone for a while. Someone will bring you something to eat. And a fresh pair of pants."

"Th-thank you." Leroy had absolutely no appetite, but he wasn't going to decline the offer. He knew he was once again a prisoner, though he had no idea who his jailers were. All he knew was that these people were dead serious, and he was going to cooperate. The hell with Darius.

Myra, Charles, Fergus, and Annie headed back upstairs.

"Looks like this guy was a bit of a pawn," Charles offered.

"I tend to agree with you." Myra was stroking her pearls.

"Ditto," Annie added.

"Now we have to wait for the others to get here."

"Should be within the hour," Izzie said as she came in from the atrium. The others followed. "Kathryn said they're going to bring the rig to one of the outer buildings. She said to tell Fergus and Charles to get out the serious hazmat suits and gas masks."

"Gas masks?" Myra looked puzzled.

"Apparently, these guys have been bound and gagged for almost two days, with no bathroom breaks, among pallets of bok choy, broccoli, and cabbage."

Charles gave a sideways look to Fergus. "And to think we get to have all the fun."

Everyone burst out laughing. "Seriously, it's going to be a hose-down. You better get the gear ready," Izzie said.

Charles and Fergus headed out to retrieve the equipment needed to handle the toxic package that was about to arrive. Charles also tossed a pair of disposable pants into Leroy's cell and slid a roast beef sandwich through the lockbox on the door. Even though his hands were still zip-tied, Leroy would be able to manage a change of britches and shove a sandwich in his mouth.

The women sat at the kitchen table. Myra looked composed. "Once Charles and Fergus sanitize the other three, we'll start with Bennie. Besides being a bit of a pervert, he seems the weakest of those three. He may cave quickly. From what we discovered and what Leroy said, Eric is arrogant but not necessarily deadly. He will most likely give in. We'll save Darius for last."

Annie was the next to speak. "What do you have in mind as their final punishment?"

"I almost feel sorry for Leroy," Myra said, and then paused. "Almost. He's just not playing with a full deck." She thought for a moment. "How are we doing in Congo River Basin?"

Myra was referring to a 5,000-square-mile wildlife refuge situated in one of the most remote areas of the jungle. It was a project she and Annie had started years ago that was now managed by a team of veterinary specialists.

Annie began to type on her tablet. She read for a moment before saying, "They need someone to look after the forest elephants."

Myra smiled. "I think that would be a perfect job for Leroy, don't you?"

Heads bobbed in agreement. Annie added, "He'll never be able to leave, and should he try, well, the shock from his ankle monitor should teach him not to attempt it again. I think he'll be okay among the flora and fauna. He can't hurt anyone, and he'll stay out of trouble unless he messes with a momma chimp."

Libby raised her hand. "May I ask how all of this works?"

Myra gave her the 411 on how they arranged for transportation for certain individuals. They would then spend the rest of their lives in a remote part of the world, doing penance for the evil deeds they had inflicted on others. "We promote and enforce the 'karma's a bitch' concept."

"Hear! Hear!" Izzie slapped the table. The others joined in, with Lady adding her two cents' worth of woofs.

"So you're going to arrange for Leroy to spend the rest of his life in a jungle looking after elephants?" Libby sounded a bit puzzled.

"Correct," Myra said.

Annie nodded as she typed a few more things on her tablet. "The transport vehicle should be here within the hour. One down, three to go."

"That's incredible." Libby was awestruck.

"We do our best," Annie said.

Alexis raised her hand and put up her fist. "Whatever it takes!" More table slapping ensued.

Charles and Fergus returned to the kitchen, wearing hooded disposable jumpsuits, gloves, shoe coverings, and ventilator face masks dangling around their necks. They were carrying a large canvas bag filled with similar items.

Annie looked at Fergus. "What's the plan?"

"The usual. We'll remove the visitors with hand trucks, cut off the tape and their clothes, hose them down, and give them disposable jumpsuits and paper shoes."

"Perfect," Annie said.

Izzie's phone rang. It was Maggie. She put it on speaker. "Hey, we're turning in to the farm. Where should we park?"

"Building five," Charles said. "Crack on!" Along with Fergus, he hauled the large canvas bag into a golf cart, climbed in, and headed to the rendezvous point.

Kathryn pulled on the airhorn of her rig, sending two blasts of noise through the air. Maggie was hanging out of the window, waving madly. "We made it!" She jumped out of the cab and flung herself on to the grass and started kissing the ground.

Kathryn came around from her side. "Such a drama

queen." She shook hands with Charles and Fergus. "I'm a bit too road-trashed for a hug."

"Don't be absurd." Charles gave her a big bear hug, followed by Fergus, who helped Maggie off of the turf.

"Fair warning—it's putrid in there." Kathryn jerked her thumb over her shoulder.

"I think the vegetables committed suicide." Maggie brushed off her pants. Not that it mattered. She was a mess from head to toe. "I have to say, I'll take a stakeout any day." Which was saying a lot, since stakeouts were one of Maggie's least favorite things to do. "But don't tell Annie!"

Fergus chuckled. "Your secret's safe with me."

Kathryn lowered the platform. She, Fergus, and Charles got on, and she raised it level with the sliding overhead door. "Ready?"

The men put their masks on and looked over at Kathryn. "Care to join us?"

"Uh, thanks, but no. Feel free to go about without me. One is in the far left corner, another in the middle on the right, and the third is behind this row of pallets." She pointed.

Maggie was busy pulling garbage bags from behind the seats. "What should I do with these?" she called up to the men.

"Put them on the workshop table inside. We'll take a look at them once we fumigate these parasites," Charles replied.

The first one off the truck was Bennie. They hoisted his almost lifeless hulk onto the hand truck. Kathryn lowered it down and wheeled the heap into the building, depositing him in a concrete stall. She went back and sent the hand truck up on the lift. The second down was Eric, who was taken to his own private stall. Then came Darius, who tried to put up a fight with whatever energy he had left. The grunts and groans were pathetic.

The three men were now ensconced in their separate concrete stalls, their hands tied together and fastened to the walls. One by one, Fergus and Charles cut off their duct-taped wrappers with surgical scissors and tossed them in a large bin with a large orange sign that said BIOHAZARD. Fergus scrubbed the men down with a harsh bristle brush as Charles hosed them clean, washing the filth down the drains in the floor. They let them dry for several minutes while Charles and Fergus changed into clean jumpsuits, sealed the stinking pile of human waste in a bin, and rolled it out the door. They put the bin in a small shed with the same BIOHAZARD markings. A proper disposal company would retrieve it later.

Charles and Fergus helped the men into their new attire, taking care that none of them would try any type of heroics. Once they were redressed, they zip-tied them to the iron rings in the concrete benches in their cells—not that any of them had an ounce of strength left to resist.

Charles and Fergus gave each of the men the same instructions: "Do not attempt to escape. You will be brought in for questioning. Do not lie."

Charles and Fergus then went into the workshop to see what Maggie and Kathryn had unloaded. There were three almost identical piles of broken pieces of plastic and shredded paper. At first glance, it was difficult to figure out what it all was. A Lego game gone awry?

Maggie poked through the pieces with a long pick. "Hey, check this out." She produced something from one of the piles that resembled a switch. "Looks like it was once a push-button switch, the kind you see on a lot of technical equipment, like monitors and computers."

"Well, perhaps Mr. Lancaster can shed some light on it, since he was the one who deposited it, correct?" Charles addressed Maggie.

"Correct. Kathryn tailed him, and I did the dumpster diving."

"You are such a sport!" Charles grinned and patted her on the shoulder.

"Oh yeah. That's me, all right." Maggie smirked.

Charles turned to Maggie. "It just occurred to me that you've been here for more than half an hour and haven't mentioned food. Are you all right?"

Maggie nodded in the direction of the hazmat containers. "Kinda lost my appetite."

"I'm sure that won't last long," Kathryn teased. "Do you know she ate two sandwiches in a row and then asked for a Thanksgiving turkey sandwich and French fries with brown gravy?"

"Well, we'll see to it that everyone has a good solid meal tonight. I assume after you shower and change?" Charles looked Maggie and Kathryn up and down.

"Please! Now!" Maggie moaned.

"We'll bring the men over to the basement one at a time. Myra is anxious to speak to all of them."

"I can only imagine!" Maggie said.

Fergus chuckled. "I'm looking forward to it. I'm sure Annie will want to have a go at them, too."

Everyone chortled, imagining what was coming.

"What are you going to do with the trailer?" Fergus asked.

"I'll have someone haul it out of here. I already contacted the buyer and seller and let them know the delivery did not go according to plan. Well, *their* plan. I told them we will make proper remunerations," Kathryn explained.

"Bravo. Well done, Kathryn!" Charles said.

"What about me?" Maggie pouted.

"You too, Maggie." Charles shook his head. Maggie was an amusing sort. "Why don't the both of you go to the house and clean up? Fergus and I will relocate them shortly."

"Sounds like a plan," Maggie cheered. She got her belongings out of the cab and tossed them into the back of the golf cart. Kathryn did the same. This time, Maggie was behind the wheel and peeled out, making a mad dash back to civilization.

With their yapping and woofing, the dogs gave notice there were visitors. Everyone got up from the table to greet the daring duo. Maggie put her arms up to stall people off. "I stink. I'm gross!"

"And we love you!" Annie was the first to grab the curly redhead.

Myra threw her arms around Kathryn. "I am so, so relieved!" Myra's eyes welled up. "Nikki is doing great, and you're back! Back with a bounty, no less!"

Once everyone had hugged one another, they introduced Libby. She was overwhelmed with the warmth and deep friendship they showed for one another, extending now to her, as well. It had been a very long time since she was surrounded with this kind of sisterhood. Yes, she loved her neighbors. Yes, she loved her home. And yes, she got lonely from time to time. She made a decision then and there to be more social. Volunteer somewhere. Do something more with her life than just tinker with technology.

Kathryn explained what was going on in the outer building where the men were being held. And that they were getting ready to bring them to the basement of the farm. Myra's and Annie's eyes were twinkling. "This ought to be fun," Myra said as she took a stun gun out from the cupboard.

Back in the cells, Charles and Fergus placed burlap bags over the men's heads. One at a time, they were brought to the house, taken down the stairs, and deposited in their own soundproof cell near Leroy's. The transition took about thirty minutes. They had to be careful so as no one would trip.

The women then went down the stairs single file, saluting

Lady Liberty as they entered the war room. Charles flipped on the closed-circuit cameras for each of the cells.

Leroy was already asleep after eating the sandwich he had been served earlier. Bennie was a heap of dough in a paper suit. Eric looked like a deer in the headlights, and Darius looked like he wanted to kill somebody.

Myra entered Bennie's cell first. Charles and Fergus stood behind her. All eyes were watching the enormous monitors in the war room.

Myra turned on the high beam of her flashlight. Bennie recoiled from the light.

"You are going to tell me exactly what you've been up to since you got out of prison," Myra stated.

Bennie could barely speak. "I don't know what you are talking 'bout."

"Bennie, Bennie, Bennie. You are here. Tied up. In a cell. Do you think you can skirt any issue I bring to your attention?"

He didn't answer. Myra pressed the heel of her shoe on his pinky toe.

"Okay, okay," he said feebly. "What do you want to know?"

"Start from the beginning. How you met your comrades and what you've been doing since. Those are not difficult questions."

Bennie described a scenario similar to the one Leroy had related: They met in prison; Eric had money; Darius bullied his way in. Eric had promised to pay everyone $50k.

"And what was your role in all of this?" Myra asked calmly.

"We . . . me and Eric . . . would locate people for Darius."

"And why would you do that?"

Bennie finally looked straight into the light. "Have you met the guy?"

"Not yet, but I am truly looking forward to it." Myra remained as calm as ever.

"Anyway, he would give us a name. Then Eric and I would meet in Arizona and do a deep dive into the dark web and find the addresses. We did it three different times."

Myra was right—Bennie rolled over like a tire down a hill.

"And what were the names of those people?" Myra asked.

Bennie thought for a moment. "First guy was Jack something."

"Jack Emery?" Myra asked as her blood began to boil.

"Yeah. That's it. We found him in Virginia."

"And then what?"

"And then nothing. We sent Darius the address."

"Did he ever say what he would do with this information?"

"Nope, and I didn't ask. You don't ask Darius questions."

"We'll just see about that." Myra felt for the stun gun in her pocket. "Continue."

"Then he sent another request. This time it was a guy in Texas. Paul something."

"Do you have memory problems?" Myra asked.

"I'm a little unnerved, if you must know." Bennie was getting a bit snarky.

"Well, good. You said Paul something?"

"Yeah, Stern or Stein."

"It's Scovil, for future reference." Myra was checking off the list she had memorized. "Who else?"

"A woman named Gina Mason. She was in Austin." Bennie coughed. "And that's all I know."

"Tell me—what was your participation in all of this? Just finding people?"

"And getting tickets and stuff to the other guys."

"Such as?"

"Eric got some phony IDs made up for us. I arranged for them to be delivered to the airport."

Annie whispered into a microphone that transmitted to an earpiece Myra was wearing. "This checks out so far."

Assured that Bennie was telling her the truth, Myra pressed on. "After you sent Darius the third name, what did you do?"

"Nothin', really. I went back to Vegas and met some woman. I think she slipped me a mickey or something, and I ended up here."

"Okay, Benjamin. Sit tight. I'll be back." Myra turned away. She, Charles, and Fergus went back to the war room.

"What do you think?" Myra asked the assembled group.

Alexis was the first to speak. "I think he's legit as far as his story. I didn't spend a lot of time with the dude, but he didn't come across as dangerous or violent."

"Okay. So what do we do with Bennie?"

Libby raised her hand.

Myra smiled. "You don't have to raise your hand, dear."

Libby blushed. "Sorry—newbie. So the guy isn't violent, but he does like looking at young naked girls."

"He was not just looking," Myra said. "He was photographing her and selling the photos."

"If we're fitting the punishment with the crime," continued Libby, "then perhaps he should have to work in hospice care for the elderly for the rest of his life. Tending to people who are sick and dying."

"That certainly would give someone an appreciation of life," Alexis added. "I'm for that solution."

Myra looked around the room. "Any objections?" No one said a word. "All in favor?"

Unanimous "ayes" filled the room.

"Excellent. We'll send him to a hospital in India. We'll contact Pearl and ask her help."

"Pearl Barnes is a retired justice. She runs a sort of underground railroad for those in need, and she helps us . . . distribute . . . certain people around the globe," Maggie explained to Libby.

"Kathryn? Please?" Annie looked at Kathryn, knowing she had issues with Pearl that went years back. Both Myra and Annie thought forcing Kathryn and Pearl to deal with one another would bridge the gap, but so far, it had been to no avail.

"Yeah, whatever." Kathryn knew her fellow Sisters would always make her be the one to deal with Pearl, until they could make amends. Kathryn would be the one to meet Pearl at the usual meadow and hand off Bennie. Kathryn punched in Pearl's number and sent a text, telling her:

Pick up package at farm.

Next up was Eric. Myra went into his cell with Charles and Fergus close behind her. She asked him the same questions she'd asked before. His answers lined up with Bennie's.

"So you provided the funds for this escapade?" Myra prodded.

"Uh-huh," he answered begrudgingly.

"Why was that?"

"I had to get someone to go to the Cayman Islands. Leroy was the perfect stooge."

"And how did Darius and Bennie fit in?"

Eric gave the same explanation: You needed a posse in jail. Darius was a leech. A scary one. Eric was in a talkative mood. "He made me pay for a three-D printer. Cost a bundle."

Charles snapped his fingers and elbowed Fergus. "So that's what all the plastic was from!"

"What was he going to do with a three-D printer?" Myra asked.

"I have no idea, and I wasn't about to ask. You don't ask Darius questions."

"Hmm. Seems to be a theme," Myra noted. "Let me see if I have this straight—you offered to pay each of them fifty K for helping you retrieve five million?"

Eric shrugged. "That was the plan. Yes."

"I see. Okay, Eric. That will be all for now." The three exited the cell and returned to the war room.

"Suggestions?" Myra asked the group.

"The guy is obsessed with money. Maybe send him to some impoverished part of the world where he has to help people fetch water every day?" Maggie proposed.

"I like that," Annie said.

The others nodded in agreement. "Okay. We'll send him to a village in South Sudan," Myra said.

"He'll then be on the same continent as Leroy," Yoko pointed out.

"I don't think there's a risk of either of them running into each other," Annie snickered.

"Good point. Just remembering my geography," Yoko said.

"All in favor?" Myra asked.

"Ayes" echoed around the room once more.

Annie addressed Kathryn again. "Tell Pearl we have another passenger for her to pick up. She can come get them at the same time."

Kathryn obliged and sent off another text to Pearl. "Done!"

Myra stretched. "All right, everyone. Are we ready to meet the big bad Darius Lancaster"

The women applauded with glee.

"You betcha!"

"Can't wait!"

"It's about time!"

This time, Annie joined Myra, Charles, and Fergus. They

were welcomed with a barrage of expletives from Darius, including the spit from his mouth.

"I don't think you are in any position to be acting like a schmuck." Myra dug into her bag of vernacular.

"And who the hell are you?" Darius wasn't giving up without a fight.

"I am the person who has you zip-tied and incarcerated. You can scream, curse, and threaten all you want, Mr. Lancaster but I can assure you that you will get absolutely nowhere."

"So what do you want from me?" Darius asked.

"The truth."

"Yeah, like what?" He was pushing his luck.

"Like making bombs."

Darius snorted. "I don't know what you're talking about."

That's when Myra took the stun gun from her pocket, held it to his balls, and pulled the trigger.

He screamed uncontrollably and cursed even more.

She nailed him again. More screams.

Myra waited a few moments before saying, "*Now* will you tell me what you did?"

"What are you talking about?" he asked feebly, curled up in a fetal position on the floor of his cell.

"The bombs, you immoral bastard." Myra's cool demeanor was gone. She zapped him again. He writhed on the ground. "I am going to ask you one more time, Mr. Lancaster Tell me!" Myra's voice was at a volume no one had ever heard before.

"Okay. Okay. I wanted to get even with the people who put me in jail."

"Jack Emery? Paul Scovil?" She held the stun gun against his scrotum.

"Yes! Yes!"

"What does Gina Mason have to do with any of this?" Myra asked.

"Gina? I didn't do nothin' to her." Darius wasn't lying. He never got the opportunity to put his full plan to work.

"I'm finished with him." Myra kicked him in the groin as a parting gesture.

They returned to the war room, and Myra laid out her thoughts. "This is what I propose: We take him to an old minefield in the desert. He will be hog-tied. The only way he can get to his food is to crawl across a mile of desert without blowing himself up."

"I like that." Annie nodded. "But what else?"

"The desert is not only filled with explosives, but is also home to scorpions and snakes. He will have to avoid those, as well, which will be most difficult after his testicles are covered in snake lure."

The room went silent. Myra continued. "After a day or so, he'll pray he finds a land mine to put him out of his misery."

Charles was twitching. "Sounds awful."

"Horrendous," Maggie added.

"Excruciating," said Annie.

"Then it's perfect," Myra said confidently. "All in favor?" The "ayes" resounded once more.

"Kathryn?" Maggie asked.

"Yep. On it." A few seconds later, Kathryn announced, "Pearl will be here in two hours."

"Well, now. Shall we have some supper?" Charles asked.

Maggie rubbed her hands together. "Yes, indeed!"

When everyone returned to the kitchen, the aroma of baked chicken filled the air. The women began their routine of setting the table, each knowing what her part was. They took their seats around the big oak table as Fergus and Charles brought over the platters of food. They held hands as Myra said grace.

"Thank you, dear Lord, for these thy gifts and the many blessings in our lives. Amen."

"When did you have time to do all this?" Libby looked at the roasted potatoes, chicken, green beans, and biscuits.

"He's quite the magician in the kitchen," Annie said.

Myra put her hand on Charles's knee and whispered across the table, "That's not the only place where he works his magic."

Hoots and hollers filled the room, along with a sense of peace, joy, and justice.

Epilogue

Pearl arrived within two hours and shuffled the men to parts unknown.

Before Libby left for Missouri, she visited Nikki several times over the next few days. They bonded, as expected. The two women formed their own Sisterhood of recovery and recuperation. A few days later, Nikki was released from the rehab center.

Before Cooper flew back to Alabama to be reunited with Julie, he and Nikki and Jack were planning on having a nice, quiet dinner with Myra and Charles. This time, they drove their car to the farmhouse. Nikki was doing exceptionally well, but was not quite ready for a bumpy ride in a golf cart.

Once they arrived at the house, Nikki was taken aback. Yoko, Alexis, Annie, Kathryn, Izzie, and Maggie were all gathered around the elaborately set table. Myra and Charles had arranged for all of the Sisters and Fergus to be there with warm, welcoming wishes. It was a surprise dinner party in honor of Nikki.

Charles had prepared his now-famous crown roast with Yorkshire pudding—though he warned everyone to never refer to it as a popover. Yoko had brought a magnificent floral centerpiece that garnered oohs and aahs from the group.

Yoko spoke up. "Full disclosure. The bride didn't think the fuchsia was fuchsia enough, so I'm recycling this center-piece." A roar of laughter filled the room.

The friends ate, drank, and celebrated Nikki's recovery and their successful mission. Rising carefully to her feet, one hand grabbing the edge of her chair, Nikki hoisted her glass in the air and led them all in in a cheer of "Whatever it takes!"